Return
to Umbria

Books by David P. Wagner

The Rick Montoya Italian Mysteries
Cold Tuscan Stone
Death in the Dolomites
Murder Most Unfortunate
Return to Umbria

Return
to Umbria

A Rick Montoya Italian Mystery

David P. Wagner

Poisoned Pen
PRESS

Sourcebooks, Poisoned Pen Press and the colophon are registered trademarks of
Sourcebooks, Inc.

Published by Poisoned Pen Press, an imprint of Sourcebooks
P.O. Box 4410, Naperville, Illinois 60567-4410
(630) 961-3900
sourcebooks.com

Library of Congress Cataloging-in-Publication data is on file with the publisher.

Printed and bound in The United States of America.
POD 10 9 8 7 6 5 4 3 2

*For my brother, Bill—this sibling thing is great;
let's keep it going.*

Chapter One

Rick Montoya took a deep breath, held it, and weighed the cold steel of the Beretta in his outstretched hands, pointing both thumbs forward. Fifty meters ahead a dark figure, purposely obscured by weak lighting, faced him directly. Rick squinted down the gun barrel, stiffened his grip, and slowly squeezed the trigger, just as he had practiced. The pistol barked loudly and jumped back in his hand. Heart beat steady, he let out the breath and dropped his arms. The distinctive metallic smell drifted up to his nostrils as he noticed heat now spreading through his grip. Lights popped on, bouncing off the low ceiling of the previously darkened room. A voice behind him was just a murmur.

"Not your best."

Rick took one hand off the pistol and pulled the ear protectors down around his neck. "What was that, Uncle?"

"I said not your best," repeated Commissario Piero Fontana. "You give me second thoughts about trying to convince you to join the police force." He put down the binoculars and pushed a button to make the paper target rumble back toward them along a wire. The silhouette had a ring of holes in the center of the figure. When the target reached them, the policeman pointed to one just to the left of the waist. "That one's yours. He would still be coming at you if he were armed, and you'd have to hope he was a worse marksman than you are."

Rick checked the weapon to be sure it was not still loaded and placed it on the table behind them. "Did it occur to you that I missed him on purpose so that you'd drop the subject of me becoming a cop?"

Piero smiled. "I had not thought of that."

A few minutes later they stood at a bar across from Rome's police headquarters where the commissario had his office. Coffee available inside the *questura* was so notorious that policemen joked it should be on the most wanted list, so this place was crowded with uniforms at all hours of the day and night. Rick and his uncle took their small cups and walked to a tall table near the window where they added sugar from a large bowl. Commissario Fontana had shed the leather jacket he'd used at the shooting range and returned to the coat which was perfectly coordinated with his light wool slacks and silk tie. The temperature on the street outside had not required an overcoat, and Rick wore only a light sweater over a sport shirt with no tie. Well-ironed jeans covered the tops of his cowboy boots.

"Riccardo, there is something I want to talk to you about, in addition to your need for more shooting practice."

Rick sipped his coffee. "I got that impression, Zio, when you called me yesterday."

His uncle smiled. "You know me too well."

"As well as you know me."

They both considered that for a moment before Piero spoke. "Your family needs you, Riccardo."

Rick was more curious than concerned. He knew from the way Uncle Piero spoke that his parents were fine, and in fact he'd spoken to his mother—Piero's sister—from Brazil on Skype the previous evening. His Italian family was not very large in comparison with his father's side, whose relatives could be found in most corners of northern New Mexico. His mother had one sister and a brother, Piero, but because Aunt Marta Dozzi lived in Perugia, Rick seldom saw her and her husband. The Italian grandparents had passed on when Rick was in high school in Rome, both in the same year, a difficult one for the three Fontana offspring. There was also a cousin, Aunt Marta's only son, but Rick hadn't seen Fabrizio Dozzi since high school, when Fabrizio was a little boy. Perhaps Fabrizio wanted to go to the States to study and needed some advice from his half-American cousin.

"It's Fabrizio."

"I suspected that, Uncle. How old is he now? Must be about twenty?"

"He's twenty-one." Piero studied his nephew before continuing. "Fabrizio has always looked up to you, Riccardo. Never had a big brother, of course, so you, the older cousin, have been special for him."

"I never saw him more that a dozen times, and he was just a little kid. He's not in trouble, is he? His policeman uncle would be the one to intervene if that were the case."

Piero waved off the idea with an uplifted palm. "He's not breaking the law, if that's what you mean, or I certainly would get involved. No, it's his behavior that is very upsetting to his mother, and when my sister gets upset enough, she calls me."

Rick, a professional translator, tried to think of an equivalent phrase in Italian for "cut to the chase," but nothing jumped into his mind. "Zio, what's going on with Fabrizio?"

The policeman took another sip of coffee. "You'll remember that Fabrizio was studying at the university in Perugia after he graduated from the *liceo*. I'm not sure what courses he was taking, but it could have been literature since he's now decided to become a writer. A few months ago he met a woman in a nightclub and they hit it off. She lives in Orvieto, and was sightseeing in Perugia with some friends. One thing led to another, and she invited him to visit her in Orvieto. That was six weeks ago. He's still there."

Rick nodded. "I can see how that would upset Aunt Marta. But a youthful fling isn't the end of the world, and—"

"The woman is twice his age, Riccardo, and married. She is also wealthy, and she's set Fabrizio up in a small apartment close to her palazzo. But Orvieto is so small, everything is close."

"Ah." Rick digested the facts, considered making a joke, but stifled the thought when he read the look on his uncle's face. "So you need someone to talk some sense into Fabrizio."

"That's correct."

"And what better person than the older cousin whom the kid has idolized forever?"

"Precisely."

Rick's deep breath was something closer to a sigh. He'd been meaning to get up to Perugia to see the Dozzi since he'd moved to Rome from Albuquerque, but something had always come up, usually work. Building up his interpreting and translating business took time, and he had to drop everything when a job appeared. Now he had gained enough of a reputation around Rome to be selective in the jobs he accepted. Coincidentally, just the previous week he'd thought about traveling to the Umbrian capital to visit his aunt, uncle, and cousin. Now, at least to see Cousin Fabrizio, he would not have to go as far as Perugia. This was a task that had to be done in person, and Orvieto was a relatively short drive from Rome.

"I suppose Aunt Marta has made an attempt."

Piero's reply was to lift his eyes to the heavens and then back to Rick.

"It's been a while since I've been up to Orvieto, and Betta has finally worked at the art police long enough to have accrued some vacation time. We've talked about getting out of Rome for a few days, this could be just thing." The thought of spending a few days with Betta definitely helped.

"So you can catch two pigeons with one fava bean." Piero used the Italian equivalent of "kill two birds with one stone."

"Exactly, Zio." Rick quickly sorted things out in his mind. "But I have a contract to interpret for a visiting group of American doctors the next three days, so I can't go up until the weekend. I assume you know where Fabrizio is."

"I know exactly where he is, at an apartment rented in the name of Tullia Aragona. There are advantages to having the resources of the *Polizia dello Stato* at hand."

"You agree, Zio, that it will be better for me to drop in on Fabrizio rather than to phone?"

"Absolutely. Surprise him in person. He won't listen to reason over the phone. I've tried. Your Aunt Marta has called too."

I'll bet she has, Rick thought. "Send me the information and I'll get a car rental reservation."

As Rick and Piero walked toward the door, five young plain-clothes policemen nodded polite greetings to the commissario and wondered who the young guy with him was. Once out on the street, the two instinctively checked the patch of sky visible between the buildings to see if any change in the weather was in the offing. The few clouds they saw, which would have constituted a promising weather system in New Mexico, were not worth noting in Rome. The commotion of coffee machines and conversations in the crowded bar was replaced with the cacophony of the street, including the sound of mopeds and cars. The imposing police building did not keep Roman drivers from behaving as they did in the rest of the city, including parking at angles not condoned by municipal regulations. The two men squeezed between two parked cars and waited for a speeding Fiat to pass before carefully crossing the street. They paused in front of the large entrance, its tall doors guarded by two uniformed policemen who stood straight when they spotted Rick's uncle.

"Sorry we are burdening you with this task, Riccardo, but you are the perfect person to take it on."

"I hope you're right, Zio."

"I know I'm right. You solved those mysteries up north, so this should be simple."

Walking back to his apartment, Rick thought that finding a murderer would be easier than getting his young cousin to give up the pleasures of a woman. Which brought his thoughts back to Betta and spending a few days with her in Orvieto. He extracted his phone from his pocket and scrolled down the numbers.

◇◇◇

The desert heat pressed down on Scottsdale, as usual, but inside the house the air felt icy cool. Two large suitcases lay open on the wide bed, their dark canvas contrasting with the white of the bedspread, walls, and furniture. The thick carpet was a soft pink, not a color or a pile that would be the first choice of most men. But the men who'd entered the room over the years hadn't noticed, or if they had, didn't care. Rhonda Van Fleet opened the drawer of one of four dressers, pulled out another clump of clothing, and dumped it in one of the suitcases. She stepped back, her bare feet making no sound as they sank into the lush pile. Looking at one almost-full suitcase, she thought how different this trip would be from that first one those many years ago. She didn't have two bags then, only a stuffed backpack that she'd carried on the plane. Life was simpler in those days, but so was she. The thought made her laugh silently.

"What is your name?"

"Rhonda. It is a family name."

"And a beautiful name. It sounds like music."

"And what is your name?"

"Luca. With one C, not like the city."

"You live in Orvieto?"

"My aunt does, I come to visit her. You are a student?"

"Yes, I will study art. And learn Italian."

"I will visit my aunt more often. I can help you learn Italian."

"I would like that."

"Can I help you with something, Mrs. Van Fleet?"

Rhonda answered without turning to the woman standing in the doorway. "The decisions on what to pack are ones I have to make myself, Anna."

The maid nodded, wiped her hands on her apron, and returned to the kitchen.

The big decision had already been made: whether to make the trip at all.

It had come after her visit to the doctor two months earlier, when what should have been a regular exam turned out to be anything but routine. As she drove home that afternoon she realized that she had to return to Orvieto, and it had to be now, while she still could. What was it she had told her? A year, perhaps more if she were lucky? But the serious symptoms would not become debilitating until close to the end. Some consolation. She had a death sentence hanging over her, but she would not go quietly. Submissiveness was not her style. Never had been. She'd turned her focus to Orvieto, spending hours on the Internet searching for threads that would connect her to that year so long ago. What she found both shocked and delighted her. Thoughts of the trip had already been dominating her waking hours. Now, with this new information, they were seeping into her dreams.

The phone rang. She padded to the table next to the bed to see the number. "Don't answer it, Anna. I'll get it," she called to the other room. She reached for the receiver.

"Hi, Gina. I was just packing."

"I haven't started yet, Mom," said the voice at the other end.

Rhonda noticed something in her daughter's voice. "What's the matter, Gina? Are you having second thoughts again? I told you there would be enough vegetarian choices on the menus in Italy. You can eat pasta, can't you? Or has that moved to the prohibited list too?"

"Don't be like that, Mom. You know it isn't that." There was a pause. "I'm just concerned about you, whether you're doing the right thing. If you're making this trip for the right reasons. You can't achieve fulfillment in your life if you dwell on negatives. You must expel the negative energy inside you that has built up over the years and cleanse your system. This trip won't do that."

"I don't need any of that psycho-babble, Gina. Your friends there in Santa Fe love that crap, but it doesn't work on me. You should know that by now."

The heavy breath was audible. "I suppose I should. But please, at least think about what you really are searching for in Italy."

"Whatever. Don't miss your flight. Francine and I will be waiting for you in the first-class lounge in Atlanta near the international departure gates. Our flight arrives an hour before yours, so Francine will likely be loaded by the time you get there. We'll probably have to pour her onto the flight."

"I'll be there, Mom."

Rhonda put down the phone. As loopy as her daughter could sometimes be, she had a point. What was the real reason she wanted to go back? It had been something she'd been wrestling with since getting the news from the doctor. At first she had told herself she needed to return to Orvieto to get closure. Closure? What the hell did that mean? She didn't need to close the book on that part of her life so she could move on; she wasn't going to be moving on for very much longer. Did she need to see those people again, look them in the face and let them see that she'd done something with her life and wasn't just another idealistic art student? She had to admit there was something to that. It was in the middle of the night when it came to her. She had to walk those streets again, the streets where she and Luca had strolled those many years ago. It wouldn't bring him back, but she needed to do it. Why, she didn't know. Gina would have some explanation, but Rhonda would never hear it because she would never tell her daughter. This was between her and Luca.

Leaving one suitcase still empty, Rhonda walked to a set of glass doors, pushed them open, and stepped out onto the tiled lanai where her gin and tonic waited. Seeing that the drink was warm, she thought about calling Anna for more ice, but instead pushed it to one side of the glass table. A rich expanse of golf fairway with mountains hovering in the distance should have drawn her eye, but she sat and opened a yellowed plastic photo album on the table. *Italia 1979* was printed in a young, feminine hand on the cover. She opened it and slowly turned the pages while her eyes moved from one yellowed picture to another, until she reached the third page. There she stopped.

Chapter Two

The *Frecciarossa* passed high above their car window like the hare getting a head start on the tortoise. Its high-speed track was set higher than the A1 autostrada as well as the older rail line, as if to emphasize the superiority of the flashy competitor. But it was not a true competition. Those rail users who needed to stop at places between Rome and Florence did not have the option to board the "red arrow," since it went directly to the Tuscan capital. Instead, they took one of the locals that used the original track-bed and traveled at a more leisurely speed. All three transportation options ran through the Tiber Valley, tunneling under the occasional hill but mostly running flat and fast through green fields near the river.

Rick kept the rental car at an even hundred and twenty kilometers per hour, passing most cars easily. Elizabetta Innocenti—known to all but her traditional father as Betta—leaned her head against the passenger seat, her eyes closed. Sleeping in the car was something Rick had never been able to do, no matter how tired he was. He stared at the countryside, remembering past family trips through Italy. They had usually gone by car, he and his sister packed in the back and complaining about how long it was taking. Except for the annual ski week, the trips were supposed to be educational experiences for the Montoya kids. If there was a museum, they were marched through it, learning about art by osmosis, if nothing else. After so many visits to churches, Rick and his sister not only knew an apse from a nave, but could have taught a survey course on medieval architecture. He'd complained at the time, but he was glad his parents had force-fed so much culture—especially now that he was back in Italy. Knowing about such things hadn't hurt when trying to impress the ladies at the university in New Mexico.

The route was a constantly changing landscape. After picking up the car at the Villa Borghese underground garage he had followed the distinctive green autostrada signs to head north on Via Salaria, the modern version of the Roman road named for the salt brought into Rome from the north. The traffic of the center lessened as the street got closer to the edge of the city, and eventually the tightly packed buildings gave way to open space. He swung onto the busy ring road that circled the city but almost immediately got off to enter the A1 autostrada, the highway linking Naples with Milan. Now the scenery turned agricultural. They entered Sabina, a section whose early tribes, more than two millennia ago, had been subdued and brought into the Roman sphere of influence. Rick had yet to meet a Sabine woman, but he spotted a couple of them driving along a dirt road as the highway began to climb into the hills south of Narni. The Tiber, working its way toward Rome, appeared and disappeared from view. A short tunnel, then a much longer one, caused Rick to turn on the headlights. Betta stirred and stretched her legs as the noise of the car engine bounced back off the walls of the tunnel.

"Rick, tell me more about this cousin of yours."

He glanced at her and back at the road. Her smile always made him happy, even when it was a mischievous one. After numerous relationships, all of which had something hollow about them, he was still trying to discover a downside to spending time with Betta Innocenti. There were others who may have been as attractive, but Betta's beauty was different, starting with her very short black hair and large green eyes. She had none of the pretentiousness of so many Roman women he knew, wasn't afraid of saying what she thought, and certainly didn't worry about what people thought of her. She had—he reached out of

Italian and into Spanish—a healthy dash of *chispa*. It was that spark that placed her at the top of his list. That and her acceptance of his sense of humor.

"There's not much to tell. I remember Fabrizio as a little kid. Kind of quiet, but that's the way children are supposed to be in Italian families. The last time I saw him was just after my grandmother's funeral, if I remember right. He was about ten. They came over to our apartment in Rome and we played with my Lego set. I've been meaning to get up to Perugia to see my aunt, but haven't found the time yet. If I'm not successful in extracting Fabrizio, I may have to put it off even longer."

The car emerged from the tunnel and sunlight poured back through the windows. The fields outside changed from dark green rows to a bright yellow carpet of tall sunflowers, their faces swiveled to catch the sun.

"Uncle Piero says that Fabrizio always asked about me, so I must have made an impression. As expected, I suppose; the little kid looking up to the high-schooler who then goes off to the university in America. Very exotic."

"Those exotic qualities have always appealed to me too."

"Thanks, Betta."

After coming over a hill, they crossed the Tiber for the last time before slowing down to get off at the Orvieto exchange. The exit ramp led to the toll booths and then out to the street that would take them the final few kilometers to the city.

The Etruscans knew a good defensive position when they saw one. Orvieto sat at the top of what might have been called a mesa in Rick's New Mexico, its rock outcropping guarded by cliffs that dropped steeply to the valley below. For millennia it was almost impossible to reach the city without the approval of its inhabitants, especially after thick walls were added to the natural defenses. Now drivers reached those city walls after navigating the steep winding road that covered much of the northern side of the hill, hoping to be fortunate enough to find somewhere to park in the twisting maze of narrow streets. But there was another way up to the town.

A couple minutes after leaving the autostrada they came to an irregular-shaped traffic circle where Rick turned off, following the P signs. A large parking lot spread out between the old railroad station and the elevated track of the high-speed trains. Rick found a space, and after locking the car, they rolled their bags to an escalator which took them under the old railroad station and out into a small square. A circular pool adorned the round piazza, its narrow jet of water bent by a slight southern breeze that swirled dust around the street. Beyond the fountain was a more modern station, with six glass gables projecting out from its single story to protect anyone waiting at the bus stop outside. *FUNICOLARE* was written in metal letters on the stone wall between the set of glass and metal doors.

Inside, a bored city employee took money at a ticket window and dispensed *biglietti*. Rick pushed euros under the glass and was rewarded with two one-way tickets and change. He turned back to Betta and noticed a digital number on the screen on the wall.

"*Subito*," he called to her, "that one is leaving in one minute." They ran to the turnstile, punched their tickets, and slipped into the red car just as its light began flashing.

"Perfect timing," he said. They squeezed themselves and their bags next to the window while the car lurched upward. Thanks to the wedge-shaped base underneath the car, the cabin would remain horizontal as the chain running along the track pulled it up the steep incline. The car immediately emerged from the station and started up the hill, olive groves visible through the trees that lined the route.

Rick and Betta looked around and caught their breath. The car was almost full. At the far end a group of elderly Italian tourists chattered away while looking out the tall windows. The middle section held a family of five including a baby in a stroller, as well as two men Rick guessed were locals. The two talked and looked only at each other, which he took to mean they'd seen the view and didn't need to check it out again.

Next to Rick and Betta stood three women whom he immediately pegged as Americans. Affluent Americans dressed in a certain way, Rick knew from observing so many tourists in Rome, and two of these three had money. Their cropped linen pants and loose tops were of light colors, indicating residence somewhere warm, and expensive, like Florida or Southern California, but a silver and turquoise belt on one said the Southwest. Their tans confirmed it. The third, a woman about Rick's age, was dressed more modestly, like most tourists her age. Her two older companions wore stylish but comfortable sandals, while she had low-cut hiking boots. Boots wore her hair long and tied behind, while one of the sandals women kept hers shoulder-length and brown, and the other in sandals had short, spiked hair that was vaguely blond. Were the two in sandals divorcees? Or—since he guessed their ages to be hovering on one side or the other of sixty—widows? The third, the younger woman, had to be a relative, and in fact there was a resemblance between her and one of the other women. As he continued to analyze the three, a guidebook clattered to the floor.

"Francine, how can you be so clumsy?" said Shoulder-Length Hair.

Spiked Hair bent down to pick up the book, but Rick reached it first and handed it to her. "Oh, thank, you," she said. Then, a pained look on her face, she turned to the woman who had berated her. "Or I should say—?"

"It's *grazie*, Francine. How long is it going to take you to get it?"

"You're very welcome, Francine," said Rick.

"You speak English very well," she said as she grasped the book. "Where did you learn it?"

"I lived in the States a few years."

"I don't even notice an accent. Whoops." The car veered slightly as it switched to one of the double tracks that allowed the two funicular cars to pass each other. She smiled when Rick grabbed her arm to keep her from falling. The younger woman watched but said nothing.

"Back off, Francine," said Shoulder-Length Hair. "He's with that girl, and she's half your age."

"You'd better hold on." Rick pointed to the bar that ran under the window. He moved back to the corner where Betta had been observing the scene.

"Some of your *connazionale?*"

"They are. And I can never turn down an opportunity to practice my English."

"I didn't need any English to understand what was going on with those three. The tone of voice and body language are enough." Betta nodded at the one with the shoulder-length hair. "That woman is a witch."

"A witch is supposed to be old and haggard, like the *Befana*."

"She's old, all right, and remember that the *Befana* brings toys to children. She looks like she would be more into getting gifts than giving them."

The car darkened as they entered the tunnel under the fortress guarding the promontory on the eastern side of Orvieto. A moment later the car slowed and arrived at the station. The doors slid open and everyone filed out. The station, a twin of the one below, opened out on a wide piazza where a small bus waited, its driver watching the people climb on, filling its seats and aisles.

The woman Betta had described as a witch pushed her two compatriots to the front of the line. "Girls, if you just stand around being polite, the Italians will fill this bus and we'll be left on the curb."

"But Mom, that would be—"

"Move it, Gina, this isn't the line at Starbucks in Santa Fe."

The comment got a smile out of the third woman, but she too did as she was told. The three squeezed to the back of the bus and found seats.

By the time Rick and Betta had studied the signs and realized it was their bus, the driver waved them away to indicate he was full. Get on the next one, his bored expression told them. The bus pulled out with their fellow funicular riders. The younger woman stared from the window and noticed Rick, her expression changing to a weak smile.

Rick took the handle of Betta's suitcase. "Let's enjoy the scenery while we wait for the next one."

They walked past the arched fortress gate toward a weather-stained statue and reached what Italians call a *belvedere*. The ride up, enclosed as it was with trees and other vegetation, had not given them a sense of how high they had risen from Orvieto Scalo, which made what they saw more impressive. The valley they had driven through spread out below, bisected by tiny twin ribbons of highway and railroad, and dotted with factories and other buildings. It was a view seemingly made for pleasure, but its original purpose was purely defensive. A force of any size coming from north or south would have been spotted easily by sentinels posted on the ramparts of the fort, giving the town time to prepare for battle. These days, the invading hordes bent on plunder were armed not with swords and lances, but cameras and euros.

Rick and Betta enjoyed the landscape in silence until he noticed another B line bus rolling into the space at the funicular station. They hoisted their bags on board and settled in the back. Soon another funicular load streamed out of the doors of the station, piled on, and they were on their way. The bus nosed out of the piazza and up a street which narrowed as it climbed before rolling into an even wider square three minutes later. They got off and faced the most spectacular cathedral facade in Italy.

The Gothic front of the Orvieto Duomo was an architectural triptych full of spires, statues, and arches. Its most striking feature was the number of colorful mosaics which filled every flat space, their bright figures contrasting with the white of the carved marble. Like all Gothic architecture, everything pointed up, reminding the faithful of the final prize, though it was difficult for Rick and Betta to keep their eyes off the art which ran from bottom to top. They walked slowly to the opposite end of the piazza where a long bench ran along the wall of the building. Squeezing between two groups of aging Italians, they sat on the stone with their bags between their legs.

Rick pressed his head back to get the maximum effect. "Even if there were nothing behind it, and the inside were bare, this is worth the trip to see."

"Ah, Rick, but there *is* more inside, including one of the gems of the *Rinascimento*."

"We will see it tomorrow."

Clumps of tourists gathered around the square staring either at the facade or at the page in their guidebooks that described it. Among them were the three women from the funicular. Francine was deep in her guidebook, reading aloud while her two companions craned their necks at the spires. Shoulder-Length Hair held her hands up as if to isolate one section, but suddenly her face darted from the church to a far corner of the square. Rick watched her say a quick word to the other two and rush toward that corner, leaving her friends shaking their heads. She ran toward someone walking alone out of the square and immediately became lost behind a group of tourists. Rick returned his attention to the cathedral.

◇◇◇

Rhonda ran through the tourists toward the man, his back to her. Suddenly she had the thought that she was mistaken, that it was not who she thought she'd seen. She stopped, and just at that moment the bell at the top of the clock tower struck the hour with a deep, metallic ring. The man stopped and turned to look up at the round face of the clock high above the square. He scowled at the clock and then at his own watch, then quickly walked off. Rhonda stared at his back.

"Everything will be all right, Rhonda. We must do this, for the cause."

"I'm frightened, Luca."

"I told you she shouldn't have come along," said the other man under his breath. "You should have left her back in Orvieto."

Luca glared at him and turned back to Rhonda. "We've planned everything to the last detail. Nothing can go wrong. You'll see. Trust me."

She looked between the faces of the two men, wanting to believe that what they were doing was the right thing. "You'll be careful?"

"Of course," Luca answered.

While she watched, the two men slipped around the corner and disappeared from sight.

Yes, Rhonda thought. It's you. And thanks to my research, I know where to find you. Her muscles stiffened and her hands tightened into fists.

When Rick moved his eyes back to the square, a tour leader holding an umbrella led her group toward the cathedral entrance and he saw the American woman in the distance, standing stiffly alone. The person she had rushed to see was nowhere in sight, and Rick guessed he had gone down one of the streets that led off the piazza.

The woman walked slowly back to join her companions who were studying the cathedral. Even from a distance Rick could notice a difference from how she'd looked when she was in the funicular and afterward getting on the bus. Seeing that person on the square had given her a jolt, but he couldn't decide if it was anger or pleasure. Perhaps a bit of both.

"It's in three parts," said Betta.

Rick took his attention from the woman. "What?"

"The facade, it's in three horizontal parts. Built at different times You can see the style change as the cathedral progressed over the centuries, but despite that, it all goes together quite well."

"Yes. Yes it does." He got to his feet. "Shall we go to the hotel? It's up this street, if I got the directions right. We'll come back here tomorrow." He slung his bag over his shoulder and took the handle of Betta's suitcase. Its wheels rattled over the cobblestones as they walked toward the Hotel Maitani.

Chapter Three

The location of the hotel could not have been better, only a few steps from the cathedral up a narrow street. Though the furnishings were mid-twentieth century, one could sense that the building had been used as an inn for much longer. It had likely undergone at least one renovation, but was getting close to needing another. Rick hoped that when it happened they would keep the marble floors, wood paneling, tall mirrors, and overstuffed chairs. Too many hotels became modern, only to find that the modern of that moment had too soon become the seedy and kitschy of the next. There was something comforting about out-of-fashion décor in hotels, a statement that they were comfortable in their own skin. The same could have been said of the hotel staff. The desk clerk had a wrinkled face under thinning gray hair and wore the traditional black suit over a white shirt and dark tie. Rick was relieved that there was no bell boy to help take their bags to the room, fearing another septuagenarian. They took the elevator to the second floor and found their room.

Betta separated the curtains of the room's only window and opened it to find a view of another building on the other side of a narrow alley. "Not much of a view," she said, "but at least it shouldn't be noisy at night." She kicked off her shoes and flopped down on the bed. "I think I may rest my eyes a bit before going out to explore the town."

Rick pulled his laptop from the bag, set it on the narrow desk, and plugged it in. "I'll check my e-mail and be on my way."

She bent her elbow and propped her head in her hand. "You'll do fine, Rick. Your uncle would not have asked you to do this if he didn't think you could convince Fabrizio."

"My uncle is a realist in his police work, but that doesn't always extend to his views about this nephew's capabilities. I hope I don't let him down."

◇◇◇

Uncle Piero's directions were written at the bottom of a street map of Orvieto, with a yellow crayon line marking the route from the hotel to the palazzo. It was typical of his uncle's thoroughness. Rick looked up at the street marker on the corner building and back down at the map, realizing that without it he would have had a devil of a time getting to where Fabrizio was staying. As in so many post-Roman Italian towns, the streets of Orvieto seemed to have been laid out by an evil madman, peppered with twists, narrow alleys, and dead ends. Stone houses, two- and three-storied, lined the cobblestones, their wood front doors right on the pavement. Who needed sidewalks when everyone walked anyway? Look around and you're in the thirteenth century. He loved it.

He returned his thoughts to the "Fabrizio problem." This would be a short initial contact with the kid, not a hard sell. *I just happened to be in Orvieto with my girlfriend, heard you were here, thought I'd drop by*—that sort of thing. Get the lay of the land, test the waters, give the situation the once-over, and any other clichéd phrase that might be applicable. Go easy on the lad. Save questions like "Are you out of your freakin' mind?" for a subsequent encounter. Play the diplomat, Rick. Use those skills that must have rubbed off from your father. Certainly don't do what your mother would do in this situation, which would likely be to throttle her nephew.

He consulted his street map again and decided his destination should be right around the next corner. A thin slice of nearly horizontal sunlight squeezed between two buildings, painting a stripe on the pavement. Rick hoped the late afternoon would be a good time to find Fabrizio at home. The kid wants to be a writer, so he should be writing at all hours of the day and night. Isn't that what writers do? When the number appeared on a nondescript but neatly painted door, Rick stood back and assessed the building. It had two doors and was wider by half than the *palazzi* that abutted it. Rick reckoned the building was two apartments, one on each floor, and he also guessed that the simple exterior did not reflect the furnishings. It was the Italian way to hide luxury behind a bland facade to discourage interest from thieves or tax assessors, who were considered one in the same. Piero mentioned that the woman was not without funds, but his uncle's litotes didn't give him an idea of how wealthy Tullia Aragona—or her husband—really might be. Rick walked to the door and rang the rusting brass bell. He was about to ring again when a voice crackled out of the box above the bell.

"Who is it?"

It was a male voice, and a young one at that. Rick was in luck. "Fabrizio?"

"*Sì*. Who is this?"

"It's your Cousin Riccardo. I was here in—" Rick heard a loud click at the other end of the line. Dammit, he thought, he's not going to let me in. Well, I didn't come all this way for nothing. About to press the bell again, he heard a noise inside. Feet. Definitely feet. He waited. The door unlatched and swung open. Fabrizio was dressed in a loose-fitting sweatshirt and jeans. His hair was long and he wore a spotty beard. The last time I saw him he barely had peach fuzz, Rick mused, feeling old. He opened his arms for a cousinly hug, but Fabrizio's head jerked back, he stepped into the street, closed the door, and took Rick's arm.

"Why don't we go for a walk?" He wheeled Rick around and down the street. "What a nice surprise, Cousin. It's, uh, so good to see you."

"Did I interrupt something?"

"No, no, not at all. So, how is Uncle Piero? I assume he sent you up here."

The kid is sharper than I expected. "I guess you have to get up pretty early to outsmart my Cousin Fabrizio," Rick said.

"Huh?"

"Forget it. That's an English expression that doesn't translate well into Italian."

"So you learned that in your interpreting business? That's still what you're doing, isn't it, Riccardo?"

"It is. And you've become a writer?" They reached an intersection, if the meeting of two narrow streets could be called that, and forged ahead.

"It takes a while to break into writing, but I'm working on it. In the meantime I'm getting experience in the real world." For the first time Fabrizio turned to Rick and smiled. "So you're supposed to talk me into going back home, right? Okay, give it your best shot."

Rick took in a breath before responding. "I get the clear impression that you are enjoying the arrangement, so it may not be easy to talk some sense into you."

"Enjoying the arrangement? Riccardo, you wouldn't believe the things this woman—"

Rick held up a hand. "I don't need any details, Fabrizio." They walked several steps before he continued. "I can also see that you are mature enough to make decisions on your own, and that you understand what your behavior is doing to your family." Fabrizio only nodded; the family reference didn't seem to phase him. "And you don't seem concerned about this woman's husband."

"Nah. Tullia never says anything about him."

"Well, then, I don't think there's anything else I can say to you." Fabrizio stopped walking. "That's it?"

"Pretty much," answered Rick. "I'm primarily up here with a friend to see the town, and I don't want to be late for dinner." He pulled out his business card. "Here's my cell phone number. If you have any free time maybe we can have a coffee. Good luck with your writing."

"Uh, thanks, Riccardo. Good luck to you on your translating."

They exchanged a hug and Rick walked off, trying to figure out what his next step would be in dealing with the Fabrizio problem. He would not give up that easily. He became lost in thought as he retraced the route back to the hotel, trying to come up with some idea to convince the kid that this was a time to think about the feelings of his family rather than his own desires. Most young men rebel in some way at this age, especially if they've been living at home all their lives. Certainly Rick engaged in some rebellious behavior in his years at the university. But this was a bit extreme, especially for an Italian family. He was pondering family when he looked up and noticed a lone figure standing looking through the window of a coffee bar. It was the youngest of the three American women on the funicular.

He had not paid much attention to her on the ride, mainly because he'd been observing the behavior of the one Betta had characterized as a witch. Also, he had learned from experience that checking out an attractive woman in Betta's presence would not go over well. But Betta wasn't with him now. The woman was about his age, perhaps a few years older. She wore her hair long, pulled back, and tied with a simple ribbon; and unlike the other two women, showed no traces of makeup. Around her neck, over a cotton sweater, she had wound a black-and-white print scarf that was vaguely Middle Eastern. The pouch of a fanny pack around her waist was turned to the front. Cargo pants completed the outfit, which clung so loosely around her body that her real figure was hard for Rick to determine. She looked up and saw him staring.

"Oh, hi."

"Hi to you," Rick answered.

"You were on the train this morning."

"The funicular."

"Right, the funicular. Are you Italian? You said you lived in the States for a while."

He was standing next to her now. "My mother is Italian and my father is American. So I'm both." She didn't answer, so he went on. "It's a requirement that I now have to ask you where you're from in the States."

She stared at him, as if she was deciding whether she should be talking to strangers.

"It's not that hard a question," he added.

Without makeup, it was easy to see her blushing. "Oh, sorry. I live in New Mexico. Santa Fe." Having found her tongue, she now held out her hand. "I'm Gina, by the way."

He took it. "I'm Rick. We have New Mexico in common, Gina. My father is from there, and I'm related to half the families in the upper Rio Grande Valley. Also, I went to UNM."

"Really? Wow, that is a coincidence. Is your, uh, friend, also from New Mexico?"

"She's Italian. Never been to the States. Where are your two friends?"

The blank stare returned for an instant. "Oh, you mean my mother and her friend. Mom is off somewhere, she didn't say where. She lived here many years ago, which is why we came to Orvieto. Francine, that's the other woman, she's drinking wine at the restaurant where we're going to have dinner. So I'm just wandering around until I meet them for dinner. I have a good street map." She pulled it from her pouch to prove it.

"It's hard to get lost in Orvieto. Pretty small place."

"I suppose so. Can I ask you something, Rick?"

"Sure."

She pointed at the glass. "I was thinking of getting a glass of juice, and I saw those oranges stacked in the wire basket behind the bar. They look good, but do you think they're organic?"

Now it was Rick's turn to be temporarily at a loss for words. "I really don't know, Gina. But the word is almost the same in Italian, so if you ask they'll understand you. Listen, I have to go. It's been nice meeting you. Give my regards to your mother and her friend."

She smiled brightly. "Thank you, Rick. It's nice meeting you too. I'd better just start working my way to the restaurant." She began to walk off but stopped and turned back. "Please don't judge my mother by the way she was on the funicular. She's dealing with some serious issues in her life."

◇◇◇

The wood door was open only a crack, throwing a thin line of light on the sidewalk outside the shop. The lamp that normally illuminated the small sign after sunset had been turned off to discourage any after-hours visitors. In his small office in the back, the owner bent over his computer, deep in concentration over sales numbers, deliveries, and taxes. He looked up when he heard a soft chime indicating the front door opening, and muttered something to himself about not wanting to be interrupted. He got to his feet, stepped quickly to the door of his office, and pushed it open.

"We're closed, now, if you could come back…" He stopped in his place and stared at the face that smiled back at him. It was a smile that showed anything but affection.

"Ciao, Amadeo. It's been a long time." Her eyes moved from the man's face to a vase sitting on an illuminated shelf on the wall near the door. Her face reflected off its glazed surface as she picked it up in her hands. She blinked and took several deep breaths as she rotated the piece in her hands.

"Rhonda? Is that you? What a pleasant surprise. I was just thinking about you the other day, wondering what had become of you." He walked toward her, his arms preparing for a welcoming *abbraccio*. He froze as the vase suddenly flew across the room and crashed against the wall, scattering bright colors in a wide circle on the stone.

"How clumsy of me, Amadeo. I'm not as agile as I used to be. You remember how I used to be, don't you? And what a lovely work of art, such a beautiful pattern. Can you ever forgive me, Amadeo?" She ran her fingers over a ceramic piece which sat by itself on another shelf. "What unique glaze work, I love the way it winds around the entire bowl." She picked it up and held it above her head. "And the decoration continues even on the base."

With both hands she flung the bowl to the ground. The man jumped to the side to avoid the flying shards. He stepped back with his hands raised, pieces of broken ceramic crunching under the soles of his designer shoes.

"Do you see what you have done to me, Amadeo? All my life I have loved beautiful pieces like this, and seeing you has made me do this. I don't recall ever breaking any pieces back then, do you? Do you remember anything at all from those days, Amadeo?"

"You were my finest student, Rhonda." He tried to remain calm.

"And how many of your women students did you say that to?"

She walked slowly along the line of shelves, her purse swinging dangerously close to the pieces displayed on them. "It seems that you have become quite successful now, Amadeo. You don't need to lower yourself any more by teaching." Her hand stroked a small vase. "Which is such a shame since you are so creative and have so much you could share with students."

His hands were shaking as he pressed his palms together. "Rhonda, please, please. We must talk. After so many years we have a lot to talk about."

He held his breath as her hand edged toward another piece of ceramic art. It stopped and she looked at his ashen face, a brittle smile still on her own, as she decided her next move.

"That might be fun. A nice chat. Just like old times. The naive student and the experienced teacher. That's what we were, weren't we, Amadeo?"

"Whatever you say, Rhonda." His muscles finally relaxed, but his mind did not.

<><><>

When they had entered what appeared to be a simple trattoria, Rick expected that dinner would be simple as well. The owner was a close friend of one of Betta's fellow art cops in Rome, and he lavished attention on the couple from the moment they walked through the door. He insisted that they try the lemon risotto, one of their specialties, and since it required time to prepare, why not start with some *carpaccio* from an excellent cut of beef he'd acquired only that afternoon? To follow the rice dish, duck breasts that had been simmering in wine much of the day would make an excellent second course. Of course the house

Orvieto Classico would go perfectly with everything, unless they preferred a red. The two of them agreed to all the suggestions, and the happy owner bustled into the kitchen. There was never even a hint that the place might have a printed menu.

Two hours later they stood in front of the restaurant, agreeing that the meal was memorable. Rick suggested that they should *fare due passi*—take a stroll—to help digest the meal. They linked arms and walked in the opposite direction of the hotel. The evening was clear and the thermometer had dropped to a perfect temperature for walking. Rick's cowboy boots clicked on the stone, in contrast with the tap of Betta's Ferragamo flats.

After a few blocks Betta broke the silence of the night. "Rick, regarding your Cousin Fabrizio. You told me what happened, but you still haven't said what your next move will be."

Rick shook his head. "I don't know what it will be. Do you have a suggestion?"

The street narrowed and squeezed itself under an arch flanked by a pair of Corinthian columns, above which two windows looked down from unplastered brick walls. A dozen meters later the stone walls of the tunnel ended and they emerged into a rectangular piazza. Unlike its brick posterior, the facade of this building was anything but plain. Arches held up a balcony running the length of the facade, with seven windows facing out to the square. Empty flag poles above the entrance indicated a government office, possibly city hall. The city coat of arms centered between the middle windows confirmed it. Next to the municipal building, taking up one corner of the square, an octagonal bell tower rose up like a giant chess piece next to an equally ancient church. An arched doorway and round stained-glass window decorated the plain brick facade of the church. Lighting for the piazza came from floodlights on the government office and carriage lamps attached to the buildings opposite. Rick was taking it all in when Betta spoke.

"I'll think of something."

Rick moved his eyes from the tower to her face. "What?"

"I'll think of something to get Fabrizio to come to his senses. Perhaps the way to do it is not with Fabrizio but through that woman. What's her name?"

"Tullia Aragona."

"Tullia. Let me think about it. Do you know where we're going?"

They had walked out of the plaza along the side of the church. It was a broad street, which meant it led to another square somewhere in the distance. "Not really, but Orvieto is so small we shouldn't get lost." He recalled that he had said the same thing to the American woman earlier. He also realized he hadn't told Betta about the encounter. "At least we shouldn't get lost for more than a couple hours."

He looked up to see a lighted window at street level just ahead. "How about a coffee?"

"Sure. And we can ask how to get back to the hotel."

"I'll buy the coffee, you ask the directions."

◇◇◇

Darkness dropped into the streets of Orvieto, and with it the traffic and noise subsided. The town, as it did each evening, eased back to its medieval past, but with electric street lamps rather than torches attached to the stone buildings. Only the occasional Vespa ruined the effect. Rhonda Van Fleet was surprised that the street she walked was still familiar after all these years. A storm sewer cover in the shape of a lion was there, as was the ironwork gate guarding the entrance to a building near the corner. Nothing changed much in Italy, which made it so fascinating, so comforting.

Despite the familiar surroundings, she didn't feel comfortable. Was this a good idea? Agreeing to meet tonight? She slowed her walk and almost turned back. Francine and Gina would already be at the villa, having a glass of amaretto on the patio. Perhaps she should catch the bus and join them. She shook her head. No, absolutely not—this was why she'd come back to Italy. It wasn't just the place, the town. It was the people. And everything was going according to plan. She reviewed again their agreement to meet that evening. Rhonda had suggested the bar, one of her favorite hangouts from those days, and was pleased to find it was still there. Again, nothing changes.

She rounded the corner and saw that something *had* changed. On both sides of the doorway round lights hung from metal brackets, lighting the arched entrance to the wine bar. They looked ancient, and perhaps they were, but they had not been there thirty-five years earlier. It had been a running joke with her *compagni* that the place was so sleazy the owners didn't want anyone finding it. Clearly the proprietors had chosen to go more upscale. She hesitated again before reaching to open the door, but this time the unease passed quickly. It disappeared completely when she stepped inside; Enzo's interior had not changed.

The tables looked the same—small and round, with metal-backed stools squeezed around them. The bar lined the right side of the rectangular room, its dark wood surface showing the same nicks and circular glass marks, larger scratches at floor level thanks to years of scuffing. She didn't see Enzo, but the present occupant of the space behind the bar looked the same, maybe a son or nephew. And the glasses stood on their same shelf, above a row of uncorked bottles. It had been the cheapest place in Orvieto for wine by the glass; perhaps it still was. There was something, though, that wasn't the same. It came to her as she took her first deep breath just inside the door. It was the smell. Italian anti-smoking laws, which nobody back then even considered, had changed the atmosphere from hazy to clear. Gone was the acrid smell of tobacco, usually cheap tobacco, that everyone had smoked then, including Rhonda.

She was still standing at the doorway when a hand drew her arm. The voice behind it was calm and soothing.

"Rhonda, let's go somewhere less crowded."

Later, the two stood on a deserted street at the edge of the city, staring over the wall into the darkened valley below. Rhonda had not spoken for several minutes, her thoughts as dark as the night which had closed in on Orvieto.

The two figures huddled in the darkness of an alley while sirens wailed in the streets around them. The smell of explosives hung in the damp air.

"How could you have let this happen?"

"Things sometimes don't go according to plan, Rhonda. Things go wrong."

"That's all you can say? Things go wrong? He believed in the cause and he believed in you, and that's all you can say?"

"He knew the risks, and you did too."

"I never thought there was a chance Luca would die."

"We all die eventually. His time came early."

She turned her head and pressed it against the cold stone. The sobs started to convulse her entire body, bending it into a fetal crouch. The man looked down at her with disgust.

"It's clear that you weren't cut out for the revolution, Rhonda. Go back to America."

She turned from the darkness and looked him squarely in the face. "Do you still think about that day?"

"It's ancient history, Rhonda. I've moved on, and I assume everyone else has as well."

"I'm trying to do that. It's why I made this trip and sought you out, to put it all behind me. But instead of helping to heal, it's opening the scar, reminding me what I was like those many years ago, and how it all changed in an instant. I didn't just lose Luca, I lost my idealism."

"What are you going to do now?" He was staring intently at her.

"That last time we saw each other you said I should go back to America. That's what you'd like me to do now, I'm sure of that. But I've returned. It took all this time, but I've returned. This will be my last visit to Orvieto, so I intend to make the most of it."

Chapter Four

It was a warm and clear morning, and the hotel staff had moved breakfast outside to the rooftop terrace. Rolls, fruit, jellies, and yogurt were arranged on a long table close to the glass doors, and a uniformed waitress shuttled coffee and hot milk from the kitchen to the tables set up on the paving stones. Only a few speckled rays from the new sun peeked over the rooftops to bother the guests, and potted white and red flowers at the edge of the terrace gave off pleasant scents that mixed with the aroma of coffee. The view directly across the street was another building, but there was just enough of an angle so that most tables could see the top of the cathedral. Rick stepped from the doorway, fresh from his morning run and shower. He spotted Betta at a table reading the newspaper and worked his way over to reach her.

"*Una bellissima giornata.*" He took his seat and poured coffee from the pitcher already on the table. "This is just what I need."

"It is indeed beautiful, especially out here."

Her smile seemed forced. He poured hot milk from the other pitcher, stirred in sugar, and studied her face. "What's the matter, Betta?" He pointed at the paper that was now folded next to her plate. "Did your Bassano *squadra* lose?"

"This isn't about soccer, Rick, it's about murder."

The cup, halfway to his mouth, returned to the saucer. "What murder?"

She found the page she wanted, folded it in half, and passed it to Rick.

He studied it, saw the article, and began to read aloud. "Police who were called to the scene, a country road about five kilometers from Orvieto, initially assumed the woman had been killed by a hit-and-run driver." He glanced at the table next to him, heard a couple speaking German, but lowered his voice anyway. "On further examination it was determined that the type and extent of injuries indicated homicide. A passport found on the body confirmed that the woman was an American, Rhonda Van Fleet." He looked up at Betta and then back at the page. "Anyone with information about the woman in this passport photo is asked to contact…it's her, isn't it?"

"The nasty one, no question about it."

"What would she have been doing on a road far from town?" He scanned the story again, but there was no information other than the basic facts of finding the body. The writer must not have had enough time before the paper went to press to embellish it with conjecture, as any Italian journalist worth his salt would do.

"That's likely what the police are trying to figure out right now," Betta said. "They probably don't even know about the other two women. Who would be prime suspects."

"Do they teach you that kind of thing in your art squad training?"

"Hardly. I learned about suspects the same way you did."

"By solving mysteries?"

"By reading mysteries."

"And I thought you were going to give me a compliment. I guess I should go to the police and tell them what we saw on the funicular yesterday."

She shook her head slowly and grinned. "So it's your civic duty to get involved. If you were all Italian rather than just half from your mother, you would set the paper aside and avoid getting involved. Or do you want to become part of another investigation?"

"You got it right with the part about civic duty."

"Well, eat your breakfast first, Signor Detective. You can't detect on an empty stomach."

After Rick left, Betta stayed at the table to enjoy the flowers and another cup of coffee. This downtime in Orvieto would be just the break she was looking forward to, with a change of scenery, culture, and of course Rick. The sudden ringing of her phone was an unwelcome annoyance to her pleasant thoughts. She fished it from her purse and checked the number. The 0424 area code was familiar, her Veneto hometown of Bassano del Grappa, but the number itself was not. A shiver ran through her that something might have happened to her father.

"Hello?"

"Hello, Betta."

The low voice was all too familiar. Relief that nothing was wrong at home was replaced by annoyance with a touch of anger. She had not seen her ex-fiancé since that violent exchange on a back street in Bassano months earlier, after which she had pushed the pain of their relationship out of her mind. Its memory returned with the sound of his voice.

"Carlo, I don't want to talk to you."

"But we do need to talk, Betta. I'm not the same person you knew, I've reformed."

Could he possibly have been drinking at this hour? The words were slightly slurred and spoken slowly and deliberately. "We most definitely do not need to talk, Carlo. We have nothing to talk about. It's over. Move on."

He continued as if she had not spoken. "You'll see that I've changed. You will change your mind. Are you still with that cowboy?"

The question sent a chill through her. "Yes, if you must know."

"I would like another shot at him too, but not for the same reasons."

"After the last time you saw Rick, I would think you wouldn't be anxious to encounter him again. Carlo, our conversation is ended. Don't call me again."

"No Betta, I won't call again. The next time we talk will be in person."

The line went dead, and Betta stared at the phone.

◇◇◇

Since moving to Italy, Rick had found himself in more than one police station. They tended to look and smell the same, perhaps to help police feel at home when transferring from one assignment to another. But the police station in Orvieto was not a carbon copy of all the others. It was in a residential neighborhood and stood across from a grassy park cut by paths and shaded by tall pine trees. The building had been a residence at some point, a large one, and now he walked through an entrance hall into what must have once been the parlor or drawing room. Ever the linguist, he made a mental note to look up the origin of the term "drawing room," which on its face didn't make sense. This room had various dented metal chairs arranged against the windows of one wall, furniture at odds with the original décor. The long desk also failed to rise to its surrounding, though a bored policeman behind it sat in a slightly more comfortable, but also metal, chair. More agitated than bored were the three people who occupied chairs along the windows, no doubt waiting to wrestle with red tape that required a visit to the authorities. Rick walked past a line of bulletin boards to the desk. As he approached, the policeman looked up, deciding if this new arrival would be a problem. Knowing that it would be requested, Rick pulled out his *carta di identita'* and passed it to the uniformed man at the desk.

"My name is Riccardo Montoya, I would like to speak to the officer in charge of the investigation in the death of the American tourist. I have some information that could be helpful."

The policeman frowned, stared at Rick's ID, and picked up the phone on the desk.

"Just a moment." He punched a few numbers. Someone answered on the other end and the cop repeated, almost verbatim, what Rick had said. He handed the card back to Rick. "The inspector asks for you to please wait."

Rick inserted his plastic ID back into his wallet and walked to the bulletin board. It was the usual mix of public announcements, internal directives, and press releases, mostly written in an almost unintelligible Italian. At one side of the board, encased in glass, an explanation of the services provided by this substation was posted, as well as the few hours when the public would be received to avail themselves of them. The *questura*, the main police station, was located in the provincial capital of Terni, well to the east. The Orvieto operation was under the command of a *commissario*, but the space provided for his name and photograph was blank. Rick was moving his eyes to another part of the board when he heard a sharp voice behind him.

"We have no need for foreigners poking their noses into police business here."

Rick stiffened and turned toward the voice, but his frown immediately turned to a smile. Before him stood a man in a tailored suit who shared Rick's age as well as his grin. "And who have we here? None other than the renowned Detective Paolo LoGuercio."

"It is a small world indeed," said the policeman as he clapped Rick on the shoulder. "But that would be *Inspector* LoGuercio, *per favore.*

"And moving up the organizational ladder. No doubt due to your exploits in the north with which I am very familiar."

"That may have had something to do with it," answered LoGuercio, "but come back to my office and tell me what has happened in your life since then." He led the way through a door, along a corridor, to a room that originally must have had a bed and an armoire but now held a desk, files, and a small table and chairs. The tall window looked out onto a small patch of grass and an ivy-covered wall. Rick was offered a chair at one side of the table. "These chairs are not very comfortable, but you must remember that this is a police station. Before we get to this nasty business of the American woman, tell me how you've been. And *la bella* Erica?"

Rick took his seat and briefly brought LoGuercio up to date, though he was anxious to learn about the homicide. He omitted his subsequent brushes with police work and concentrated on those people the policeman had encountered when they'd met in the Tuscan hill town of Volterra. "Beppo Rinaldi," he concluded, "is doing fine, still chasing down art thieves, and Erica Pedana is in America. My translation business grows, so I have no plans to leave Rome."

"And your uncle continues in a position of prominence in the police there."

"You remember that family connection. *Bravo.* And your career has certainly not been stagnant, Paolo."

The inspector shifted in his chair. "It could be better. When I left Volterra they sent me south, not my choice but of course one does not have choices in this business. And my connections among the hierarchy were minimal. The assignment did not go well. Without going into detail, let's just say that a position was found for me here. Orvieto is a pleasant town, but a backwater for police work. By chance the *commissario* was transferred a few months ago and a replacement has yet to be named. So here I am when this murder happens. There is already pressure locally, and since I am the acting *capo* at the moment, it's all falling on me. If this crime isn't solved quickly, they may be sending me to someplace even more remote. Not that they are jumping to send me help with this murder, I've already been told to use my own resources. Depleted resources. To make things work, I've had to give up my conference room to the *Guardia di Finanza* who are conducting some kind of operation in the area. So I'll have to run this murder investigation out of my office."

He opened his jacket and pulled out a pack of cigarettes. Rick had not recalled him smoking in Tuscany, though they hadn't spent that much time together. Smoking was prohibited in public buildings in Italy, but who was going to complain?

"Which brings us to the reason for your appearance here today, Riccardo. Tell me what you know." LoGuercio had been sitting across from Rick, but now he got to his feet and walked to the desk, lighting a cigarette as he walked. He took a notebook from among the papers and extracted a pen from his jacket pocket.

"I saw the victim yesterday. Twice, in fact." He described, in as much detail as he could recall, the encounter with Rhonda Van Fleet in the funicular car, as well as what he witnessed from a distance in the piazza in front of the cathedral and the quick exchange later with the victim's daughter. LoGuercio took notes as he listened, glancing up only when Rick mentioned that he was traveling with a lady friend. "I hope that helps," Rick concluded.

"It helps considerably. As you know, hotels and *agriturismi* are required to send the police the names and identity information on their guests. Since finding the body last night we have begun to search those records for her, but now we know there are two more American women. It is most likely they were staying in the same hotel." He re-inserted the pen in his jacket and leaned back in the desk chair. "If we track down the other two, Riccardo, you will be called upon again to help us with your interpreting skills. I trust you would be willing? "

"Anything to help an old friend." Rick quickly slid his card across the table while trying not to show his excitement that he'd be involved in another murder investigation. "Tell me, Paolo, what do you know so far? The story in the paper this morning was quite sketchy. If you don't mind sharing, of course."

LoGuercio emitted a cough too deep for someone his age and put his cigarette out on an ashtray at one corner of his desk. "You are the nephew of a respected *commissario* who has assisted the police in the past. Why would I mind?" He opened a file on the desk and held up two sheets of paper. "We've just begun, of course. The forensics report won't arrive until later in the day. The technician called to the scene would only say she was sure it was homicide due to the types of injuries. None of the usual bruising or broken bones that come from being struck by a car, so that was ruled out. Also, the only marks on the ground next to the pavement were made from her body impacting it from above. No marks from the body being rolled or dragged along the ground, as often is seen in a hit-and-run. And no recent skid marks. But what conclusively ruled out a hit-and-run were the stab wounds, several of them to the abdomen. One doesn't normally get stab wounds from being hit by a car. But it's likely she was dumped in the spot from an automobile, though already dead from an unfortunate encounter with a sharp blade."

"Stabbed, and dumped like a bag of trash? The murderer appears to be especially vicious, or was in a hurry to dispose of the body. So you don't know exactly where the murder took place. It could have been here in town or out on some country road."

"One of many questions left unanswered, Riccardo. My assumption is that she was murdered, stuffed into the trunk of a car, and driven to where her body was dumped. At least we are sure it wasn't a robbery, since we found her purse intact and she was still wearing jewelry. Expensive jewelry."

"You got quite a lot of information from searching around in the dark."

The policeman shrugged. "We had lights. But the—" He was interrupted by a short buzz from his phone and raised a hand to Rick in apology as he picked it up. "He is? I suppose it's to be expected. I'll be right out to get him." He carefully placed the receiver down. "The head of tourism for the city is here. Concerned, I'm sure, about the effect of this crime on the image of Orvieto. This is one of those times when I wish they'd sent a new *commissario* by now. He could take the political heat." He reached out and took the ashtray in his hand. After dumping its contents in his waste basket, he put it in a desk drawer.

Rick got to his feet. "You'd better get used to it."

LoGuercio pushed a hand through his thick, black hair. "I suppose so."

He walked Rick out to the waiting room where a tall man in a dark suit stood in front of the desk, deep in conversation with a much shorter man. The tall man looked up, smiled at LoGuercio, and held up a finger to indicate he would be with him momentarily. He then returned to the short man. They spoke in low voices, but from their faces and gestures Rick could see that the discussion was anything but subdued.

LoGuercio leaned toward Rick's ear. "Besides being the city counselor with the tourism portfolio, Signor Livio Morgante, the taller man, is a successful businessman. He owns a pharmacy on one of Orvieto's main streets."

"Everyone needs aspirin," said Rick.

"And as if I didn't have enough trouble, the man with him is Luciano Pazzi, a so-called journalist. He is here to see me, I'm willing to bet, but now that he's run into Morgante he'll try to pump him for gossip on something else. Probably some local scandal, real or created inside the mind of Pazzi. The man is a menace."

The pharmacist raised his arm in a gesture Italians use to indicate that they'd heard enough. He strode toward Rick and LoGuercio, leaving Pazzi standing with a smirk on his face.

Morgante sported unfashionably long hair for someone who Rick guessed to be in his late fifties. The length and the dye job spoke of a man who'd decided his hair was a key factor in keeping him young. A wide smile and good looks added to the carefully cultivated aura of vitality, which was also the aura of a politician.

"Inspector LoGuercio, I hope I didn't interrupt anything." He looked from the policeman to Rick.

"Not at all. Signor Montoya was just leaving. May I present Riccardo Montoya, who may be able to help with the investigation. I trust you are here about the murder, Signor Morgante?"

The pharmacist gave LoGuercio a pained assent before shaking hands with Rick. "Just visiting Orvieto, Signor Montoya? I see you are an American, is there a chance you knew the victim?"

Rick and LoGuercio exchanged puzzled looks. "Why do you think I'm American? I hadn't said a word, so it couldn't have been my accent."

The man flashed what must have been a practiced campaign grin. "Your Italian is flawless, so I wouldn't have known anyway. No, it was the name Montoya, which I suspected was Spanish, at least in origin. But knowing there are many Spanish names in

America, I saw your footwear and came to the conclusion that you are from that country. Did I guess correctly?"

"The cowboy boots have blown my cover before. But in fact I proudly share both American and Italian nationalities and live in Rome. I'm up here for a few days. To do some tourism, which Paolo tells me is your specialty."

"It is the specialty of Orvieto, Signor Montoya. There is much to see."

"So I should be off to see it and allow you gentlemen to talk." Rick shook hands with both men and walked to the door.

His departure was followed closely by Luciano Pazzi. The journalist was now sitting in one of the metal chairs at the side of the room. Waiting patiently.

◇◇◇

Betta looked up at the cathedral from her place on the long, stone bench, its surface indented and shined by decades of tourist posteriors. Other early-risers, in twos and threes, were glad to have the seating, as hard as it might be. She studied the multicolored facade through a set of small binoculars and chatted with an elderly couple next to her. Noticing Rick walking into the far end of the piazza, she waved to get his eye. He returned the wave and walked to her.

"I didn't know you'd brought binoculars, Betta."

"I didn't, these nice people let me use theirs. It really helps to appreciate all the detail."

She gave the binoculars to the gray-haired man and thanked him before getting up to take Rick's arm. The couple smiled, as if recalling a fond memory, when Rick and Betta went toward the doors of the church. As they walked she listened carefully as he recounted his meeting at the police station. The square was not crowded; it was much too early for the Roman tour buses, and the tourists staying in the city's hotels were still enjoying their second cup of morning coffee. Afternoons, when sunlight bathed the west-facing front of the cathedral, was the best time to enjoy the spectacular facade. At this hour, shadow covered the steps they climbed to reach the entrance. Inside was even darker.

Both dipped their hands lightly in the font inside the door and crossed themselves. As the architect had intended, their eyes were drawn the length of the nave to a tall, arched window where light poured down through the stained glass, covering the altar.

"I can't believe you actually knew this policeman. No, now that I think about it, perhaps I can believe it. Why don't you become a cop and be done with it?"

"You sound like my uncle," Rick said, his eyes taking in the space.

The total lack of pews made a bare interior appear even larger. The only obstructions between the side walls were rows of thick columns that separated the nave from the two side aisles. Unadorned wood beams crisscrossed in support of the high roof above the nave before reaching the more ornate transept. Stone was the main material in this main part of the church—unadorned, cold, and permanent—in alternating black and white stripes. The layered pattern continued on the columns themselves, giving them the look of stacked Oreo cookies, though Rick opted not to share such a sacrilegious image with Betta. They were on their way to the Madonna di San Brizio chapel to see frescoes by Luca Signorelli, which she told him were among the great masterpieces of the Renaissance.

"You're going to interpret for the inspector when he interviews the other two women?"

"Once he tracks them down."

"That should be easy. *Mannaggia.*"

Rick's eyes jumped from the ornate transept ceiling down to Betta. "What's the matter?"

She pointed at a sign perched on a wooden easel. "We need tickets from the tourist office across the piazza to get into the chapel. It would have been nice to put the sign at the entry door." She turned.

"I'll get them, Betta. You stay here and read your guidebook so we know what we're looking at."

She waved her hand. "You paid for the funicular tickets, Rick. It's my turn. We agreed."

They walked back to the door and into the sunlight where more tourists had appeared and were peering up at the spires. Rick watched five old men, dressed in coats and ties, who stood in a circle listening to a sixth. Some important point, likely political, was being made by both word and gesture. Was there a town square in Italy that didn't have its own regular group of pensioners? Perhaps they were assigned their spots by the local authorities.

A small white car with the city coat of arms, the sole vehicle in the pedestrian-only square, almost blocked the steps into the tourist office. As they walked around it a man stepped from the door and called out.

"*Mi scusi*, I should not have parked so close, let me—Oh, it's you, Riccardo."

Rick introduced Betta to Livio Morgante, the man he'd just met in the police station. Morgante repeated his request to be excused for his parking job. "And you are starting your day of tourism in the shadow of our masterpiece." Their eyes moved with his to the cathedral. "It took over three hundred years to complete, if a cathedral can ever be called finished, under the hands of several architects. The mix of mosaics, sculpture, and architectural elements in the facade is unlike any other church in Italy, perhaps the world. But it is spectacular inside as well. Scholars come from all over the world to study the frescoes, though one does not need to be a scholar to appreciate them." They were words expected of the tourism chief, but despite the biased view, Rick and Betta nodded in agreement.

Morgante suddenly turned serious. "It causes me great sadness that a visitor who comes here to see such beauty, as this American woman did, could find such ugliness."

"Crime can and does happen anywhere, Signor Morgante."

"That may be true, Riccardo. We want all our visitors, without exception, to have an experience filled with beauty, whether they are staying here in town, renting villas in the countryside, or passing through."

"That will be the case with us, I'm sure," said Betta, trying to reassure the man. It appeared to work, for a smile returned to his face.

"But you two must let me give you a tour of the cathedral. I don't get to show off Orvieto often enough to visitors, I leave that to our professional guides. And it would be a small way to show my appreciation for the assistance you're giving to our police."

Rick held up a hand in protest but Morgante waved it off. "No, I insist. *Purtroppo,* I cannot be your guide at this moment, I have to get to my pharmacy. But I could do it today at, let's say, six o'clock? Would that work for you?"

Rick and Betta exchanged nods. "That would be much appreciated," Rick answered. "Let me give you my cell phone number in case something comes up."

Rick handed him his card, got one in return, and Morgante bade them goodbye before slipping into the city car and driving off, carefully avoiding the tourists. Rick and Betta watched the Fiat disappear into a side street.

"I can see why he is concerned about the murder, Rick. He's very passionate about his city."

Rick was looking at the card, which had the same Orvieto coat of arms as what was on Morgante's car and the building they'd passed the previous night. "Yes, you're right. But I noticed you neglected to complain about having to walk all the way back here to get tickets for the chapel."

"Next time, when I get to know him better."

They were interrupted by the muffled sound of the Lobo Fight Song, and Rick fumbled in his pocket to get his phone. It was not a number he recognized. "Montoya...*Si,* Paolo... ah, that's good...right now?" His face turned sheepish. Betta rolled her eyes, nodding her head. "Of course...we're in front of the cathedral...fine, see you then." He snapped the phone closed. "That was Paolo LoGuercio. They just tracked down the other two women to a rental villa north of Orvieto."

Rick looked at the phone, still in his hand. There was a frown on his face.

"What's the matter?" Betta asked.

He put the phone away and looked at her. "I may be getting too suspicious."

"If you're going to help out with this investigation, being suspicious is a good thing, Rick. What is it?"

"Paolo just called to say that the women rented a villa, and Morgante mentioned tourists in villas. Strange coincidence."

"He talked about all tourists, no matter where they are staying. You are right, you may be getting too suspicious. Besides, LoGuercio probably told him."

"Yes, you're right."

"So the inspector wants you to help him interrogate the two women?"

"Interview is a better term; interrogate sounds like we will be using blunt instruments."

"You won't?"

"Sorry to disappoint you. Can you see the sights on your own for a couple hours? I should be back for lunch, but I'll call you."

She patted his chest. "I'll be fine. Go do your civic duty."

From the distance came the distinctive sound of a police siren, its pulsing different, to the Italian ear, from those of a fire truck or ambulance. A few moments later the blue sedan burst into the square, slowing down immediately to a crawl to work its way through the pedestrians. Rick raised a hand and it drove to the spot where Morgante's car had been parked. LoGuercio unfolded from the front passenger seat and smiled at Betta before turning to Rick.

"Riccardo, now I really feel guilty for stealing your free time."

"Betta, this is Inspector Paolo LoGuercio. Paolo, Betta Innocenti."

LoGuercio bowed gallantly as he took her hand in both his. "It is indeed a pleasure, Betta." He inclined his head toward Rick and spoke in a stage whisper. "Riccardo, explain to me how such a woman as this would waste her time with some bumbling foreigner."

"I'm still trying to figure that out."

Betta laughed. "You two had better be on your way. The first few hours are always the most critical in a criminal investigation." Tourists who had been gazing at the church now watched the three people standing next to the idling police car. "I think these people are hoping you're about to push Rick down on the hood and put handcuffs on him."

"Ah, and she is also familiar with police work."

"She works for the art cops, Paolo. You have to agree that they do police work."

The inspector's tired eyes widened. "The art police. Well, we certainly know about them, don't we Riccardo? But she is correct, we should be off." He extended his hand. "Betta, it has been my great pleasure. We shall see each other soon, I trust. Unfortunately it will include Riccardo's company, but there is nothing I can do about that."

A few minutes later the car was flying down road to the valley, lights flashing. Each time a car appeared in its lane, the uniformed driver would send out a short yowl from the siren and roar past it. Rick and LoGuercio sat in the backseat, holding tightly to the handles above the doors.

The policeman fumbled with the cigarette pack in his pocket but left it there. "She's certainly different from Erica."

"Your powers of observation have not diminished, Paolo."

Chapter Five

Villa Felicità was the ironic name of the renovated stone farmhouse Rhonda Van Fleet had rented for herself, her daughter, Gina, and her friend Francine. Its foundation was dug into a sloping hill so that windows on both the upper floor and one side of the lower level looked out over the valley below. Wood and glass doors on the lower floor opened to a patio covered by a pergola woven with grape vines, their wide leaves shading the brick pavement from the afternoon sun. Beyond the patio stretched a rectangular pool, just big enough to do laps if the renters decided to abandon temporarily the *bel far niente* to engage in a bit of physical activity. It was a difficult choice, given the comfortable chairs on the patio and the view they afforded of the Umbrian countryside.

Though Rick and Inspector LoGuercio didn't realize it, the villa was visible, high in the distance, from several bends in the road. The driver had brought the speed down to what would be normal for an Italian driver on a deserted country road, making it easier for the two men in the back to converse. LoGuercio told Rick what he knew about the two women, which was no more or less than the basics required for the registration forms: names and passport information. Francine Linwood was the victim's friend. As Rick expected, the daughter had a different last name than her mother. Either she was married or had been, or even more likely, her father was a husband pre-dating Mister Van Fleet. They would find out more when the women were questioned.

"We're almost there," LoGuercio said. "The spot where the body was found is just around this bend. We can stop and look at it on the way back if you'd like. If we're fortunate, something these women tell us may give us reason to examine the scene again."

Crime tape, tied to bushes at the side of the road and poles stuck into the ground next to the pavement, delineated where the body had been found. A lone, young policeman watched the car approach and then raised his hand in a loose salute when he recognized it. The driver waved as he drove past. LoGuercio pointed at a sign a few meters from the crime scene.

"That's the bus stop for the line that goes between Orvieto and Acquapendente. It would be the one they would use."

The car slowed as the driver scanned the road ahead. "Here it is, sir." The Fiat turned off the pavement onto a gravel road and began a climb through tightly packed pine trees before bursting into open fields. At that point the driveway could have gone directly to the villa, but instead, perhaps for dramatic effect, it meandered through a few more slow curves. The gravel widened into a parking area in front of the house where a silver Mercedes was parked next to a police vehicle. A uniformed policeman standing between them looked up and walked toward the new arrivals.

"They're inside, Sir," said the policeman after LoGuercio and Rick emerged from the backseat of their car. "My English is not very good, but I think they understood. As you ordered, I only told them that their companion was found dead and that you were coming to talk to them."

The two women were sitting opposite each other in the living room, both dressed in exercise suits and sandals. The one with short gray hair who Gina had told Rick was named Francine, sat staring into the void, a glass of red wine close to hand. Gina sat cross-legged on the soft chair, her eyes closed, and Rick realized that she was meditating. It was a strange way to deal with the death of one's mother, but perhaps it worked for some people. The two looked up when the men entered the room. Both were visibly surprised to see Rick, Gina more than Francine.

The living room was what one would expect after seeing the quaint outside of the villa. The floors were brick and the walls white stucco with patches where the stone and mortar from the outside peeked through to the interior. A low ceiling was criss-crossed with dark wood beams, likely the originals, but one could never be sure in Italy. The rustic style of the structure continued with the furniture—simple yet comfortable, mostly natural wood with seats and backs covered by stuffed cushions.

"Gina, my sincere condolences for your loss."

She looked up at Rick, confusion on her face.

He turned to Francine. "Ms. Linwood, my name is Rick Montoya, I—"

"You were in the funicular yesterday." The gray-haired woman's comment matched her puzzled face. Her head snapped toward Gina. "You know him?"

"We talked on the street yesterday while you were having a drink. Before dinner."

"I'm completely confused," said the older woman. "Are you a policeman?"

"No, ma'am, this is Inspector LoGuercio, who is in charge of this investigation. He has asked me to help him ask you some questions, since his English is not perfect."

LoGuercio stepped forward and shook hands stiffly with both women, who were now on their feet. "I extend my condolences," he said in somber and heavily accented English before giving Rick a look which indicated that would be his limit.

"Thank you, Inspector," Francine.

Gina shook his hand but did not speak. Instead she settled back into the soft back of the chair and took several calming breaths. To the relief of LoGuercio, who stood in silence, Rick took charge.

"The Inspector understands your shock at the death of your mother and friend, but you will certainly agree that the investigation must move quickly. The two of you are essential in helping him get started, so if you can give us a few minutes of your time it would be appreciated."

"Of course," said Francine, looking between Rick and LoGuercio. Gina nodded but remained silent.

Rick used his most soothing voice. "We noticed the lovely patio as we drove up, perhaps we could use that. Gina, why don't we start with you?" He gestured toward the glass doors.

"You mean you want to talk to me alone?"

"That's the way they do it," Francine said with some impatience.

"Francine is correct," Rick said, and then turned to her. "Do you mind if I call you Francine? Please call me Rick."

She agreed, and the use of first names calmed Gina down somewhat. Francine sat back down as Gina led the two men through the door and out to the patio. On the round wood table two ceramic mugs sat on paper napkins and Rick suspected the women had been enjoying their morning coffee when the police appeared at their door. Without prompting, Gina sat at the table, followed by Rick and LoGuercio. They sat with their backs to the rolling valley view, which was just as well. Gina needed their full attention. She had pulled a tissue from somewhere in her clothing, dabbed her eyes, and slipped it back in place.

"Gina, I'll be interpreting everything that you say for the inspector, as well as everything he says, for you. It doubles the time needed for our interview, but there's no way around it, I'm afraid. Why don't you begin by telling him about your mother?"

Rick told LoGuercio what he had asked, and Gina began to speak. Rick stopped her every few sentences, and after a while the routine achieved a certain rhythm. As she spoke she became more calm, and during the interpretation breaks she sometimes closed her eyes, either composing her next sentences or simply meditating. Rick wasn't sure.

"My mother lived in Arizona. Scottsdale, to be exact. Many people would consider her fortunate, if wealth is the most important factor for happiness, but in fact her life was anything but easy. She managed to find three husbands, one of whom was my father, and when the marriages ended in divorce she was left each time with favorable alimony. Very favorable. After the third divorce I think she realized that she wasn't meant for marriage, so she put all her energy and time into her pottery, something she'd gone back to after her first marriage ended. She had learned the craft when she studied here, but you probably know that."

Rick stopped her and quickly interpreted for LoGuercio before turning back to Gina. "No, this is news to the inspector. She was here in Italy?"

"Here in Orvieto. Some kind of exchange program when she was in college. She had taken Italian courses so she already spoke the language. I hadn't heard her speak it until this trip, and it sounded quite fluent."

LoGuercio said something to Rick after hearing the Italian, and Rick nodded.

"She had friends here, Gina? Was she going to meet people she knew back then?"

"If she was, she didn't tell me, but that wouldn't be surprising, given our relationship. We haven't talked much in years, and as you know I live in a different state. I was surprised when she invited me along on this trip, since it was clearly some kind of nostalgia thing for her. But given her health issues, I couldn't refuse."

"Health issues?"

"Of course, you wouldn't know about that either. She was diagnosed with terminal cancer recently. That's why she wanted to return, while there was still time. She hadn't been back to Italy since she was here in college."

Rick remembered what he'd seen in the square in front of the cathedral. "Your mother never told you she was going to look up anyone here, but do you think she did?"

"Absolutely. She saw someone in front of the church just after we got into town yesterday, though we couldn't see who it was. And then she disappeared just before dinner at the restaurant."

"Tell us about yesterday," Rick said, at the request of the policeman.

"We were finally getting over our jet lag, after two nights of falling asleep in the afternoon and then waking up in the middle of the night. So we had enough energy to venture out further than the trattoria five minutes from here. Mom insisted we take the bus into town instead of driving the rental car. She said it was the best way to get a feel for the people, and we would have trouble finding a place to park legally anyway. The bus line ended at the little square where we got on the funicular. On the ride up is when we saw you."

Rick nodded, but said nothing.

"The bus dropped us at the cathedral, which is where we started our sightseeing. That's where Mom saw someone, but since she didn't tell us, maybe it wasn't who she thought it was. She wouldn't tell us. We walked around the town for the rest of the afternoon, and had early dinner at a restaurant there. I don't remember the name, but Francine should. She has a better memory than me."

"You said your mother disappeared before dinner."

"Right. That's when I met you. Mom said she had something to do, and we didn't press her on what it was, knowing she would have told us if she'd wanted to. She eventually showed up at the restaurant. She tried not to show it, but she was a bit agitated."

"How long was she gone?"

"About a half hour. Maybe forty-five minutes."

"Then what happened?"

"After our meal, Mom told us she was going to meet someone, an old friend she'd run into earlier. Francine and I assumed it was the person she saw in front of the church, but it could have been who she saw before dinner, if indeed she'd met with someone."

"So you and Francine came back here?"

"Yes, Francine had it all worked out. We got on the bus where it had dropped us off, at the bottom of the funicular, and our stop is close to the driveway up to the villa."

"We passed it on the way here." He didn't mention the crime-scene tape. "The rest of the evening…?"

"Francine and I had a drink out here and I went to bed. It was about ten."

"You didn't hear your mother come in?"

She shook her head. "She took the best of the bedrooms, of course, which is the one here on the ground floor. Our rooms are upstairs. If she came in I didn't hear her." Her eyes narrowed in thought. "But she wouldn't have come back and then gone out again, would she?"

"We don't know, Gina."

After Rick finished interpreting he asked LoGuercio what other questions he had.

The policeman shrugged. "At this point we usually ask if they have any idea who could have killed the victim, but I'm not sure she can offer anything."

Rick turned back to the woman, who had been trying to understand a word or two, but without success. "Gina, do you have anything else you can offer that could be of help to the inspector? Does something come to mind?"

Her lips quivered and Rick wondered if she was going to break down. "I wish I could, Rick. If only I could. I can't believe that someone she knew could have done this, she must have just found herself in the wrong place at the wrong time, and…" She pulled out the tissue.

Rick looked at LoGuercio who was holding up a hand to indicate they'd heard enough for the moment. He took the hint. "You've been very helpful, Gina, and if you can think of anything that might help, even some tiny detail, you can call me. I'll leave my cell phone number with you both." He got to his feet. "Could you ask Francine to come out, please?"

She nodded and gave both men a wooden smile before going back inside. Rick sat down and watched LoGuercio flipping through the pages of his notebook.

"You handled the woman very gently, Riccardo, and I think that helped to get her to open up. We will talk with her again, but for the moment there is much to be done. We must find out who Signora Van Fleet knew when she was a student here years ago. I suspect that at least one of them is still living in Orvieto. We Italians tend to stay close to our birthplace, unlike you Americans. Unless we're policemen."

As LoGuercio was speaking, the door had opened and Francine Linwood appeared on the porch. She had taken advantage

of the time to change into a different outfit—a long, loose skirt
and a blouse, with sandals—as well as put on some makeup. She
carried a coffee mug. Rick stood and motioned her to the chair
just vacated by Gina. Rick was about to explain the interpreting
drill but she spoke first.

"Where did this take place, Rick? Is her body in some morgue
somewhere? When can we arrange to have her sent back home?"

"Since this just happened," Rick answered, "I'm not sure if
the police have advised the embassy. They will assign a consular
officer to deal with these issues." He left her other questions
unanswered.

"If there is an issue about next of kin, Gina is it. Rhonda's parents are long gone, as you would expect for someone of our age."

Rick quickly interpreted for LoGuercio and turned back
to Francine. "So you and Gina are it? No other close friends?"

For the first time, Francine showed some emotion, covering
her mouth with her hand and blinking. "I think I was her closest friend. Much more so than even Gina. They weren't quite
estranged, but nearly."

"Francine," said Rick, "we regret that you have to go through
this questioning, but it has to be done."

Her answer was a wave of the hand and nods. LoGuercio
took out his note pad.

"How long had you known Rhonda?" Rick asked.

Francine's chest slowly rose and fell as she took in a long
breath and let it out. "Let me see. We go back a long time, we
were in college together, and were in the same sorority. One of
the years we were roommates. I remember when she went off
to this exchange program here—did Gina tell you about that?"
Rick nodded, and she continued. "The sorority sisters joked back
then that she did it to marry some rich Italian count. That didn't
happen, of course, though she later did well—in a monetary
way—with the husbands she had."

While Rick interpreted she took a drink of whatever was in
the mug.

"Rhonda was very different when she returned from the year abroad. I guess that would be expected, and I understand it more now that I'm here. The different culture, the history, the food; it would change anyone."

"You've been close to Rhonda ever since college."

"No, in fact we lost touch for many years. I married someone and lived on the coast, but it didn't work out and I ended up moving back to Arizona. We ran into each other in 2000, I remember since it was just after my divorce. I went into her pottery shop—did Gina mention that Rhonda had a shop?" Again Rick nodded. "I went into her pottery shop and we recognized each other. You know how women are, after a few minutes it was like we'd never been apart. She had also just gone through a divorce, even nastier than mine, so we quickly found that we had as much in common as when we were back in school."

"How did this trip come about?"

"It was Rhonda's idea, of course. She'd been talking about it for a long time, but then she found out about some serious health issues, which made the trip more urgent. I'm sure Gina told you about Rhonda's cancer. How ironic, since now she's gone. She also decided that she had to return to Orvieto, where she'd spent that year when she was a student. We were going to stay in a few other cities, but that changed when she got the news from the doctor."

"So just Orvieto."

"This was it for me and Gina, but Rhonda was going to spend a few days in Milan by herself after the villa. She didn't tell us why."

Rick's translation caused a flicker in LoGuercio's eye as he took notes.

"We arrived three mornings ago, stayed in Rome one night, then picked up the car and drove here. We were still exhausted, so yesterday was our first foray into town. We took the bus, at Rhonda's insistence, and it turned out she was right. Parking would have been a nightmare, and it was fun coming up on the funicular. That was when we saw you, of course."

She smiled and brushed back a tuft of the short hair.

"And what happened after that?"

"The bus dropped us in the square in front of the cathedral. Rhonda was so excited to see it, since I guess it's kind of the symbol of the town, so it brought back a lot of memories. We were taking in that gorgeous facade when she slipped away and talked with someone. Someone from her time here, of course."

"Had she told you before the trip that she was planning on meeting anyone from her exchange year?"

"No. But Rhonda keeps her relationships to herself. Kept, I should say."

"Did you see the person in front of the cathedral?"

"No, but now I wish I had. After that, Rhonda was still excited, being back in Orvieto and all, but seemed a bit distracted. We walked around and saw other things: churches, old buildings, some other beautiful plazas. And shops—we went into a lot of stores. She was very interested in the ceramics shops, since that's what she makes—I mean, made—back home. And what she studied when she was here. There were a lot of shops selling ceramics."

"And then?"

"We had dinner. It was early by Italian standards but we were hungry and Gina was starting to fade. We went to some place that was in a basement, brick ceilings and floors. I forget the name but Rhonda said it has something to do with rope, or rope makers. We were the first ones in the restaurant, but by the time we left it was about half full."

She held out her hand as if to hold a thought. "Wait, I forgot. She took us to the restaurant but instead of going in, she said she had something to do and would meet us there later. Gina went for a walk, but I went in and ordered a bottle of wine. When Rhonda showed up I didn't even bother asking her where she'd been. I knew she wouldn't tell us."

She looked up when a slight gust blew in from the grassy area around the pool, bringing a few stray leaves with it. The breeze picked up the earthy smell of the geraniums planted in terra cotta pots at the edge of the brick. A few of their red blossoms fluttered down like confetti, joining the leaves in a dance around the patio before the gust vanished and they fell lightly to the ground.

"When we left the restaurant, Rhonda told us she was going to meet a friend and that we could get the bus back to the villa. From the way she said it, there was no question in my mind that she wanted to be alone, so I didn't even suggest we go with her. She pointed us in the right direction, and I took over from there since Gina is useless with directions. We got back here about nine o'clock, but I don't wear a watch so I'm not really sure of the time without the usual cues I have at home, like TV programs. We each had a glass of wine and then Gina went to bed. She was completely beat. I had another glass and turned in myself, hoping to sleep through the night, which I did. We were having our coffee this morning when your policeman arrived."

Rick interpreted, got a question from LoGuercio, and turned back to Francine.

"You said that Rhonda didn't say who she was going to meet last night. Did she at least say it was the person she ran into in front of the cathedral?"

"She wouldn't tell us, but it was normal for Rhonda to be secretive. Especially if it involved men. I thought at the time, which is terrible to think of now, that after dinner she was meeting some man. I even thought that she really hadn't met anyone in the square and she was really going to meet Donato."

"Donato?"

"He's the caretaker for the villa. I don't remember his last name. Some long Italian word."

LoGuercio frowned and wrote in his notebook when he heard the name.

"So she didn't even confirm that it was a man she was going to meet?"

"I don't believe she did, Rick, now that I think about it. I suppose it could have been a woman. It's just that, knowing Rhonda…" She didn't finish the sentence.

LoGuercio looked at his notes after hearing the translation. "Most of what she said, Riccardo, confirms what we heard from the daughter. You can tell her now where we found the body. Perhaps that might spark something in her memory, and I want to see her reaction."

Rick turned to Francine, who had been watching the two men talk. "To answer your earlier question, he is not sure where the murder took place, but the body was found on the road near your bus stop."

"You mean right down at the end of the driveway? Someone was waiting for her when she got off the bus? It could have been us if the murderer had been there a few hours earlier." She pulled nervously at a large silver and turquoise ring on her left hand and her eyes darted between the two men. "Are we in danger?"

Rick wanted to answer directly, but decided he should leave it to LoGuercio.

"Tell her we don't think she has anything to fear. It is almost certain, based on what she and the daughter told us, that this crime is connected to the victim's previous time in Orvieto. And tell her again we don't know where the murder actually happened. But if she likes, I can assign a policeman to the villa."

Rick interpreted, and his words seemed to calm Francine.

"Yes, the inspector is right. It has to be someone she knew before. No need to put a man here whose time would be better spent helping to find the killer."

"If you change your mind, you can call me and I'll tell Inspector LoGuercio."

"Thank you, Rick, I appreciate your concern." For the first time her lips formed into a tired smile.

Rick got a nod from LoGuercio which he took to mean that the interview was over. They both got to their feet, followed by Francine, and the policeman shook her hand and thanked her in accented English. She said he was welcome, and expressed hope that the investigation would be successful. Rick didn't bother interpreting.

"So you live in Orvieto," she said to Rick.

"No, I live in Rome and work as a translator and interpreter. I came up with a friend to do some tourism and got drawn into the investigation."

"She must be the cute girl you were with on the funicular. If I were her I'd be annoyed that you'd abandoned me."

She turned and walked to the glass door. Following her inside, they found Gina still sitting on the sofa, tightly holding a coffee mug. Rick left two of his cards with his cell phone number, asked them to call if they remembered anything else that could be helpful, and he and the inspector saw themselves out.

◇◇◇

"I have much to do," said LoGuercio as he flipped through his notes. The car retraced the route back to Orvieto, but at a slower speed, making Rick wonder if LoGuercio had said something to the driver. There was no need to hold on this time. "Starting with this caretaker, Donato." He tapped on a line of his notes. "Wouldn't it be easy if he confesses to meeting our victim last night and doing her in? I could go back to petty crime, you could return to sightseeing full time, and our tourism chief could get off my back."

"It's never that simple, Paolo, in life or in crime. And the killer has to be someone she knew when she was here as a student, almost certainly the person she ran into in the piazza or someone she saw later. The two women don't appear to be capable of murder, or even to have a motive."

"Nor do they have an alibi. Either or both of them could have been waiting at the bus stop when she got off. My men are tracking down the driver of the bus on the final run last night. According to the schedule, it would have reached the stop near the villa at about eleven-twenty last night en route to Acquapendente."

"About a half hour after the women went to bed. Or said they went to bed."

"Precisely."

"Do you really think she was attacked after getting off the bus?"

LoGuercio shook his head. "I do not. The scenario of being murdered somewhere else still makes sense. She must have told the murderer where she was staying. He offers to drive her there, and kills her at a secluded spot somewhere on the way. Then he puts her body into the trunk and drops it at the side of the road to make it appear that she was killed after getting off the bus."

"So you can start looking for possible locations between Orvieto and where the body was found, to look for the actual murder scene."

LoGuercio gestured at the low hills on either side of the car. "It could take a while."

Five minutes later the car slowed into a turn and began the climb up to the city.

"Over there," LoGuercio said, while pointing to one side of the road, "are some fascinating Etruscan burial grounds which you really should visit. A stone city of the dead in the shadow of Orvieto's cliff, a very evocative place. Are you planning on seeing some Etruscan ruins this trip, Riccardo?"

"I think I had my fill of things Etruscan the last time we met, Paolo."

"Perhaps you're right. There is enough history here that is of a more recent vintage. Which reminds me that with all this going on I have not heard enough about what you have been doing since Volterra. Are you and the lovely Betta free for lunch? Despite the demands of the job, even a policeman must pause to take in nourishment."

"Especially when there is no *commissario* to keep you working at your desk at lunch time."

LoGuercio grinned, and it struck Rick that it was the first time since they'd met earlier in the day that he'd seen the man smile.

"I am shocked, Riccardo, that you would think such a thing." He pulled out his notebook, scribbled something on a blank page, tore it out, and passed it to Rick. "I will reserve a table at this place for the three of us at one o'clock."

Chapter Six

Betta read from her red guidebook while Rick stood, arms crossed over his chest, and took in the stone beauty of Orvieto's Palazzo del Popolo. As she spoke of individual aspects of the building's architecture—the tall arches of the ground floor, trifore windows on the representational second floor, and pointed battlements on the roof—his focus moved accordingly. His eyes stayed on the battlements, called *merli*, which also means "blackbird" in Italian. The rows of jutting stone did indeed look like huge blackbirds from below. Rick knew that *merli* in Guelph towns, whose government supported the pope, were designed in one way, while the Ghibelines, who backed the emperor, had a different shape. He could never remember which was which, but since Betta's guidebook had noted the various popes who had taken refuge in Orvieto over the centuries, he guessed these to be Guelph. Betta put a red string in the page and closed the book.

"The stairway is the most impressive feature," she said, looking up.

Ten people abreast could have climbed the stone stairs to the landing before swinging around to climb another set to reach the wide balcony under the arched windows of the second floor.

"What year did they start construction of the building?"

She opened to the same page. "Eleven fifty-seven."

"No handicap ramps required in those days."

"Unfortunately not."

"Since they don't have a *capitano del popolo* anymore, what do they use the building for now?"

"Conventions, meetings, big events. There's a large hall on the second floor."

"I'll bet the Albuquerque Convention Center has one that's larger."

"What?"

"Nothing. Did you notice those kids over there drawing the building? Let's go take a look."

They walked to the far end of the plaza where about a dozen students of college age sat on fold-up stools armed with sketch pads and pencils. Thanks to the internationalization of clothing styles, it was difficult to tell young people of one country from those of another just from their dress. Jeans, loose-fitting shirts, and casual footwear were worn by everyone. But something about their body language gave Rick the sense that these kids were Americans. There was an adult, somewhat older than Rick, who prowled behind the group, making comments as he did. He also had the aura of an American, but was trying valiantly to look Italian.

"Art class?" Rick said to him as they both looked over the shoulder of one of the students. The man didn't seem surprised to hear a question in English.

"Drawing. But with a bit of architectural history. We try to cram as much history in the program as we can."

"Some kind of semester abroad program?"

"That's right." The man extended his hand. "I'm Gus Suarez. Your first visit to Orvieto?"

Rick shook the hand. "Rick Montoya. No, I was here a few years back. Is the program connected to one university?"

"Arizona State. It's where I teach. But we get students from other colleges."

"Arizona State?" The professor might not have noticed the change in Rick's voice, but Betta, who was standing nearby, certainly did.

"Has the program been around a while?" Rick asked.

"Quite a while, actually. I think it was started in the nineteen seventies. Do you know someone back in the States who might want to apply?"

"I just might. Is there an office here in Orvieto where I can get information?"

"Sure." He took a pen from his pocket, as well as a pad that looked more appropriate for sketching than note taking. "Here's the address and the name of the director. Bob is there much of the day, either teaching classes or in his office. Of course you can also go online."

"Thanks, Gus, I'll do that."

Rick and Betta strolled away while the professor went back to his charges, all of whom were immersed in their work. Their eyes had stayed on either the building or their own drawings while the two men conversed.

"This could be a break for the murder case, Betta."

"I thought you'd been talking with the guy about architecture."

"Not at all. These kids are in a university exchange program which has to be the same one our murder victim participated in years ago. I've got to call Paolo."

He pulled out his phone and dialed while Betta watched twenty elderly Italian tourists shuffle into the plaza from a side street. Their guide, a neatly dressed man in his twenties, walked backwards as he spoke in a strong, high voice. Except for a few old stragglers in the back, the guide managed to keep everyone's attention, despite not seeing what he must have been talking about.

Rick tapped his phone off. "Paolo gave us the green light to talk to the exchange program director about the case. When I read off the address he told me where it is. Not far from here, in fact."

"Doesn't he want to be along?"

"He would, but he's on his way to interview the caretaker of the villa."

Betta frowned and shook her head. "But you can't do that. You're not with the police."

Rick took her hand and they started walking toward the far end of the piazza. "No, but you are."

◇◇◇

"He's there, Sergeant."

LoGuercio hung up the cell phone and tucked it into his jacket pocket. The trip would not be a waste of time, and Donato would not have time to flee, though the inspector doubted this was his murderer. As Riccardo had said, that would be too easy.

The dark blue police car slowed as it reached a row of four plain, two-story houses just off the road. They had been built by the same *ingegnere*, from the same set of plans, down to the stone walls separating one from the other. No need for an expensive architect here. A few feet of grass and dirt separated the pavement from the simple fences in front of the houses. As these were the only structures on this stretch of highway, there was no call for a sidewalk, assuming anyone wanted to visit the neighbors. Each house had a dirt driveway that cut through grass and hedges to reach a one-car garage. Behind, between the houses and a heavily wooded hill, small patches of vegetable gardens squeezed between more low walls.

"It's the last one, Sir."

The car pulled off the pavement and came to a stop in front of the fourth house in the row. As LoGuercio got out of the backseat he saw a man rushing around the side of the house and walking briskly toward him. He was in his late twenties and wore a stylish cotton sweater and blue jeans, both accenting his physique. In an affected, almost feminine gesture, he brushed back a shock of long black hair from his forehead. LoGuercio noticed that it had been a few days since this face had seen a razor, either in a nod to fashion or an indication of his standards of hygiene. The man was almost breathless when he got to the policeman's car, just outside the gate.

"Can we talk out here, Inspector? I don't want to upset my mother."

LoGuercio leaned against the fender of the car and sized up the man before him. "Of course, Donato. This shouldn't take long, if you can answer my questions satisfactorily."

"I'll do my best."

"Let's begin with where you were last evening."

The caretaker answered without having to think about it. He had been ready for the question. "I was here. I had dinner with my mother and we watched TV before going to bed at about eleven."

"You both stayed up until eleven?"

"Well, uh, no. Mama goes to sleep earlier than I do."

"You didn't go out at all after dinner?"

"I told you I went to bed at eleven, didn't I?"

LoGuercio couldn't decide if the man's tone was from anger or nervousness. He would have one of his men interview the neighbors to ask if they heard any cars leaving or returning from the last house during the night. It would be no use questioning Donato's mother.

"Tell me about all your contacts with the three Americans."

Donato looked quickly at the window of his house. "I was there when they arrived. On change-over day I check to see that the cleaning crew has done their work and the villa is ready for the new renters, and then I'm there when they drive up. There was a drip in one of the showers, which I fixed. When they got to the villa I gave them the key and showed them how everything worked. Where to turn the lights on, how to run the dishwasher, that kind of thing."

"This is in English?" LoGuercio folded his arms across his chest as he waited for the answer.

"One of the reasons I got the job is that I had studied English in the *liceo*."

LoGuercio's arm snapped out, its fist catching the man in the chest. Donato lurched back and managed to keep his balance. His face showed surprise and fear. The driver kept his eyes on the ground.

"That doesn't answer my question, Donato," the policeman snapped.

"About half and half, Sir. The woman who was killed, Signora Van Fleet, she spoke Italian and wanted to use it. That annoyed the other two, especially Signora Linwood. I had greeted them in English so they knew I spoke it."

LoGuercio nodded, as if nothing had happened, and his voice returned to its previous soothing tone. "After you showed them how to wash the dishes, you left?"

"That's correct, Inspector." He stole another glance at the window.

"Did you see them again?"

"The next afternoon. Even though the renters are given my cell phone number, in case there's a problem, the owner wants me always to come by to be sure everything is to their satisfaction. Happy clients tend to come back the following year."

"The women were there, I assume?"

"They were, but I only spoke with two of them. The young woman was sleeping."

"And after that?"

"It was the last time I saw any of them, Inspector. I was planning on going over today. To offer my condolences, of course."

LoGuercio shook his head. "I'd rather you didn't have contact with them just yet, Donato." He handed him a card. "If that shower starts leaking again, call me and we'll take care of it."

As he drove back to the city, LoGuercio went over in his mind what the caretaker had said, and just as importantly, how he'd reacted to the questions. It was all just what he'd expected. He'd never questioned anyone in a murder case who hadn't been nervous, so that part was no surprise. The bit of initial bravado, again, was nothing he hadn't seen before in both suspects and innocent witnesses. He was concerned, of course, that Donato had no real alibi for the time of the murder. That just added him to the list of people, starting with the two American women, who couldn't prove their whereabouts at the time of the murder. LoGuercio stared out the window of the car as it made the sweeping turn for the climb to the city.

◇◇◇

When the Italian state was created in the nineteenth century, and Rome was selected as the permanent capital, a real estate crisis was created on the banks of the Tiber. Where would they put everyone needed to administer the new united Italy? A temporary solution was quickly found. The pope had refused to recognize the existence of this upstart new kingdom which had swallowed up what had been his Papal States, including Rome itself. When the pope went into voluntary exile in the Vatican, the new government acted. It took over hundreds of papal properties in the Eternal City, perfect for the offices of bureaucrats streaming in from all parts of the boot. It would be a temporary solution, to be sorted out when time permitted. A century and a half later, many of those buildings, including former monasteries and convents, were still filled with the desks of government workers. Ornate rooms inside those buildings, once used for prayer and reflection, now took on a different use. Speeches and discussion on decidedly non-religious subjects echoed through them under the gaze of haloed saints painted on walls and ceilings. Tucked in the back of those rooms, when the audience was international, were glass booths. Inside them toiled interpreters like Rick Montoya.

So Rick knew his convents, and as ex-convents went, this one in Orvieto was not that impressive, starting with the door. Even the *portone* to Rick's apartment in Rome was larger. A rectangular brass plate, with words in both English and Italian, identified the building as the site of the university program. The only vestige of the structure's former vocation was a cross carved into the keystone above the arched doorway. Rick was reaching for the handle when the door opened and two young men started to exit. When they saw Betta they stopped and gestured for her to come in, unabashedly checking her out as she passed.

"May I come in too?" Rick said in English, getting their attention. The two grinned and stood aside while he entered.

After passing a bulletin board covered with small and large scraps of paper announcing events around the city, they came to a corridor that stretched left and right. Ahead was an open area which might have been where the sisters in centuries past walked, quietly saying their rosaries. Today small groups of students sat on the patchy grass, chatting and laughing. One of them noticed Rick and Betta, got to her bare feet and walked to them.

"Can I help you find someone?"

She must not have noticed my cowboy boots, Rick decided, but was pleased the girl had used Italian. To encourage her, as he always did in such situations, he answered in the same language.

"Do you know if Professor Romano is here? We'd like to speak with him."

"I think he is," said the girl. "His office is the last one down the corridor on the right."

They thanked her and walked in the direction she had indicated, passing one empty classroom before coming to a door at the end of the arched passage marked "Director." Rick tapped on the door and a voice called from inside.

"*Avanti.*"

Rick and Betta exchanged glances and she walked first into the room. It was a spartan office, furnished with a wood desk facing the wall, a couple of chairs to one side, and a tall floor lamp which lit most of the ceiling but little below it. A single, high window did its best to add more light to the room. The only decoration, save for a poster of the Orvieto Cathedral over the desk, was a lonely potted plant near the door. Professor Romano was dressed casually: blue jeans and what may have been the only Hawaiian shirt in Orvieto. No hair remained on the top of his head, and what there was along the sides and back had been grown long and tied in a small ponytail. It was a hairstyle Rick had seen many times in New Mexico, and it never failed to amaze him. Romano finished what he was writing on the computer in front of him and twirled around in his chair. He pushed a puzzled look from his face and turned it into a welcoming smile as he rose from the chair.

"Robert Romano. How can I help you?" It was said in heavily accented Italian.

"I am Detective Innocenti, Professor," replied Betta, "with the police." She pulled her identification from her pocket and allowed the man to look at it before stuffing it back. "Do you have a few moments to talk? This is Signor Montoya."

His puzzled look had returned at the word "police," and became more pronounced when Rick was introduced. "*Per favore*," he said, gesturing toward the two empty chairs while closing the door to the office and retreating to his own seat.

"Professor Romano," Rick said in English, "I am Detective Innocenti's interpreter, should it be necessary. But you appear to speak Italian well." It was a compliment without foundation.

Romano settled into his chair and spoke in English with a halting voice. "You are very kind, Mr. Montoya. Despite my name, my Italian is sufficient only for dealing with waiters and shopkeepers. Speaking with a policewoman is another matter. So I would very much appreciate some assistance. Montoya? I know several Montoyas in Arizona."

"There are pages of us in the phone book in Albuquerque, where my father is from."

The professor stared blankly, curious about how the guy from New Mexico had made his way into his office. But curiosity about the police matter won out. "How may I be of assistance to the detective?"

They quickly settled into the interpreter's routine. Romano did not seem to notice that Rick was mostly asking the questions and then translating them and the answers for Betta.

"She wanted me to tell you immediately," Rick began, "that this has nothing to do with any of your students or the program now."

Romano glanced at Betta. "Thank you for that." To Rick he said: "But why…?"

"There was a murder committed last night in Orvieto, and it was an American woman. She was an exchange student in the city about thirty-five years ago, and the police think she could have been enrolled in this program."

"That's terrible, just terrible. If she was participating in a university semester abroad program, not some high school exchange program, ours was almost certainly the one she was on. There haven't been any other American universities here, at least not that I know of. But wait a minute. I think I can look it up in our database." He swiveled back to his computer. "What was her name?"

Rick told him and then translated the exchange for Betta.

"What we need from him, Rick, is the name of anyone still in Orvieto who would have known her back then."

"I'm on it, Detective."

While they waited for Romano to search his records, their eyes wandered about the room, but found little of interest. There was not even a filing cabinet, a virtual requirement of any Italian office, making Rick think that the university had gone paperless. Thousands of trees allowed to live long and happy lives, while the professor kept his fingers crossed that the system wouldn't crash.

"Here she is, Rhonda Van Fleet. At that time she was Rhonda Davis, so she must have updated her information with the alumni office. Studied fine art here from October of 1979 until May of 1980."

"What courses did she take?"

Romano shrugged. "The records don't go into that kind of detail. But I don't think the curriculum has changed that much. Italian language and culture, art and architectural history with an emphasis on Umbrian, and then whatever specialty she was interested in. Could be painting, ceramics, sculpture; it's up to the student's interest."

"Apparently it was ceramics. She became quite an accomplished potter, we understand."

"Did she? Many of our alumni have gone on to distinguish themselves."

Betta's look, directed at Rick, was as good as a poke in his ribs.

"The detective would like to know if there might be anyone here now who was involved in the program at that time. She knows it was a long time ago, but—"

"Yes, in fact there is. Doctor Tansillo." The man's head turned sharply from Rick to Betta, causing his ponytail to twitch. "Luigi Tansillo was the administrator when the program began. Every year we celebrate the anniversary, and every year he appears and joins in the toasts. He loves chatting with the students and telling stories about the old days. It would not surprise me if he remembers Rhonda Davis."

◇◇◇

Rick looked up at the cloudless sky. It was the kind of weather that Livio Morgante and his employees in the Orvieto tourism office had to be relishing—perfect temperature and no chance of precipitation. Even the smallest bar managed to squeeze a few tables into the street in front of its doorway, luring passersby to stop for a cup or glass. The chairs provided a perfect perch to watch a pedestrian parade with as many Orvietani as tourists. Young and old office workers had found excuses to stroll the streets for a few minutes in shirtsleeves and sunglasses before returning reluctantly to their cubicles and computers.

The route to the restaurant, which Romano had explained in excruciating detail, took Rick and Betta back past their hotel along Via Maitani, named for the most prominent architect of the Duomo. The naming was appropriate, since the street ended at the square in front of the cathedral. A rectangular slice of the colorful facade became wider as they neared the piazza, finally bursting into full view when they came to the corner. Fewer people stood in cathedral square than when Rick had driven off with LoGuercio that morning, and now most of them were tourists. The locals had already begun drifting off to restaurants or homes for their midday meal, leaving the streets to the visitors. Once again Betta and Rick stopped to appreciate the work of Maitani and others. It was impossible to pass the facade without doing so.

"I know what you're thinking, Betta. Yes, we will get inside to see those Signorelli frescoes. Perhaps this afternoon."

"Unless you have to go with Paolo to interview this professor Tansillo."

"The inspector can do that without my help."

"But if he asks you to accompany him you wouldn't turn him down."

"How could I? My uncle would never forgive me if I shirked my civic duty."

They had begun to walk when Betta stopped him, grasping his arm with her hand. "Have you called Piero about this case?"

"Excellent point. He will be so pleased that I've gotten involved with a murder investigation that he may not show his disappointment with my lack of success with Fabrizio." He took out his phone. "I'll call him now."

Betta pushed her hands into her jacket pockets and waited while Rick dialed.

"My dear nephew, I trust you have good news."

"The weather is beautiful, Zio, Orvieto is a jewel, and we had an excellent dinner last night. Betta is right here and sends warm regards."

"So you were not able to convince your cousin to stop this foolishness." Rick could not help but notice a disappointment in the man's voice.

"Not during my first encounter with the lad yesterday, but that was just an initial foray. I didn't want to come on too heavily until I got a feel for the situation."

"Which you now have?"

"I'm afraid so. Let's just say that Fabrizio is getting some good ideas for his future as an author, assuming he writes romance novels." Betta frowned and shook her head.

"That's what I was afraid of. Well, do your best."

"But I was calling about something else, Zio."

"The murder of the American woman?"

Betta laughed and Rick raised his arms in exasperation before returning the *telefonino* to his ear. "You know already?"

"It's the kind of crime that comes across my computer screen, Riccardo. I saw that your man from Volterra is in charge of the investigation. Are you already assisting him?"

Rick sighed. "Yes, Zio, I am."

"That's good, since I just recommended to him that he get you involved. Just so you don't forget what you're really up there for."

"Your recommendation will sound like an order."

"That's fine. From what I've heard about his previous assignment, LoGuercio needs to follow orders."

"He mentioned something to me about his work in the south not going well."

"That is an understatement. He could have been dismissed."

His uncle did not want to go into details, and Rick knew better than to push it. "Betta and I are going to have lunch with him now."

"*Buon appetito*. Keep me informed on the case. And of course on Fabrizio."

Rick didn't know which had more of Piero's interest.

◇◇◇

The restaurant was more elegant than Rick expected, but on further consideration, the policeman would not choose a pizzeria to meet out-of-town visitors. It reminded Rick that he didn't know LoGuercio well. When their paths had crossed in Volterra, the encounter had been intense and short, and Rick had returned immediately afterward to Rome. He'd liked the man, but there hadn't been any time to get to know one another. This, their first meal together, would be the opportunity, and Rick looked forward to it. His mother's skill at getting someone's life story in a few minutes of conversation had unfortunately not rubbed off on Rick, but Betta was with him, so she would take care of it.

The atmosphere that greeted them was an indication the food would not disappoint. The clientele was mostly businessmen, though not dressed as formally as they would have in Milan or Rome, with a few elegant women mixed in. Tables were separated enough to allow private conversations, and the string quartet music coming from hidden speakers was kept low. Rick told the head waiter that their reservation had been made by Inspector LoGuercio, and they were quickly shown to a round corner table for three where the waiter pulled out the chair for Betta and whisked away the "reserved" card. Rick had barely settled into his place when mineral water appeared, along with three menus. They were beginning to scan the choices when LoGuercio came through the door, spotted them, and strode to the table. His suit seemed even more rumpled than when they'd parted earlier, and his face still had not seen a razor. Rick stood and they shook hands.

"Hope you haven't been waiting long, I got tied up working on the case."

"Don't keep us in suspense, tell us what's happening," Betta said with a sweet smile while the two men sat down.

"It was just my luck that the forensics person is in Terni working on a case and couldn't get here until this evening, so I decided to send the body immediately to Rome for a complete forensics investigation. It may be there in the next couple hours, if there isn't too much traffic on the autostrada. So we'll have to wait a bit to get a full report, if we're fortunate, by the end of the day."

"What do you hope to find that you don't already know?" Rick asked.

"There are a number of things that can come out of the complete autopsy, including a more rigorous examination for fingerprints. We did find what seems to be a good print on the belt of the woman, and a more complete examination will show if it is hers or someone else's. Rome should be able to come up with other details we wouldn't have spotted at the crime scene, though perhaps we shouldn't be discussing them just before lunch."

Rick and Betta agreed, and the three took a time-out from crime to study the menus. It was not a long list, but had enough tempting dishes to make choosing difficult. All three, independently, opted to begin with *prosciutto e melone*, it being the season for good cantaloupe. For a pasta course, LoGuercio suggested Rick and Betta try the tortellini with the local mushrooms and black truffles, and they quickly agreed. He chose something a bit more substantial, the *pappardelle al ragu di lepre*; freshly made ribbon pasta with a hare sauce. After the choice of a wine, LoGuercio returned to the previous subject.

"It was quite a process to get Rome to do the autopsy. I had to get help from the public prosecutor who's been assigned to the case to cut through the red tape.

"Red tape there would be expected since Rome is where the term was invented," said Rick. "It comes from the pieces of red ribbon that hung from the seals of papal documents."

Betta sighed. "He loves to talk about word origins, Paolo. It's something I have to put up with constantly."

"You have to take the good with the bad, Betta," said Rick. "But regarding red tape in police headquarters, Paolo, I happen to know someone who could help. I just spoke with him."

The policeman's reaction was not what Rick expected. "I've been ordered already to have you assist on the case. Apparently they don't trust me in Rome to do the right thing."

"I don't think you should look at it like that, Paolo. Since you had already brought me in, just think of it as my uncle giving you his blessing."

LoGuercio stayed silent.

Betta took a piece of *focaccia bianca* from the basket in the middle of the table and put it on her bread plate. "Rick, you make it sounds like Uncle Piero is a cardinal in the curia."

"Not an inappropriate analogy," LoGuercio observed.

The wine arrived at the table, a Torgiano Rosso from the tiny village of the same name, just south of Perugia. After the cork was carefully removed, it was tasted by Paolo, approved, and the three glasses filled by the waiter. Paolo offered a welcoming toast to the two visitors from Rome and they tapped glasses.

"Did you find out anything useful at the university, Riccardo?"

"Do you mean, did the *detective* find anything? I was only the interpreter."

The policeman held up a defensive hand. "Of course. *Mi scusi.* Betta, did you get anything useful from the man?"

She took a small drink and patted a drop of the red wine from her equally red lips. "Only the name of the program director when Signora Van Fleet was a student. Professor Romano, the man we talked to, seemed to think the former director might remember her."

LoGuercio took a bread stick from the basket and waved it like a small flag. "Excellent. We shall visit this aged professor after lunch and hope his memory is as good as Romano thinks it is."

The waiter silently placed a small dish in front of Betta, followed by those for her companions. Each held a slice of bright orange melon, cut from but sitting on its rind, draped with paper-thin slices of prosciutto. Wishes of "*buon appetito*" were exchanged and they ate. After agreement that few taste combinations compared to the salty tartness of the ham with the sweetness of the fruit, conversation swung away from food.

"Paolo," Betta said after a few bites, "Rick has not been able to tell me much about you. He didn't even know what town you're from. Hearing your accent, I would guess somewhere north of here, but I'm not sure how far north."

"Ferrara," he answered, while slicing his melon. "And from your accent, Betta, you are from still farther north."

"Somewhat. Bassano del Grappa, the jewel of the Veneto."

"You sound like you're working for your hometown tourist office," said Rick while looking past Betta. "Like Paolo's friend Morgante."

LoGuercio groaned. "He's already called me once since I saw him at the station this morning, demanding a progress report. He found out there was a hotel cancellation by someone who thinks there might be a murderer on the loose here."

"There is, Paolo."

"Thanks, Riccardo, for reminding me. By the way, we can't take the caretaker off the suspects list. He has no alibi. I have trouble picturing him as our murderer, but we can't discount the possibility."

"Motive?" It was Betta.

"A romantic encounter that went bad? They argued. It got violent. Who knows? He considers himself a ladies' man, of that I'm sure. I wouldn't be surprised if his services for the villa renters sometimes go beyond fixing a leaky faucet."

They watched the waiter remove their empty plates, and replace forks, just as the pasta dishes arrived. The distinctive aroma of truffles wafted from Betta's and Rick's *tortellini*, mixing with the earthy smell of mushrooms. The combination nearly overpowered the *profumo* of the pungent, dark sauce on Paolo's *pappardelle*. The portions, as expected in an elegant *ristorante*, were small. The waiter sprinkled cheese on each of the plates and quietly retired to allow the three to taste their food.

"Is there a Signora LoGuercio, Paolo?"

Her question took both men by surprise. They had expected a comment on the pasta, which was, as expected, excellent.

"There *is* a Signora LoGuercio." He paused for dramatic effect. "My mother, back in Ferrara. But I'm guessing that wasn't what you meant. I was engaged for a while, but my *fidanzata* decided the life of a policeman's spouse would not be for her, so she returned to Emilia-Romagna. That happened while I was working in the south."

Rick remembered what his uncle had said. That southern assignment for LoGuercio must have scarred him in more ways than one.

The policeman swallowed a taste of pasta. "Is there by chance a sister at home back in Bassano, Betta? If she is even half as—"

She waved an empty fork. "I don't have a sister, Paolo, but there are some very attractive friends." She looked at Rick. "Gisa?"

"A perfect match," answered Rick, before taking another small bite of *tortellino*. He was making it last. "Gisa is good looking, intelligent, has a great personality. Not in the same class as Betta, of course, but more than a lowly policeman could hope for in a female companion."

As Rick hoped, the comment brought a smile to LoGuercio. "So how did you two meet? If you don't mind a question from a lowly policeman."

Betta expected Rick to continue the repartee, but instead he turned serious and described the trip to Bassano del Grappa where he and Betta met while helping to solve a pair of crimes. Usually the wine made him more jocular, but this bottle was having the opposite effect. He made it sound like she had been, if not the key person in the Bassano investigation, at least an equal partner. When Rick finished, with the conclusion that fate had brought them together, she was too stunned to speak.

Paolo didn't notice her reaction, but Rick did. He reached over and put his hand on top of hers before looking toward

LoGuercio. "So that's how we met, my friend. But now she's followed me to Rome." He leaned closer to the policeman and lowered his voice. "Paolo, I think she's stalking me."

Betta took two short breaths and tapped her chest with the free hand. "Thank goodness the Rick I know is back. I was worried there for a moment."

Conversation returned to their food. Bites were exchanged and tastes analyzed. Wineglasses were refilled. A vote was taken on which pasta was more tasty, but since each of them chose their own dish, the *tortellini* won easily. The next decision was what, if anything, to have next. Betta said a *secondo* for her was out of the question. The men, perhaps in deference, agreed to pass up the main course, but something to clear the palate? The helpful waiter suggested *sorbetto* of either lime, strawberry, or peach. They agreed it was an excellent suggestion, and asked that each of their bowls have a small scoop of each flavor. The waiter, as good waiters do, complimented them on the choice and disappeared into the kitchen with their empty pasta plates.

LoGuercio leaned back in his chair. "Riccardo, could you accompany me to the interview of this Professor Tansillo? It is an American university program he ran, so you may think of things to ask him that would not occur to me."

Rick turned to Betta, who wore a classic "I told you so" look on her face.

"You don't need my permission, Rick," she said. "Also, this afternoon I would love to poke into some of the shops for which Orvieto is famous. If you'd rather do that than help Paolo with the investigation…"

"No, Betta, thank you. And Paolo has a point, American universities are not organized in the same way as Italian ones. I may be able to—"

A deep voice broke in. "You'll forgive me for interrupting your meal. I know that even police inspectors in the midst of an investigation have to eat."

Rick and the policeman rose from their chairs, napkins in hand. At table-side stood a large man dressed in a well-tailored suit. A perfectly trimmed salt and pepper goatee surrounded a pair of large lips open in a smile. The little hair he had above the ears matched the beard. LoGuercio immediately showed discomfort.

"Mayor Boscoli, may I present Riccardo Montoya and his friend Betta Innocenti. Riccardo has been assisting me in the investigation."

Bernardo Boscoli shook hands with Rick and Betta, eying them carefully as he did.

"Are you a policeman, Signor Montoya?"

"No, sir. The inspector asked me to help interpret when he was questioning two people involved in the case. I'm a professional translator and interpreter."

"Riccardo was kind enough to use his English skills at the American university program where the victim had been a student."

"She was in that program? I didn't know that."

"Neither did we until Riccardo uncovered it."

The mayor nodded his head several times. "This is very good. But you don't think she could have been killed by someone in this program, do you Inspector?"

"Not with the program now, but during the time she was here. If we can find someone who knew her in 1980."

"Yes, that would make perfect sense. Are you getting close to finding the culprit, Inspector?"

"It is still very early in the case, Mr. Mayor."

Boscoli thought before answering. "Of course it is. If there are developments, I would appreciate being informed." He looked back at a table where a man was placing his cell phone down on the tablecloth. "Vincenzo has finished his call. It sounded important so didn't want to eavesdrop on the man. I was a pleasure to meet you, Signor Montoya, and you, Signora Innocenti."

Rick and LoGuercio sat down after the man walked away.

"First the head of tourism and now the mayor himself." LoGuercio rubbed the back of his neck as if he had slept on it wrong. "Everyone wants to be kept informed."

"It's natural that they would," said Betta. "It seems like you could give updates to the mayor, and he could pass it on to Morgante and anyone else on the city council."

"Unfortunately it doesn't work that way, Betta. Morgante and Mayor Boscoli are not just in different political parties, they are adversaries. Morgante wants to be the next mayor. So they don't talk much, except when they clash at city council meetings."

"At this point," Rick said, "I think I'd vote for Morgante. Seems like an affable fellow. Betta and I ran into him this morning in front of the Duomo and he offered us a personal tour of it this afternoon."

"He probably wants to pump you for information about the investigation. I may have given him the impression that you're involved."

"He won't get anything out of me." Rick finished the last drops from his wineglass. "Has Boscoli been mayor long?"

"As long as I've been here," LoGuercio answered. "He's also a lawyer, and a very prosperous one. Owns a lot of buildings in town, mostly commercial property."

"I've never met a destitute lawyer. Who is the guy having lunch with the mayor? One of his political allies?"

"If someone's having lunch with the mayor he likely wants something from the city." LoGuercio glanced quickly at the other table where the two men were deep in conversation. "A local businessman named Vincenzo Aragona."

LoGuercio didn't notice the exchange of looks between Rick and Betta.

"What kind of business?" Betta asked.

"Wine. He owns the Sonnomonte Vineyards east of town. Not Orvieto Classico but some other grape, apparently he exports a lot of it. He's very active in the chamber of commerce, which is probably why he's lunching with our illustrious mayor."

Rick turned and tried to surreptitiously size up Aragona. His suit was as well cut as the mayor's, but unlike his dining partner he had a craggy face which may have come from spending time outside. It was difficult to picture the man picking grapes, but riding a horse through the fields could work. Large hands and a serious bulk went along with the image. Rick had not pictured Tullia Aragona's husband to be small and weak, but neither did he expect a bruiser like this man. He did not follow the scripted image of the cuckolded spouse.

The *sorbetto* arrived; white, orange, and red spheres in porcelain dishes. After serving them, the waiter positioned a small plate of thin sugar cookies in the middle of the table.

"Paolo," said Betta after her first bite of the sorbet, "have you contacted the police in the woman's hometown in America?"

"I sent a fax this morning, written by one of my sergeants who claims to have good English skills, with the basic facts of the case as we knew them then. Hadn't heard back when I left to come here, but it's early in the morning in Arizona."

Rick was trying to decide whether to finish off one flavor before starting on the next, or taking a spoonful from each in a circle until it was all gone. He opted for the latter.

"Paolo, if it would help, I can call the authorities there and explain what's happened. They may have some ideas, though I doubt it."

"Certainly. We can do that after we go see Professor Tansillo."

Betta had finished the lemon and was starting on peach. "You didn't mention the fingerprint to the mayor, Paolo. It might have made him happy that some progress has been made."

LoGuercio shrugged. "I suppose I could have. But we really should keep that kind of detail within the investigation. Boscoli knows everyone in town, and he might be tempted to share the news, and it would spread quickly. The murderer might hear that we have the print and disappear."

"If he hasn't already," Betta added, before finishing her sorbet.

Chapter Seven

Twenty kilometers from Orvieto, the small historic center of Bolsena sat on a hill overlooking the volcanic lake that shared its name. The tranquility of the clear water, broken only by the occasional sailboat, gave no hint to the violent eruption that had formed its bowl in prehistory. Today the shore was dotted with small hotels and restaurants, their Roman clientele less bellicose than the legions which millennia earlier had camped along its waters on their way to Gaul. The culinary draw was the same then as now: a variety of freshwater fish which quickly went from net to grill. Unfortunately, Rick and LoGuercio were not going to Bolsena in search of the catch of the day; their fishing would be inside the memory of Professor Luigi Tansillo.

The police car carrying them had survived the difficult part of the drive, a series of cutbacks taking them over the escarpment just west of the Orvieto. The road mercifully smoothed out at that point, winding over hills before starting a slow descent to the lake. Just after they crossed from Umbria into Lazio its water appeared briefly in the distance before disappearing as the car swung behind a hill. A few kilometers later the view was unbroken, the lake spreading majestically before them as they drove closer to the town. The driver slowed as the road narrowed and space between buildings grew smaller. They passed an ancient church and the ruins of a castle built there for its panoramic defensive view of the lake. According to a banner hanging from the stone ramparts, the fortification now served as a museum.

The car drove slowly down through the town before reaching the street running along the lake shore. In season it would have been bumper to bumper, especially in the evening. Parking areas allowed visitors to leave their cars and stroll along the water, but the lakeside path was now empty, save for a few elderly couples taking an afternoon walk. The driver checked the numbers on the buildings, passing deserted restaurants and hotels before reaching a two-story duplex built close to the pavement. A balcony on the second floor offered a view of the lake.

"This should be it, Sir." The car came to a stop at the curb in front of the building.

Rick and LoGuercio got out of the backseat and walked to the fence, beyond which ran a thin strip of grass between it and the building. Each of the duplexes had its own gate that opened to a path of slate stones leading to a door. They found the one with the name Tansillo and rang the bell. Rick expected a voice from the inside asking who was there, but instead the gate buzzed open almost immediately. As they made the short walk to the door it was opened by a gaunt man with thick white hair. He wore a shirt with a tie, under a sleeveless, brown sweater. A thin wrist and hand reached out to LoGuercio.

"You must be the inspector." The voice was raspy, that of a man who had spent years of his life smoking. The lines on his face confirmed it. "And this gentleman?"

"Signor Montoya, who is assisting in the investigation."

The wrinkled smile that Tansillo had given to LoGuercio was extended to Rick, along with a handshake.

"Please come in. My wife passed away several years ago, and with her went the neatness that characterized our home, so you will have to forgive me. The most pleasant place to receive visitors is on the terrace upstairs. The temperature today is relatively benign, and you can enjoy the view." He extended his arm in the direction of a stairway.

"That would be fine, Professor," said LoGuercio, and he and Rick followed behind the man as he climbed.

The room in the front of the second floor held enough books to start a community library. Three of its sides—the fourth being the windows and door facing the lake—were lined with shelves from floor to ceiling. A chair and ottoman, their leather cracked with age, sat in one corner. A metal lamp curled over the back of the chair, and next to it was a battered wood table, on which an open book was spread, pages down. Wedged in another corner was a desk, most of its surface covered with books. The only items not made of paper on the desk were a goose-neck lamp, a telephone, and some writing instruments, all of which dated from the previous century. The professor smiled when he saw Rick staring at the rows of books.

"My field probes into a rather obscure niche of Italian literature, Signor Montoya, sixteenth-century literary Mannerism."

"I've always thought of Mannerism as a movement in art and architecture."

Tansillo nodded. "Most people do. Shall we go outside?" Before opening the door he took a heavy cardigan sweater off the back of the desk chair and slipped it on.

A few leaves had wedged themselves into the corners of the square patio, but otherwise it was swept clean. Four metal chairs with plastic cushions angled toward the lake, its surface visible over the low balcony. Two trees on the other side of the street would have partially blocked the lake view in the summer, but now patches of silver could be seen between the branches. A light breeze blowing off the water carried the musty smell of dead leaves.

The professor pulled his chair around so that his guests could continue to enjoy the view. "What I was told over the phone did not have much detail, Inspector. You wanted to ask me about a former student in our program?"

LoGuercio cleared his throat. "That's correct. The body of a woman was found early this morning, and we believe her death to be a homicide. The woman, an American named Rhonda Van Fleet, was in your program in 1980."

Tansillo closed his eyes in thought. "I don't recall anyone named Van Fleet."

"She was Rhonda Davis then, Professor," Rick said.

The man stiffened. "Good God, Rhonda Davis? Of course I remember her. She was murdered? Who would do such a thing?"

"That's what we're endeavoring to find out, Sir," said LoGuercio. "What can you tell us about her?"

The professor turned his head and stared out at the lake, as if this would help him remember. "She came into the program late, in October or November. I recall that because there was some question as to whether we should let her in. She'd been doing some kind of internship—in some other city—that didn't work out. But someone had left early, so we had an opening." He shook his head. "Strange how I can remember that, but couldn't tell you what I had for lunch yesterday."

"What kind of a student was she?"

"One of the best from those early years. Pottery was her field, and she immersed herself in it completely. Always seemed to have clay on her hands. Turned out some beautiful pieces."

"So all work and no play?" Rick asked.

"No, no. I didn't mean to give that impression. She was very much into the nightlife in Orvieto. Of that class, probably the most active."

"I realize it has been many years," LoGuercio said, "but do you recall any enemies, people she didn't get along with?

Tansillo frowned. "Why would—ah, of course. Someone who could have done this. No, I don't remember anything like that. Rhonda had a strong personality, overbearing at times, but her friends accepted her for what she was." He tilted his head toward LoGuercio. "But surely you don't suspect that one of her fellow students from that year would come over here and murder her."

"No, sir. But she must have had Italian friends. Can you recall anyone?"

A gust blew in from the water, stirring up the leaves on the terrace. The professor pulled his sweater tighter around his neck as he concentrated.

"Bianca Capello. Yes, Bianca was in Orvieto at that time, before going off to Milan to study at the Bocconi. Wanted to go into banking. Her English was very good, so she would help with orientation when new groups arrived. I'm almost certain that one of the years Bianca worked for us was Rhonda's."

"She is in Orvieto now?" LoGuercio had scribbled the name on his pad.

"I believe so, Inspector. She worked for a bank somewhere in the north for years, but moved back here and started a real estate business. It was right about the time I retired from the program."

"Is there anyone else from that time still in Orvieto?"

"Signora Vecchi, but I'm not sure if she would remember much." He grinned, showing an uneven line of teeth. "She is even older than I, gentlemen. She ran a boardinghouse where the female students lived. At that time we separated the women students from the males, not that it made any difference."

"We'll track her down. Anyone else?"

The professor shook his head slowly. "No, I think that's—no wait, of course. Amadeo. Amadeo Crivelli. Confound me, I should have thought of him immediately. Amadeo was the pottery instructor. Part time, of course, he had his own pottery business, then as now."

"He must have known Rhonda Davis very well, since that was her area of study."

"Very well indeed, Signor Montoya. I recall him telling me that Rhonda had a true talent. Amadeo became very successful with his line of pottery. He lives in Todi, owns a ceramics shop there and one in Orvieto, both featuring his work." He suddenly slapped his hands on his knees. "Gentlemen, I just realized that I have been remiss by not offering you something. When my wife was alive she would have seen to it. A bit of sherry, perhaps? Or I can make some coffee."

LoGuercio slipped his notebook into his pocket along with the pen. "That's very kind of you, Professor, but we must be on our way back to Orvieto. You have been very helpful."

He got to his feet, followed by Rick and the host, but all three stood where they were and looked out over the water.

The afternoon sun had come from behind a low cloud and was bouncing its rays off the water.

"Can you tell me what became of Rhonda after college?"

After a nod from LoGuercio, Rick answered. "She was a potter in Arizona and apparently was quite successful at it. Less successful in marriage, unfortunately; three of them ended in divorce. She came on this trip with her daughter and a friend who told us she wanted to see Italy one last time."

The professor put his hands on the railing and stared toward a tiny island in the distance. "I can't help wondering if she knew what awaited her in Orvieto."

◇◇◇

While Rick and LoGuercio drove back from Bolsena, Betta strolled the streets of Orvieto. The training period with the art police in Rome had offered her little time off during the day, so she welcomed the chance to walk through a shopping district when the businesses were actually open. Not that she needed anything; the only item in her mind was a postcard to send home to her father. In a country where national chains had not taken over completely, shops were unique from one city to the next, giving each town its own feel. Orvieto and Betta's native Bassano were known for their ceramics, but here the emphasis was on a local style of pottery passed down through the centuries. It featured floral patterns, often with a green tint, and swirls of delicate animal figures, especially roosters. Lots of roosters. Interesting, she thought, but certainly not on the level of our artists in Bassano.

The street was near the Duomo, and as would be expected for such a location, most of its shops catered to the tourist trade— from day-trippers up from Rome to international travelers. It was a *zona pedonale*, allowing shoppers to wander freely from one store to the next without fear of being run down by cars or motorbikes. Betta walked slowly, admiring the colorful ceramic plates and masks decorating the doorways of the shops. She came to a *tabaccaio*, the establishment in Italy which traditionally sold not just tobacco products but postage stamps. Sheets of plastic cases holding postcards hung from this doorway, and she stopped to pick out one for her father. Most of them featured the Duomo from various angles, a few pictured the art inside the cathedral, others had shots of the city taken from below its cliffs. She pulled one showing a detail of the Luca Signorelli Last Judgment frescoes from its case and walked in for a stamp. Her father, who owned an art gallery, would appreciate seeing Signorelli's masterpiece.

The inside, like most tobacconists in Italy, was small to begin with, and adding to that were shelves with magazines and smoking paraphernalia, making it positively cramped. A woman was standing near the counter, talking on her cell phone. Betta noticed more postcards on a low shelf and leaned down to see if she liked any of them better than the one she'd brought in from outside. She heard snatches of the woman's conversation, something about when she'd be back, which would be soon. Talking with her husband, Betta assumed. The woman ended the call and started to put her cell phone in her purse when the man behind the counter spoke.

"There you are, Signora Aragona, that will be—"

Betta gasped and her shoulder jerked upward, catching the woman's arm. The cell phone clattered to the floor and slid under the counter. Both women reached down to get it and their heads collided.

"I'm so sorry," said Betta, rubbing her head. "Please let me get it." She bent down, reached under the counter, and found the phone. After blowing off a bit of dust that had stuck to it, she handed it back to the woman.

"It's quite all right, my dear, there isn't much room in this place." She turned to the man, who had watched the scene in horror. "You need a larger shop, Vito."

He shook his head and was struggling to find a response when Betta spoke. "It was my fault, Signora. I hope your *telefonino* was not damaged."

"I've dropped it before and it survived. But are you all right?"

She looked at Betta's head. "With that short hair you don't have as much padding to your skull as I do."

The woman, who was fighting valiantly to avoid turning fifty, appeared to have come directly from the beauty parlor, and not a cheap one. Her hair, dark with a few accents of blond, fell perfectly to the shoulders. The coiffure alone, leaving aside her expensive clothes, shouted high maintenance.

"I'm all right," Betta said. "It was clumsy of me."

"No harm done." She paid the man and strolled out the door.

Betta threw down some euro coins for her postcard and followed.

◇◇◇

The driver dropped Rick and LoGuercio at an intersection of the street where Bianca Cappello's office was located. It was a pedestrian street, and even though the police car could have driven directly to the address, or anywhere else in town, LoGuercio preferred to walk the two blocks rather than squeeze through all the foot traffic. In addition, he and Rick were ready to stretch their legs, even if it was only for a few dozen meters, and LoGuercio wanted a cigarette. The store fronts on this street had more appeal to locals than tourists: a jeweler, a fruit seller, a pharmacy, a shoe store, a *salumaio*, a women's clothing shop, a bank. The only one that caused the two men to stop was the *salumaio*, its window filled with cheeses, fresh pasta, and other delectables. For a moment, thanks to a basket of porcini mushrooms, Rick's mind shifted from the murder case to dinner. LoGuercio's voice pulled it back.

"Her office should be a couple doors away. On the other side."

As with every real estate office in Italy, this one's window was covered with framed pictures of properties for rent or sale. Basic information such as price, square footage, and location appeared underneath the photos. An elderly man standing on the street reading the notices looked at Rick and LoGuercio as the two reached the doorway. The policeman reluctantly stubbed out his cigarette and they entered the office.

The room was the size of Professor Tansillo's balcony. It had two desks, one occupied by a woman working the mouse on a

PC and peering intently at the screen through half glasses. She looked up when she heard the door open and assessed the two who came through the door. Rick watched her face and could almost hear her mind working. *Are these men possible clients or are they bringing a problem?* She rose from her chair.

"How can I help you?" She took off the glasses and they hung by a thin gold chain over the front of her striped silk blouse.

"Signora Cappello?"

"Yes?"

The police identification card came out. "I'm Inspector LoGuercio and this is Signor Montoya. We'd like to ask you a few questions if you have the time?"

She motioned to the two chairs in front of her desk. "Of course, Inspector, please sit down. What is this about?"

They settled into the chairs, a modern metal and leather design which fit in with the rest of the décor. "You may have read the news of the murder that took place last night."

She shuddered. "Yes, of course, the American woman. I talked about it this morning with my assistant." She waved a hand at the empty desk. "I didn't see the newspaper but she told me about it. It's terrible to say, but we were wondering if it could have a negative effect on business. We rent apartments and villas to Americans all the time, and—"

"Was this woman's villa one of your rentals, Signora?"

"No, no. I . . but I didn't know she was staying at a villa. Is that why you're here? You thought she had rented from my company?"

LoGuercio didn't answer immediately, instead pulled the notebook and pen from his jacket pocket. "No, we didn't, Signora Cappello." He uncapped his pen and glanced at Rick who took the hint.

"Signora," Rick began, "we think you may have known the victim."

"I don't think so, my assistant said the name in the—" She stopped when Rick held up a hand.

"The name in the paper was Van Fleet, but when she lived here many years ago, before she married, it was Rhonda Davis."

The reaction was immediate. She gasped, and one hand went to her mouth while the other gripped the arm of the chair. Had to be genuine, Rick concluded, unless she was very good at acting. She took several short breaths before being able to speak.

"I can't believe it. Rhonda was here in Orvieto? I didn't know she was coming."

"Had you two kept in touch?"

She stared at the desk before realizing that she'd been asked a question, then looked at Rick and shook her head. "No. Not for a long time. The first few years, after she went back to America, there were letters back and forth, but after that we lost contact. Was she still living in Arizona?"

"Yes, she was. Would she have been trying to find you?"

She held her palms up and shrugged. "She could have. But I believe I'd written to her about taking a job in Milan, and after that we lost touch. I spent twenty years working in a bank there before I returned to Orvieto to run this business. She must have assumed I was still in Milan." She was struggling to maintain her composure, but her hands trembled.

"Would she have been searching for someone else?" LoGuercio asked.

"Inspector, you don't think someone she knew back then could have done this, do you?"

"We're just trying to find out as much as we can about the woman," LoGuercio answered. "Who else from that time could she have wanted to see again?"

Her eyes closed in thought. "Professor Tansillo, of course. He ran the program back then. A kind man, but more of a scholar than an administrator."

"We talked to him. He gave us your name."

"I see. The only other person I recall from those days was Amadeo. Amadeo Crivelli. He was the pottery instructor. Did Professor Tansillo mention him?"

"He did," said Rick. "Is there anyone else you can think of?"

She shook her head while trying to remember. "I don't think so. It wasn't a large program, and most of the instructors were professors who came over for a semester or two from Arizona. Amadeo was one of the few Italians."

"And your position in the program?"

"I had just come back from nursing my sick grandmother outside Milan and had gotten a job at the tourist office. The office was glad to let me work part time for the program, helping the American students find their way around the city, learn the sites, and generally get acclimated. My English was good and most of them had little Italian, so whenever they had some question about Orvieto, they came to me. It was before I went off to the university myself, so we were about the same age. I made some good friendships." The thought brought her hand back to her mouth. "Rhonda was one of them."

"What can you tell us about Signora Van Fleet when she was a student here?" asked LoGuercio, his voice calm, almost soothing.

A hint of a smile showed on Bianca Cappello's face. "Rhonda was very different from the rest. Never afraid to say what she thought, even though it might offend someone, which it often did. Liked to socialize, especially over a bottle of wine. And she liked to socialize with Italians, in particular Italian men, which shocked some other students in the program, especially the women. Those were different times."

"Were any of her relationships with those men...?" Rick searched for the right word.

"Serious? I don't recall any. I remember talking with her about that, and she told me she had no intention of getting serious with anyone. Apparently she'd been disappointed in the past and didn't want it to happen again." She blinked and rubbed her eyes. "I can't believe I'm remembering this. It was so long ago."

"We're glad you can remember it," LoGuercio said before leaning to the edge of the chair and putting his card on the desk. "If other things come to mind, please call me."

She glanced at the card and placed it next to the keyboard. "Of course, Inspector. Is there anything else I can help with now?" The demeanor of the efficient businesswoman had returned.

"It's routine, of course, but can I ask you where you were last evening?"

Her face was a blank until she realized the implication of the question. "Oh. Of course. I…I was at home. I worked here until seven, our closing time, then made my own dinner and went to bed. It had been a busy day, and I was very tired."

"You live alone?"

She didn't answer for a moment, perhaps deciding whether it was any of the policeman's business. "Yes, I do. My mother moved in after my divorce and lived with me until she passed away a few years ago."

"This has been a shock," LoGuercio said, "so we won't ask any further questions at this time. It is likely that after more thought, other things may occur to you that could help us with the investigation. You have my number."

They all stood and the two men expressed their condolences for the loss of her friend.

"Thank you," she said. She seemed to want to say something else and they waited. "I know you aren't required to do this, but if you could tell me when you find who did this, before it gets in the news, I would be grateful. Rhonda was a dear friend."

By the time they stepped outside, Bianca Cappello was once again studying the screen of her computer.

"Not a dear enough friend to stay in contact," LoGuercio said when they got to the street. "But her reaction to the news was genuine enough." He stopped and took his cell phone from his pocket. "Let me find out if they've located Crivelli." He dialed and moved away from two women strollers who had paused to gaze at the merchandise inside a clothing store.

Rick walked to a shoe store to see if the latest fashions being offered to the shoppers of Orvieto was the same as what he'd been seeing in Rome. As with so many shoe stores in Italy, the entrance to the store itself was at the end of a line of display windows, women's shoes on one side, men's on the other. The cold weather would be arriving soon, which meant that on both sides, shoes with heavier heels and higher sides had appeared in the line-up, as well as boots. He searched for a pair of cowboy boots, but the only ones to be found were on his feet. If they knew how comfortable they were, Rick thought, everyone would be wearing them. He turned and started back toward the street when a male figure in a long, white coat rushed past the store down the street. He watched as the man disappeared through a door a few businesses down the street.

"Did you see that?" Rick asked when LoGuercio was putting his phone away.

"See what?"

"Livio Morgante just went by in his pharmacist coat."

"Yeah, his pharmacy is right over there." He tapped the pocket where he kept his phone. "We're in luck, Riccardo, Crivelli splits his time between his shop in Todi and the one here, but he's in Orvieto today and it's only a couple blocks from here. He's expecting us."

"That's great. Let's go." They started off toward the corner where they'd been dropped earlier. "Paolo, about Morgante—"

"Forget Morgante. You know, Riccardo, I have to get you some kind of identification. I don't know what I would have told that woman if she'd asked who you were. You need something to show you are official."

"I'm not official, Paolo." He pulled something from his wallet. "But how's this?"

"What is it?"

"Pass to get into the *questura* in Rome when I go to see my uncle. He got tired of having to come down to the entrance to get me."

"This could work." LoGuercio took the small plastic card and looked at both sides. "It's got your picture, and even an official seal. Not a very good picture."

"You should see my passport photo." Rick slipped the card back into his wallet.

"Hold your thumb over where it says "Building Pass" when you show it to anyone."

"I'll do that," said Rick.

They turned a corner onto the street leading to the Duomo, and the number of tourist shops immediately increased, as did the number of tourists. Their demographics had changed from the high season of July and August, when schools were closed and families with children roamed Italy. Now it was an older, graying crowd, unencumbered by kids. To the delight of the merchants, these visitors were also more inclined to purchase higher-ticket souvenirs. Ahead Rick spotted a ceramic sign hanging on chain links from a cast-iron pole: Studio Crivelli.

"Before we go inside," Rick said, "when I saw Morgante—"

"I'm certainly glad he didn't see me or he would have been breaking my *coglioni*."

Rick held LoGuercio's arm to stop him. "Paolo, when he walked by us he went straight to Bianca Cappello's office."

◇◇◇

Tullia Aragona, despite what she'd said on the phone, did not appear to be in any hurry to get home. She meandered along the street, her purse over one shoulder and the small bag from the *tabbacaio* swinging from the other hand. Every store window got her attention, though she spent more time in front of shoe stores and those selling jewelry. Betta hung back, keeping one eye on merchandise displays and the other on Tullia. As she did, she asked herself why she was following the woman. Perhaps she could gain some insight into what made her tick, and thereby help Rick resolve the Fabrizio problem. But maybe it was just the policewoman coming out in her, wanting to get involved. She watched the older woman disappear into a dress shop and realized it could be a long wait.

As it turned out, it only took ten minutes. She emerged from the shop carrying a small bag, likely not something that needed to be tried on, like a blouse or belt. The other smaller bag was not evident, so she must have stowed it inside the new one. Tullia checked her watch—its round, silver face so large that Betta could almost read it from a distance—and continued down the street. Her pace picked up. Betta followed a safe distance behind, helped in keeping inconspicuous by pedestrian traffic.

After fifty meters the woman turned off the shopping street into a smaller one. When Betta got to the corner she could see that it was almost an alley, but it bent just past the corner. On a straight street, it would be almost impossible to stay hidden, but if there were more bends she could continue to follow without being noticed. When Tullia disappeared, Betta stepped onto the stones of the narrow street and followed. As it turned out, there were no more bends, but it didn't matter.

Betta stopped and peered around the edge of the building where the street made a slight turn. Tullia stood in front of a tall metal gate facing a large man who Betta immediately recognized as the other man at the mayor's lunch table. Vincenzo Aragona's thick index finger repeatedly jabbed the air in front of his wife's face as his voice rose in anger. Betta flattened herself against the stone of the building and watched through an opening between the stone. Even without seeing the two clearly, their voices were easy for her to understand.

"You've decided to come home? Why don't you end this charade and just spend all your time in that little apartment?"

"And why don't you just move into that room in the winery? You spend most of your time working anyway. It's as if you don't have a wife."

He pointed at her shopping bag. "It's my work which allows you to patronize the most expensive boutiques in Orvieto. You don't seem to be complaining about that."

"I'm surprised you noticed, Vincenzo."

"You have to stop this…this arrangement. People are beginning to talk."

"And your precious status in the community might be harmed."

"You will regret this, Tullia." His voiced was reduced to a growl.

"I'm going inside, you can stay out here and shout at yourself."

She turned toward the gate and he grabbed her arm, pulling her roughly toward him before putting his face a few inches from hers. "I mean what I said, Tullia. I have enough to worry about at the moment, I don't need something else."

She peeled his fingers from her arm and rubbed it in pain. For the first time fear showed in her eyes.

Betta edged back from the corner and walked quickly away, stunned by the vicious edge to Aragona's words. Tullia was in a situation any woman would dread and Betta wondered how she would cope. She knew, from recent personal experience, that it would not be easy.

Chapter Eight

It crossed Rick's mind that all the ceramics stores on the street might be owned by the same person, and that person had saved money by hiring one decorator for all his shops. Every one had large pots stacked outside the doorways, plates hung on the sides of the doorways, and shelves stacked with smaller ceramic pieces to entice the shopper once inside. The designs of the ceramic decoration also varied little from one place to another. Apparently the tourists didn't mind the similarity, or even liked it. They squeezed past the outdoor wares and poked through the shelves, sometimes emerging with some treasure inside a bag decorated in the same colorful design. There was one shop which proved the exception: Studio Crivelli. Apparently Crivelli styled himself as something of an avant garde artist, and a minimalist one at that. A simple sign was the only indication to passersby that something was being sold inside, its color and material hinting that it could be ceramics. At least there wasn't a brass plate next to the door warning "by appointment only," as Rick often saw outside galleries in Rome. The wood door was painted a bright turquoise, reminding him of the gates to adobe dwellings in New Mexico. It was open, and Rick followed LoGuercio through the door.

Inside, Studio Crivelli continued to revel in its contrast with the other ceramics stores. Rick counted a mere two dozen pieces, most of them on shelves and lit by tiny spots set in the ceiling.

Larger ones, the size of umbrella stands, sat on the floor under the shelves, each with its own hidden lighting. None of the historic designs of the other shops here, thank you very much—Crivelli's ceramics were starkly modern, with bright lines of color that swirled around the surfaces. Though each was different in the way it mixed its colors, the fundamental style was the same.

At the rear of the room a table made of an ebony plank sat on two equally dark sawhorses. After noting a pair of shapely legs under the table, Rick raised his eyes and saw that they belonged to a girl in a short dress with spiky blond hair. The only item on the table was a thin tablet, propped on its own stand, with a similarly thin keyboard. No telephone, but he guessed that any tablet worth its salt would include that function. The girl stood up, pushed the dress down slightly over her hips, and smiled.

"You must be Inspector LoGuercio and Signor Montoya. Signor Crivelli is expecting you." She raised her arm with a ballerina-like movement, gesturing in the direction of a door that was slightly ajar at the back of the room. LoGuercio thanked her, and they walked to the door and pushed it open.

While the space would not be described as cluttered, the minimalist décor of the showroom had not been extended to Crivelli's office. The furniture was modern and colorful, mostly plastic and metal, including four chairs that surrounded a coffee table. The art on the walls was abstract impressionist, in keeping with the style of ceramics. A few small pieces of pottery sat on a corner of the desk, perhaps anxious to get into the other room to a position of honor under the spotlights. Crivelli stood when his two visitors entered.

He was a large man with a red face crowned by thick white hair in need of a cut, or at the very least a brushing. His beard had the same color, but in contrast with the hair it was neatly trimmed, causing Rick to wonder if the man had two barbers, each for a different part of his head. The blue blazer hung well on his body, indicating it was tailored rather than off the rack. A dark tee-shirt and blue jeans completed a wardrobe intended to project the image of a successful artist. He came around the desk and extended his hand.

"Inspector, welcome to Studio Crivelli, but I imagine you are not here to look at ceramics. And this must be Signor Montoya. I don't believe policeman usually wear cowboy boots. Please sit down."

The boots did it again, Rick thought. And so much for trying out my police building pass.

"I hope you'll accept a coffee. I usually have one next door at this time of day, and I took the liberty of telling Angelica to bring it when you arrived."

"A coffee would be welcome," said LoGuercio. Rick nodded his agreement.

Crivelli settled into the chair and crossed one leg over the other, exposing a beige sock inside a dark brown loafer. "The sergeant who called didn't tell me what this is about. If you were the *Guardia di Finanza* I might be worried, but since you are the regular police…"

"We are not interested in looking at your books, Signor Crivelli, we are investigating a murder which took place last night."

It was the direct approach intended to elicit a reaction from Crivelli. What LoGuercio got was a puzzled frown.

"The murder of that American woman? I read about it in the paper this morning. Do you think she was in one of my shops? I don't recall seeing her, though the picture in the paper looked vaguely familiar. I could have seen her in the shop, but Angelica handles most customers."

At that point Angelica herself appeared carrying a plastic tray with three small cups and saucers, as well as a sugar bowl, all in the same bright style of the other ceramics in the shop. She placed it carefully on the table and retired, each delicate movement followed by the eyes of the two visitors.

"Signor Crivelli," said Rick after stirring sugar into his cup, "the woman looked familiar because she was a student here many years ago when you were the pottery instructor. Her name then was Rhonda Davis."

Crivelli put his cup back down without tasting it. "*Dio mio,* Rhonda? I was thinking about her just recently, wondering what became of the girl. She was one of the most talented students I had during the years I taught that course. Not that there were many with talent, but she was outstanding in both creating forms and decorating them. It would have been wonderful to see her again." He had been staring at a painting on the wall while he spoke, but now his head jerked up. "Inspector, could she have been intending to find me?"

"We have to assume she would have wanted to seek out people she knew from that time. Professor Tansillo gave us your name. She hadn't written to you to say she was coming, I assume?"

"No, no, of course not. I had no contact with her after she left Orvieto all those years ago. Nor with any other of my students, for that matter. So you think that the person who did this was someone she knew then?"

"We're looking at all possibilities," answered LoGuercio. "Tell us what you remember of Signora Van Fleet—that was her married name—when she was a student."

Crivelli rubbed his bearded chin with the back of his hand. "She arrived late to the program, which annoyed me since I had gone through the basics with the others and had to repeat it for her. If I recall, she had been doing an internship in Milan at Richard Ginori, the porcelain makers. Something happened and so she applied for admission to our program here."

"A problem with the internship in Milan?" Rick asked.

Crivelli shook his head. "No, it was something else. Something personal, I think, but I don't recall what."

"Are there other people who might still be in Orvieto who knew her when she was here?"

"Signor Montoya, I did not interact with others in the program. At that time I was struggling to get my own business started, and I took the job with the university to help make ends meet." His white beard framed a toothy smile. "As you can see I've done well. But inside the program back then I had contact only with the students during my class, and with Tansillo to get my check."

"You did no socializing with students or other professors?"

Crivelli snorted, as if Rick's question was a joke. "Good heavens, no." He finished his coffee and returned the cup to its saucer before looking at LoGuercio. "Isn't this when I'm supposed to tell you where I was when the murder took place? I read a lot of *gialli*, especially those by British crime writers."

"Go right ahead."

Rick wondered if Crivelli noticed the annoyance in Paolo's voice. The man was beginning to grate on both of them.

"I live in Todi, as you must know already, where my other shop is located. But I have a small apartment upstairs that I use if I'm kept late in Orvieto. That was the case last night. I had dinner with friends and slept here. So there is no one to corroborate my alibi for the entire evening, I'm afraid. Not even my wife, since she was in Todi."

"May I ask with whom you had dinner?"

"Of course, Inspector. I dined with Mayor Boscoli and his wife." The grin returned. "I'm sure he will be glad to confirm that if you call him."

◇◇◇

"He's a real charmer, isn't he?"

Rick didn't answer immediately. He had pulled out his cell phone and noticed a missed call and message, but didn't recognize the number. He'd check it later. "I'll agree with that, Paolo. Being a snob appears to work for him, his business looks like it's based on snob appeal. Small production, probably limited-edition pieces. If you're a discerning collector, your home cannot be considered complete without a signed Crivelli vase."

"Did you see the way he dropped the mayor's name?" LoGuercio said. "I've already got Mayor Boscoli on my case, I don't need Crivelli to be complaining to him."

"I'm sure the mayor has more important items on his agenda that telling you how to solve a murder."

"You could have said that about Morgante. And speaking of Morgante, Riccardo, what are your thoughts about him running to Bianca Cappello's office?"

They had turned up a side street in the direction of the police station, squeezing into a doorway to let a car pass. Ahead there was a break in the buildings lining the left side of the street, opening to a small square that allowed a wider view of a stone palazzo at the far end. Based on the styles of palazzi he passed regularly in Rome, Rick guessed the building was from the seventeenth century. A small, stone balcony, supported by columns reaching to the street, looked down from the third floor.

"She was distraught about the news of her friend's murder and called the pharmacist. He rushed over with some potion to calm her down."

LoGuercio nodded and rubbed his eyes. "Could be that. And it's an interesting that you said that here." He stopped Rick with his hand and pointed to the building. "See that? There was a case of a distraught woman that took place right up there. She found out her husband was having an affair and climbed out on the balcony and started screaming, threatening to jump. It drew a crowd. People came from the whole neighborhood. Her husband was a prominent businessman, so that made it an even bigger event."

Rick studied the balcony and saw that it was a long way to the pavement. "What happened?"

"She jumped and died."

"That's terrible. You tried to talk her out of it?"

LoGuercio's eyes stayed on the building. "Me? No. I wasn't there."

"Didn't someone call the police?"

"They probably did, but it happened in 1710. I may have the year wrong. Sometime back then."

Rick shook his head.

They were in front of the police station when he remembered the phone message. "Paolo," he said after listening to it and closing his phone, "that was from Francine Linwood. She has something she wants to tell us."

"We can't drive there now, I'm supposed to contact the prosecuting attorney, and you were going to make that phone call to the police in Arizona."

Rick stuffed his phone in his pocket. "She's here in town. You make your call to the prosecuting attorney and I'll walk over and see what she has to tell us. It shouldn't take long. When I get back we'll call Phoenix."

"That will work." LoGuercio walked to the door of the police station and went inside.

Rick pulled out his phone and checked the time. "Damn." He punched a number and put the phone to his ear as he walked. It went to messages. "Betta, things are running longer than I expected, I have to talk with one of the American women again. It's going to be impossible to meet Morgante at the cathedral. I'll call him and tell him. Hope you're having fun. Ciao." He took Morgante's card from his wallet and dialed the number. Same thing, to messages. "Signor Morgante, Riccardo Montoya. I'm afraid we've gotten busy with the case and won't be able to accept your kind offer to see the cathedral today. Hope that doesn't inconvenience you." He hung up and picked up his pace.

Francine Linwood had called from a bar on one of the small squares in Orvieto, so small that Rick had to use the GPS on his phone to find it. The afternoon sun was beginning to drop behind the tile roofs of the surrounding buildings, slowly shrinking a rectangular patch of sunlight on the similarly rect-angular paving stones. Eight small tables with umbrellas were arranged outside the door of the bar, most of them occupied by people whom Rick guessed to be locals. Of those, half were older couples, dressed more formally, the other half younger people more interested in reading their cell phones than live conversation. Francine sat alone with a wineglass and a dish of peanuts in front of her. She seemed to be staring at a tower in the distance, but Rick couldn't be sure. Her eyes were covered by sunglasses, even though the spread of afternoon shadows had made them unnecessary. The shadows had also begun to lower the temperature, but she had come prepared; a shawl of bright Southwest colors draped the chair next to her. She spotted Rick and waved. From the smile he concluded that the information she wanted to impart was not that serious. Or she was already three sheets to the wind. He made a mental note to look up the origin of that phrase, though he suspected he already knew.

"Hi Francine." He took the chair across from her and looked around the square. "Very picturesque spot you've found. Away from the bustle of the tourist crowds."

"Close your eyes and you're in Italy," she said, removing her sunglasses and taking a drink. "The sign in front of this place says bar, but inside everyone's drinking coffee. What's that about? But the barman was able to find me some chilled white wine. Very good, too. Can I get you some? My treat."

"Thank you, I'll pass." He stretched out his legs next to the table and rested one boot on top of the other. "Are you holding up all right?"

She picked up the glass. "With a little help from my friend here, I'll make it." She took another sip. "Where is the inspector? I was expecting to watch you in action again, in both languages."

"He's busy with the case. Where's Gina? Did you leave her back at the villa?" If Francine did come by herself, Rick thought, I hope she took the bus.

"She wanted to be alone and meditate, so I dropped her off at the cathedral. We each deal with grief in our own way." She held up the glass to illustrate her point.

"What did you want to tell the inspector, Francine?" He hoped his impatience was not too obvious.

"Well, Rick…" She paused and carefully chose one of the peanuts to put in her mouth. "As much as anything, I wanted to ask him about the investigation. As Rhonda's best friend, I think the authorities owe it to me to keep me informed. Has he told you what's going on?"

"Not very much," Rick lied. "I think there may be some suspects, but remember, it hasn't been even twenty-four hours since the murder happened. I'm sure the inspector is working as quickly as he can."

"Suspects? I hope I'm not one of them." She emitted an alcohol-induced giggle.

"Is there any reason you should be a suspect?" Rick didn't expect much of an answer.

"Why would I murder my closest friend?" She took another sip from the glass. It was almost empty. "Gina had more of a reason to murder Rhonda, though I don't think she had it in her to do it." Her teasing smile was an invitation to Rick and he was forced to oblige.

"What motive would Gina have?"

"The obvious one, of course. She will now inherit a pile of money and won't have to teach yoga anymore. But knowing her, she likely will stay with it. Calming, and all that."

The tone annoyed Rick. "What about you, Francine? Are you in the will?"

His question surprised her but she composed herself quickly. "I never thought of that. I suppose I could be thrown a few crumbs, for all I've done for her over the years." She looked at her wineglass, trying to decide whether it was time to pick it up again. "But knowing Rhonda, I doubt it. It will all go to her dear daughter. To assuage her guilt."

"Guilt?"

"Rick, dear, you may have grown up in a loving family but Rhonda and Gina never got along very well once Gina became a teenager. In most mother-daughter relationships the kid grows out of it, but Gina never did, thanks to Rhonda. She was never cut out to be a mother. Not that I should talk. Even after the diagnosis, and on this trip, she treated her daughter the same. You saw a bit of that on the ride up into town yesterday."

"Gina seems to be reasonably stable, despite that."

Francine coughed, as if some of the wine had gone down the wrong pipe. "Gina has always been introverted, which may have helped her overlook her mother's verbal abuse. Not to be a psychiatrist about this—though I've had considerable experience with shrinks—but Gina probably blamed herself for the way her mother was toward her."

"So both mother and daughter felt guilt for the way the mother treated the daughter?"

"It is strange, isn't it?" Francine shrugged. "Are you sure you won't have something, Rick? But of course, you want to get back to your little friend. What's her name?"

"Betta."

"Cute name," said Francine, and drained her glass. "Well, I'm going to have another wine and enjoy the atmosphere. Rhonda would have wanted it that way."

Rick decided there was nothing more she was going to reveal, and he could think of nothing else to ask. He said goodbye and started across the square. After a signal to the waiter, Francine pulled her shawl from the other chair and draped it over her shoulders.

⟨⟩⟨⟩⟨⟩

The phone call with the Phoenix police got them nothing. Rick spoke with a detective named Rede who promised to check the fingerprint sent earlier against their records. While Rick was on the line the detective did a quick computer check on Rhonda Van Fleet and found nothing more than a few parking and speeding tickets. Francine Linwood's only offense in their system was a DWI a few years earlier that had been dismissed by the judge when the arresting officer did not appear for the hearing. Rick thanked him and hung up.

LoGuercio was not impressed with Francine's story about Gina's relationship with her mother, assuming such things went on all the time in America. Rick chalked it up to the influence of American movies and TV shows and left the station frustrated. He'd wasted his time talking with Francine, and again on his phone call to the States, when he could have seen the cathedral with Betta. In addition, LoGuercio was becoming more and more frustrated with the lack of leads in the case, and held out little hope the autopsy would reveal anything helpful. Rick was somewhat cheered by a call from Morgante, who didn't appear to be at all annoyed by Rick canceling the tour of the cathedral, inviting him and Betta to have a glass of wine before dinner. Rick was looking forward to spending some time alone with Betta, but decided courtesy required that he accept. Also, there could be a way to find out why Morgante was going into Bianca Capello's office.

The walk back from the police station took Rick along the side of the cathedral into the square in front of it. The last rays of the afternoon sun lit the top tier of the facade, and he couldn't help stopping to admire it. He recalled the Sandia Peak east of Albuquerque, where the angle of the sun was constantly changing the hues and patterns viewed from below. It was the same way with the shapes and colors on Orvieto's cathedral.

Rick was walking the final meters to the hotel when a short man leaning against the wall stubbed out a cigarette and came toward him. With long dirty hair and a rumpled suit, he looked vaguely familiar. He gave Rick a yellowed grin and extended his hand.

"Signor Montoya."

"Yes," said Rick, unable to avoid the handshake. "And who would you be?"

"Luciano Pazzi. I am a journalist. I expected that you would be staying in one of our best hotels, and inside they confirmed it. They also said you were out, so I decided to wait."

Rick now remembered. Pazzi was the man in the police station talking with Morgante when he'd come out of LoGuercio's office. He was the man everyone knew and disliked, and just from looking at him Rick could understand the dislike. Had LoGuercio given the journalist his name? He doubted it, but Pazzi looked like the kind of reporter who would have other contacts inside the police who would tell him what he needed.

"Why would you want to see me, Signor Pazzi?"

The smile returned. "It is my understanding, Signor Montoya, that you are assisting in the investigation of the murder of the American woman. As an American, you will, I'm certain, understand the importance of the press in finding out the truth. The public has a right to know. I have some questions about the crime and the police's response to it. If you would be so kind."

Rick looked down at the man, unsure whether it was the hair or face that was more in need of soap. "Your concern for the public is admirable, Signor Pazzi, but I don't think I can be of any assistance. I know little of the investigation, and even if I did, the inspector would not be pleased if I shared it with the press. And my main concern at this moment is seeing all that Orvieto has to offer."

"There is more to this city than the churches and museums, Signor Montoya. Once you scratch below the surface you can find the most curious activities. You wouldn't believe what goes on in this town."

"That is your specialty, Signor Pazzi?"

"I suppose one could say that." He reached inside his jacket and pulled out a frayed card. "If you change your mind, please call me. I could make it worth your while."

He gave the card to Rick, turned, and walked toward the cathedral. Rick watched him go, then mounted the steps of the hotel, went through the door, and walked across the lobby to the reception desk. He was deciding whether to ring the bell or just go back and pick up his key himself when he heard Betta's voice.

"I'm in here, Rick."

He waved and went in her direction. "*Ciao, bella.*"

The sitting room across from the desk was cozy, furnished with soft chairs arranged to seat several small conversation groups each with a floor lamp covered by a chintz shade. Betta sat at the far end, the same paperback book she'd been reading open on her lap. Rick walked past a foreign couple who eyed him with bewildered looks. From their dress and hairstyles Rick concluded they were British.

He leaned down and kissed Betta on the cheek before collapsing onto the sofa next to her. "Those people over there are confused. A guy walks in wearing cowboy boots and starts talking Italian with a beautiful young woman who calls him Rick, clearly not an Italian name. They'll spend the rest of the evening trying to figure it out."

Betta glanced at the couple and back at Rick. "How did it go with the woman? Did she confess to the murder?"

Rick sighed. "I'm afraid not. It was a bit of a waste of time since she really wanted to ask me what was happening in the investigation more than give information herself."

"She wanted to know if you are getting close to finding out that she was the one who did it. Surely you could see that. Did she try to work her charms on you?"

"Hardly," he said. "It was a waste of time." He pointed his finger toward the hotel entrance. "But just now, in front of the hotel, I had a curious encounter with a journalist. He was in the police station this morning and LoGuercio warned me that he can't be trusted. After a quick exchange with the man, I'd agree." He tried to come up with a good Italian equivalent to "sleazy," but all he could think of was *squallido*, which didn't do justice to Pazzi.

"How did he find you?"

"I suspect someone in the station leaked my name."

"He is probing into the murder investigation?"

"Exactly. Needless to say, I didn't bite. But I should be asking how *your* afternoon went."

"Me? Nothing of great interest. Did some shopping but didn't buy anything except a postcard. That's all."

Rick looked into her green eyes. It was six months ago that they'd met in her native Bassano, and a few months since she'd moved to Rome to join the art squad at the ministry. He'd helped her find an apartment, shown her the city, spent evenings and weekends with her, shared countless meals. He'd come to know her better than any woman in his life other than his mother and sister. So he was quite sure that she now had something to tell him and wanted to be coaxed to reveal it.

"All right, what happened?"

"I went into a little store to buy postcards, and overheard the clerk addressing a woman there as Signora Aragona. I figured it had to be her."

Rick's eyes widened. "What's she like?"

"Attractive. Takes care of herself. I think she was coming from the beauty parlor when I met her. A bit brash. I could sense she would not be ashamed about having a young *amante*, even proud of it."

Rick sighed. "Too bad you couldn't have talked to her in that store. You could have convinced her to give up a relationship with a young man based purely on physical attraction."

"That would be a bit hypocritical on my part, wouldn't it?"

Rick opted to ignore her humor. "What happened next?"

"I followed her."

Betta described in detail where Tullia had gone, ending with what she had seen on the street in front of the Aragona palazzo. When she finished she was clutching Rick's hand.

"Rick, this is a violent man. I suspect—no, I'm sure—this is not the first time he's been this way with his wife. There's no telling what he's capable of."

Both of them thought of Betta's abusive ex-fiancé, but neither voiced their thoughts. By mutual consent, Carlo was someone they hadn't spoken of since she'd moved to Rome.

"Fabrizio doesn't know what he might have gotten himself into," Rick said. "I wonder what Aragona meant with that last thing he said to her."

"You mean that he had enough to worry about without needing his wife having an affair?"

"Right. He's probably having problems at the office, like every other businessman in Italy. I think Piero would have told me if he knew anything unusual about Aragona, but I'd better call him." He unlocked his hand from hers and pulled out his cell phone. After dialing he waited while it rang.

"*Salve*, Riccardo. Good news?"

"I'm afraid not, Uncle, but some news none the less." He briefly recounted what Betta had said about the encounter with the Aragonas. "Besides letting you know what just happened, I wondered if you have anything on Aragona himself. Not necessarily criminal record, but just—"

"I understand. Let me see what I can find out. I suspect the issues for the man are the usual ones, domestic and otherwise, and nothing will turn up, but I'll check."

"And I'll contact Fabrizio again. I'm not sure what I'll tell him, but I'll think of something."

"Please do. I have to go, I'll get back to you if I find anything on Aragona."

Rick looked at an ornate clock on the wall. "I haven't told you. Morgante invited us for a drink, we're supposed to meet him in about a half hour. He suggested dinner but I told him we had plans. We don't, but I really just wanted to have you to myself."

"And I'd like to have you to myself, to find out what's happening in the case. I'm ready; do you need to change?" She held out the room key.

"Just my shirt. I'll be right down."

He got up and walked toward the hallway, noticing that the British woman who had watched him enter was now sitting alone. Her husband must have needed to change his shirt as well. As he walked by, he touched the tip of an imaginary Stetson and slipped into his best Texas accent.

"Howdy ma'am. Mighty fine hotel they have here."

She was still staring when he reached the stairs.

Chapter Nine

Being the chief of tourism for the city had its perks, and one was access to places that would normally cost a tourist large sums of euros. This included a top floor hotel suite that overlooked the Piazza del Popolo. As Morgante led him and Betta out to the balcony, Rick wondered if the man was given a list of the city's hotel vacancies every morning, and if so, whether this one was at the top. The balcony was more of a terrace, complete with table and chairs, a pair of chaise lounges, and lemon trees in colorful ceramic pots. Anyone staying here would be tempted to have all their meals out here and never leave the suite. The three stood at the railing and looked at the Palazzo del Popolo at the other end of the square, its gray stone turned a faint yellow by artificial illumination. The area in front of it, unlike when the art students sat and sketched, was empty. A few locals crossed the square, oblivious to the ancient building, more interested in getting home in time for dinner and their favorite TV show.

"The cathedral may be the soul of Orvieto," Morgante said, "but this square is the heart. Over the centuries, in time of crisis or celebration, the Orvietani have come together here, and they still do. Now the space is also the stage for music and theater, bringing in visitors from around the world. You must return next year during the season; we have already scheduled some wonderful concerts." He tapped his hands on the railing. "But we can't get ahead of ourselves. Tell me what you have seen already on your first day here."

Betta answered. "Since Rick has been helping out with the case, we haven't seen much more than a quick look at the inside of the cathedral and the Palazzo del Popolo. What would you recommend?"

"There is so much to see, of course, starting with the Duomo. And speaking of that, I still would like to show it to you personally. By chance, the day after tomorrow I will be doing a VIP tour of it for our local chamber of commerce. Next year the city is hosting a tourism convention and we need all our civic leaders to be well versed on our monuments so we can put our best face on Orvieto. If you can, please join us. It will be about nine in the morning."

Rick and Betta exchanged glances and nods. "We'd love to," said Rick. "We don't have to return to Rome until the afternoon."

"Excellent," Morgante said. "And you can mix with Orvieto's elites, such as they are."

Rick suspected the line was an indirect reference to his political rival, Mayor Boscoli.

"Now for other things to see in Orvieto," the man continued. "Besides the Duomo, there are more churches well worth visiting. San Andrea is built on the ruins of an Etruscan temple, so lots of history there. San Giovanale, at the far end of town, dates to the start of the eleventh century and has a wonderful feel to it, as does San Agostino across the square from it. But you must visit the Pozzo di San Patrizio, the well built by Pope Clement VII when he fled Rome during the sack of the city in 1527. And there are many fascinating museums, of course. I always recommend the Museo Civico Archeologico, because the subject is a particular interest of mine."

"You are very proud of the city," said Betta. "I assume you were born here?"

They were interrupted by the arrival of a waiter. His tray held a bottle of wine in an ice bucket, three glasses, and a small plate of canapés. While they watched, he opened the bottle, poured a splash of its yellow liquid into one glass, and passed it to Morgante. After getting a nod, the waiter poured wine into the other two glasses, served Betta and Rick, and filled the third before retiring.

Morgante raised his glass. "*Benvenuti a Orvieto.* And what better way to welcome you than with a glass of Orvieto Classico." Rick and Betta expressed their thanks before their host answered Betta's question.

"I was born in a small town just outside Orvieto, so I can't claim to be a true native, but I moved here at an early age and I feel like one. The only time I spent away was to go to the university to study pharmacology, and even then I lived at home and commuted into Rome. I worked at the pharmacy, and after a few years the owner retired and I had a chance to buy him out. Fortunately I had money saved up and was able to make him an offer. Orvieto has been good to me over the years. When my wife died, half the city was there, including most of my customers at the pharmacy." His eyes wandered out across the piazza before coming back to Rick and Betta. "And you two? You have moved from your native cities."

Rick and Betta gave Morgante an abbreviated account of their backgrounds, Rick's more abbreviated due to his more complicated bi-cultural life to date. Then their host steered the conversation to the investigation.

"I have heard that you are helping the inspector beyond just interpreting when he questioned the two American women. I thank you for that. Do you think he's getting closer to finding the perpetrator of this terrible crime?"

The three had taken seats at the table where the wine bottle, covered with a white napkin, rested in an ice bucket. They adjusted their chairs to enjoy the view. Rick wondered how much Paolo had told Morgante about the investigation. The man was clearly probing, so perhaps he hadn't gotten much from him.

"Inspector LoGuercio has not shared his conclusions with me, but I know he is gathering evidence and interviewing people who may have known the victim." He decided not to remind Morgante that fewer than twenty-four hours had lapsed since finding the body.

"I'm sure LoGuercio is doing his best," Morgante said. He took a drink from his glass. "I expected that the police would send someone to take over the investigation. We had a *commissario* running the police operation here, but he was recently transferred and we're waiting for a replacement." His gaze moved to the piazza and back to Rick. "You have a relative who is a *commissario*, LoGuercio told me."

It annoyed Rick that Morgante knew, though he wasn't sure why. Normally he didn't mind that someone knew his uncle was in the police, but not this time. It wasn't very professional on LoGuercio's part to give out that kind of information to Morgante, but perhaps he was justifying having Rick in the case.

"That's correct, my uncle. And from the little I know about the police hierarchy, I would imagine that if they thought Inspector LoGuercio was not up to the job they would have sent someone immediately. Don't you think so?"

Morgante nodded his head in thought. "I suppose you're right. My hope now is that the news of this murder gets off the front pages quickly. Many of these crimes never get solved, they just fade away. I hate to say it, but for our city, that might be as good an outcome as any. The terrible murder in Perugia a few years ago stayed in the media forever. We don't need that here in Orvieto."

◇◇◇

After their big lunch and the tasty nibbles with the wine, Betta and Rick decided to eat lightly at dinner. They'd passed a pizzeria on the way to their meeting with Morgante, and agreed it would fit the bill if they could find it again. Orvieto wasn't that big, but the streets all looked the same, especially the smaller ones. The arrival of the evening didn't help, it gave all the building fronts a similar shadowy look. As they turned a corner, the place magically appeared, so Rick was spared the shame of having to ask directions.

The décor was wall-to-wall wood. Light-colored pine tables and chairs matched walls festooned with antique wooden farm utensils. The clientele was a mixture of all ages, sometimes at the same table, almost giving them the impression they had stumbled upon a family reunion. As they were shown to the table, Rick checked out the food in front of the diners they passed, and decided that the pizza looked good. Their table sat underneath what looked like a butter churn, which they hoped was firmly attached to the wall lest it come crashing down on their food. Rick ordered *una spina* for each of them and they settled in to study the menus. After a moment, Betta pushed hers away.

"You are certain that it was Morgante who went into the woman's office?"

"Absolutely. He was wearing his white coat and I could see his face. I suggested to LoGuercio that he could have been bringing Signora Cappello something to calm her nerves after receiving the news of her friend's death. Pharmacists do such things."

"Do you believe that?"

"Not in the least. I didn't notice any medications in his hand, though he could have had something in his coat pocket. But by the way he was rushing to her side it seemed like she was more than a regular client."

"So you think they may be...lovers?"

"Could be. Or not that serious. Maybe they're just likers."

The draft beers arrived with thick heads in tall glasses. The waiter paused with his hands behind his back and waited to hear what they'd like to eat. Rick was surprised to hear Betta order a *quattro stagioni* before he asked for his *margherita*. The waiter nodded and left. Rick and Betta tapped their glasses and drank.

"That's good," said Rick before licking some foam from his lips. "Can you guess where I had the best draft beer ever?"

"Germany?"

"No. I was too young to drink beer the time my parents took me to Germany."

"Probably Albuquerque." She still had trouble pronouncing it, but she was getting there.

"Good guess, but no. It was Rio, the last time I visited my parents. There is a little restaurant called the Bar Lagoa, where they have the coldest and freshest draft beer you'll ever drink.

We were sitting outside, and it was warm, as it often is in Rio, even at night. The cold beer on a hot night was wonderful."

"You were at this bar, in a city known for its sensuous women, with your parents?"

"Of course."

He took another swig and his face turned serious. "Betta, I'm a bit *giu* about how things are going here in Orvieto. Only your presence keeps my spirits up. Nothing is happening on the murder inquiry." He raised a hand to stop her from speaking. "I know, I know, it's only been one day, but as my uncle always says, most cases are solved within twenty-four hours. If the killer is not found almost immediately, the chances of finding him drop dramatically. If nothing happens tomorrow, this case will start going cold fast."

"Rick, the autopsy results aren't even in yet."

"Do you think anything will come of them?"

"You never know."

Rick stared at his beer glass, now half full. Or was it half empty? "And the other problem is Fabrizio. It appears that the situation is more serious than we thought, and my cousin is blissfully oblivious to his possible danger. And he doesn't answer his phone."

"Try calling him again, Rick. He may have been in the shower when you called from the street."

Rick pulled the phone from his jacket folded over the back of his chair and hit a button while Betta watched and waited.

Rick shook his head. "I'm going to have to go back to his place and hope he's in. I'll send him a text." He tapped the small screen while she took another pull from her beer. "Sent. 'Will come by your apartment at ten. Hope to find you there.' That should do it."

"If he doesn't want you to come, Rick, you should hear from him."

Their pizzas arrived. The colorful quadrants of Betta's "four seasons" held prosciutto, artichokes, olives, and mushrooms. Rick looked at it and nodded in approval.

"Very lively. But I am more traditional. The classic margherita is the ultimate test of the skill of the *pizzaiolo*. He must add just the right amount of cheese, proportioned with the tomato sauce, and of course the basil has to be present but not overpowering."

"Since you are an expert, I trust you know the origin of the margherita?"

Rick recoiled. "What do you take me for, some tourist? Of course. It was created in Naples to honor the visiting the Queen Margherita, its ingredients mirroring the colors of the Italian flag."

"Bravo."

They picked up knife and fork and cut into their respective pies. The pizza and beer did not take their minds off the issues at hand, as they both had hoped.

◇◇◇

Rick walked Betta to the hotel, picked up the directions for Fabrizio's love nest, and headed out again into Orvieto's night. The temperature had dropped, which may have been the reason the streets were more deserted than earlier. More likely it was simply the time; the locals were sitting cozily in front of their television sets and the tourists were back in their hotel rooms after a long and tiring day of soaking up culture. Rick kept his hands in his coat pockets, pulling one out occasionally to consult the map. Light came only from the occasional street lamp, as most windows of the houses on the streets had already been shuttered. Between their thick stone walls, windows, and heavy wooden shutters, the centuries-old homes could hold in the warmth very well. Rick recalled the traditional houses of his northern New Mexico relatives and wondered which building material was more energy efficient, stone or adobe bricks. Or more expensive.

The street where Fabrizio lived was empty of both people and parked cars. Rick walked along trying to find the number, but it was not as easy as the previous day when the afternoon sun aided in the search. To make things worse, the one street light over Fabrizio's part of the block was burned out, so Rick had to get close to each number to read it. He eventually found the right door, and was about to walk up and ring the bell when he noticed a bit of light spilling out on the street. When he got closer he could see that the door was slightly ajar. Not what would be expected on a chilly fall evening. Rick reached out and pushed the door inward, where it bumped softly against the wall. He stepped inside.

"Fabrizio? Are you in there?"

There was no answer. A lone glass fixture lit a steep stairway to the second floor.

"Fabrizio. It's Riccardo."

He thought he heard some movement coming from the second floor, but he couldn't be sure. As he started up the steps he wondered if he was making a mistake. Fabrizio could be in the midst of an encounter, if that was the word, with Tullia. But the other possibility was that something was wrong, and that thought kept him climbing. The small landing at the top of the stairs had two doors, one straight ahead and the second just to the right. The one directly ahead of him was partly open, and Rick could see what appeared to be a living area. He pulled the door open the rest of the way and stood in the doorway. The room was furnished with the kind of cheap but functional furniture that one would expect in a rental: a sofa with side tables, a wooden shelf on which sat only a dozen books, and a small desk and chair. On the desk a flat laptop computer sat open, its screen dimly lit. A print of the Italian countryside was the only attempt to decorate the walls. Squeezed against the back wall, near a doorway leading to a tiny kitchen, was a table with two chairs.

Rick was about to walk to the computer when the door behind him crashed against his back, knocking him to the ground. He splayed out his arms to break the fall and slid a few feet on the tile floor, managing to keep his chin from scraping. Behind him he heard the door slam shut and the sound of footsteps pounding down the stairs. Angered, he got to his feet, threw open the door, and started down after the intruder, but lost his footing on the third step. Only by grabbing the wood railing did he keep from taking a tumble. By the time he recovered and got outside there was no one to be seen on the dark street.

He rubbed his palms together, decided they were no worse for the wear after the encounter with Fabrizio's floor, and went back inside and up the stairs. The door on the right was now open, revealing a room with one low bed pushed against the wall, and a tall armoire near the window. The bed was made, not what Rick would have expected given Fabrizio's age, but he guessed it was the influence of Tullia Aragona. Off the bedroom was a small bathroom with shower and sink, equally neat. He went back into the living/dining room and saw that the screen of the computer had timed out and was now dark. He also noticed a yellow pad next to it, scribbled with notes. So Fabrizio also used the old-fashioned method for organizing his author's thoughts. But where was he? And who was the intruder who had unceremoniously knocked Rick onto his face? He couldn't help concluding that the visitor had something to do with Signor Aragona's displeasure with the arrangement. Could it have been Aragona himself?

The sound of footsteps arose from the stairwell and Rick looked around to find anything that could serve as a weapon. The intruder could be returning, and this time more ready to take on Rick. As his eyes peered into the kitchen a figure appeared in the doorway.

"Riccardo, sorry I'm late. I see you found your way in."

Rick ran his fingers through his hair and tried to relax his tense muscles. "Do you always leave your door open, Fabrizio?"

His cousin walked into the kitchen and put two bottles of mineral water from the plastic bag into the small refrigerator. "I don't usually lock the door if I'm just going out for a minute. Orvieto's not a big city, I don't worry about burglars."

Rick sat down on the sofa and rubbed his hands together. The skin now felt a bit raw from his fall, something he hadn't noticed during the excitement. "Perhaps you should worry, Fabrizio. I think there was someone in here." He decided not to go into the details of his encounter with the intruder, perhaps a bit embarrassed by being blindsided. "Somebody ran down the steps when I was here in the living room. Does anything appear to be missing?"

Fabrizio's mouth was open in mute surprise, and his eyes darted to his computer.

"Somebody was in here?" Relieved to see that his computer was safe, he surveyed the rest of the room. "Not much to steal here, really. I don't own much, and the rest of the stuff came with the apartment. I guess my clothes could be gone." While Rick waited he walked quickly into the bedroom and returned. "Everything's the same, as far as I can tell. You must have surprised him before he could take something."

"Maybe he was here to see you," Rick said, and waited for the comment to sink in. There was no reaction. "The reason I wanted to talk to you is that your uncle and I are concerned that Signor Aragona could become fed up with this arrangement and do something to end it."

"Do you think he knows? Tullia says he's always at work and doesn't pay any attention to her."

"As you said, Flavio, this is a small town. He knows, believe me."

The concern returned to the kid's face. "What do you think he'd do?"

Rick stretched out his legs and folded one boot over the other. "How about come around and tell you he wasn't happy?"

"Tullia says he never does anything himself." He realized what he'd said and cringed. "Do you think he sent someone here, and that you showed up and scared him off?"

"That's one possibility. The important thing is for you to be careful. A better thing would be for you to pack up your computer and clothes and head back to Perugia."

"I can't do that, Riccardo, Tullia needs me." His voice sounded like he was not just trying to convince Rick, but himself as well. "She called me this afternoon to say she wouldn't be here tonight. She was crying, but she wouldn't tell me why."

Thanks to Betta, Rick was sure he knew why.

◇◇◇

As he walked back to the hotel Rick went over his conversation with his cousin. The kid was almost there, almost ready to give up and head home; only the headstrong tenacity that went along with his age was keeping him there. It made Rick think about his own age, and what he was doing when he was Fabrizio's, and it made him feel old. Perhaps the thought of someone breaking in would push his cousin to leave, once the ramifications started to sink in. Better than waiting for another incident, more serious, to force the decision.

With his mind wandering, his feet did the same, and he got confused as to where he was. Fortunately, in Orvieto all streets and numerous signs put up for the benefit of the tourists lead to the Piazza del Duomo. When he reached it he checked his phone to find it was almost eleven o'clock. Lights lit the facade, and a few stragglers stood enjoying the show as Rick turned up the street to the hotel. He tapped on the door of the room and Betta let him in. She was dressed in jeans and a sweat shirt, and held her book in one hand. After closing the door she put a marker in the pages and returned to where she had been sitting on the bed.

"From how long you were gone, he must have been there. Tell me how it went."

Rick took off his jacket and hung it next to hers on a hook near the door. "Not like I expected." He told her what had happened, leaving out only the detail of being knocked sprawling to the floor. Betta listened to the whole story before speaking.

"Do you think it was Aragona?"

"Hard to say. After seeing him in the restaurant I tend to think that he would send someone to do his dirty work, but I'm not an expert on the behavior patterns of desperate husbands."

"Do you think this might push Fabrizio to hit the road?"

Rick sighed. "If only it would. I was thinking about that on the walk back to the hotel."

He looked at Betta's bare toes poking out from the jeans, remembering that he'd heard somewhere most women thought their feet to be the ugliest part of their bodies. That's silly, he thought. His eyes went to her face, full of concern as she thought about Rick's cousin, whom she'd never met.

"Betta, this is not fair for you. We're here to have an enjoyable few days away from work and enjoying the culture of Orvieto, and I've dragged you not only into my family problems, but a murder investigation. We haven't been together much at all."

She stood up, put her arms around his waist, and kissed him softly on his cheek. "Rick, don't be concerned about me, I'm fine. Just getting away from the office has worked wonders for me. Spending a few days in Orvieto with you is more than I could have asked for."

"I feel the same way, Betta. And nights. Don't forget the nights," Rick added, just as his cell phone rang. He pulled it from his pocket and checked the screen. "I think it's from the States, but I don't recognize the number."

"You'd better answer it."

Reluctantly he put it to his ear. "Montoya."

The voice was almost a whisper. "Rick, this is Gina. Someone is outside. I think they're trying to break into the villa. You must help."

◇◇◇

Because of the hour, few other vehicles were on the road, allowing the police car to take the inside lane on the curves and gain maximum speed when it broke onto the straightaways. Rick and LoGuercio rode in the backseat, holding tight to the hand grips and watching the heads of the two uniformed policemen in front jerk left and right. Only fifteen minutes after the car picked up Rick did it slow down at the driveway of the villa. As instructed by his boss, the driver pulled over, blocking access to the road for any vehicle trying to leave the villa. Another police car silently pulled in behind them.

LoGuercio gathered the five uniformed policeman from the two cars in a circle around him, Rick at his side. "All right, when we get up to the house, you two will go with me around the side of the house to the left. And you, Sergeant, will take the other two and go around the right side. We'll meet in the back by the pool if we don't find anyone. Have your weapons in hand. Be as silent as you can as we get closer to the house, we want to catch this guy. Don't use the flashlights unless you need them."

Rick was holding his hand over his cell phone. "Are you sure you don't want me to go with the Sergeant, Inspector?" There was annoyance in his voice.

"You'll stay in front of the house and keep the Signora calm, Riccardo. Okay, let's go."

They began walking up the driveway in silence. A three-quarter moon gave just enough light to see the driveway as it bent right and left as it climbed the hill. By the time they reached the parking area in front of the villa, Rick's eyes had become adjusted to the semi-darkness. He could see the outline of the villa and the Mercedes parked by the front door. He also noticed a structure he had not seen on the previous visit. A small, low house, which he guessed to be a maintenance storage shed, squatted at one side of the parking area. Likely it was where Donato stored his gardening equipment and other tools to fix what needed fixing.

Without speaking, the policemen split into two groups and moved as planned. Rick watched them disappear. The villa appeared larger in the darkness, perhaps due to the black shadows from a moon now unencumbered by clouds. He hadn't remembered what was around it, but saw that trees ran along both sides, shading and cooling the roof during the day, now offering darkness to anyone wanting concealment. The tall pine trees they had driven through on the way from the road formed a natural colonnade on two sides of the wide gravel lot.

Rick put the phone back to his ear. "We're here, Gina," he whispered. "I'm out in front."

"Thank God."

"So if you hear someone outside now, it will likely be the policeman searching the grounds. You're still locked in your room?"

"I haven't moved since you called back. The lock is so puny, Rick, if he gets in—"

"He won't get in now, Gina, the place is surrounded by police. So just stay where you are. Is Francine still sleeping?"

"I can hear her snoring. She was probably asleep when her head hit the pillow. I doubt if she even got undressed. Booze does that to her."

"They should be done checking in a few minutes. Then I'll come inside and we can talk."

"Keep talking now, Rick. Don't hang up, I'm scared."

He could tell that from her voice. "I will, but I'm afraid my voice will be heard. Let me get farther away from the house."

Rick thought that an intruder could be hiding among the thick growth of trees that circled the parking area, watching the action, but more likely he was long gone. Gina had become calmer when she knew they were on the way, helped by Rick's reassuring voice on the line. When they were almost there, he had started to wonder if she had imagined the whole thing. Or worse yet, had called to get attention.

Despite the cowboy boots, he stepped as quietly as he could across the lot toward the shed. The side of it would offer a barrier so that his voice wouldn't be heard. Like on the portico of the villa itself, ivy hung down from the roof of the little building. It was probably the vines that kept him from noticing it during the day. Perhaps the camouflage was intentional, to keep the high-end villa renters from seeing something that detracted from the beauty of the grounds. The shed was well hidden between the hanging ivy and a row of terra cotta pots sitting on the brick walkway that circled it.

"Rick, are you still there? I think I hear something outside the window."

He ducked under the branches of a tree next to the shed, the phone pressed to his ear. "Gina, I told you to—"

The terra cotta pot crashed against the side of his head. The phone fell from his hands and clattered on the brick. He fell to one knee and his hand flew instinctively to his head. Dirt, but no blood. At the same time he realized that the darkness was not due to the lack of moonlight. He heard someone running away but couldn't see him. He couldn't see anything but a few orange flashes at the corner of his eyes. Were his eyes open?

He tried to focus, but his mind wouldn't cooperate. It slipped back—back to some vaguely distant past—another smash on his head, shouting, and footsteps running. Albuquerque? Yes, that's it. A bar on Central Avenue. Despite the pain, he smiled, pleased with himself that he had such a good memory. It would take more than a bump on the head to rid him of that.

He passed out and crumpled to the ground.

When his eyes came back into focus he was sitting against one of the posts that held up the portico at the entrance to the villa. Rustic lamps on either side of the doorway lit the scene, and Gina, dressed in a bathrobe, knelt before him holding a cold cloth to his head.

LoGuercio stood behind her. "You were right, Riccardo, I should have let you go with the sergeant."

"Or you should have issued me a helmet. Did you get him?"

LoGuercio shook his head.

He reached up to touch his head but Gina pushed it away. "It's going to leave a mark," she said, as if he didn't know that already.

Rick shifted to English. "I'd like to be able to say 'you should see the other guy,' but I'm afraid I can't. What a jerk I was to pick that place to talk to you."

"What are you saying?" LoGuercio said, not liking to be left out.

"She said how brave I was to take on the intruder, and I told her that I had to, because the rest of you had disappeared." Rick noticed LoGuercio's frown. "All right, I was noting that my choice of spots to lurk may have been a slight error in judgment."

"That's better." The inspector pointed at one side of the parking area. "We think he ran that way, through those trees past the shed. There's a road about a hundred meters in that direction and there are some tire tracks next to it that look fresh. The car's long gone. Now if you had—"

"I know, don't remind me. And whatever you do, don't tell my uncle."

"Have the *commissario* find out that his nephew is a total *scemo*? Why would I do that?" He rubbed his eyes. "I need some sleep. Tell the signora that I'm going to leave a policeman here on guard for the rest of the night. And then let's get back to Orvieto."

Rick did as asked, said goodnight to Gina, and climbed into the car. They had decided not to wake Francine; Gina would tell her what happened in the morning. As they drove down the driveway Rick leaned back into the headrest and remembered he had some aspirin back at the hotel. He closed his eyes.

"It has something to do with the murder, doesn't it?"

"Of course, Riccardo. Otherwise it would be too much of a coincidence."

"He was looking for something."

"Either that or our murderer only attacks women from Arizona."

Chapter Ten

Betta was still sleeping soundly when Rick quietly slipped out of the room and walked down the stairs to the lobby. Outside the night chill remained, and he was glad he wore a sweat shirt over his usual tee. He crossed the street, put his leg up on the wall, and began his stretches, causing his head to throb slightly. A bit of pain wasn't going to keep him from his morning run. Rick finished his warm-up with jumps and twists before starting off down the street. A street light looked down at the running figure and created a long shadow, its last duty before ending the shift and shutting itself off. He started up the street, away from the cathedral, and then turned in an alley to work his way to the edge of the town. The street ran parallel to the walls, offering a view of the valleys below. Tufts of fog drifted between the hills as if searching for a hiding place from the sun which would soon appear over the eastern horizon.

The morning run had been a part of Rick's routine since his college days. Its benefits were mental as well as physical, allowing him to go over the events of the previous day as well as look ahead to those of the next. This morning his thoughts were stuck on the problems at hand, but as he had done in the past, he tried so push them from his mind and replace them with something else. Betta? That made him smile. Might as well concentrate on the surroundings, in this case Orvieto. He never got into the "zone" that athletes claim comes over them, he always looked around as he ran and tried to notice the small things. Like all

Italian cities, there were many small things here to notice. As if on cue, a black-and-white cat skittered across his path.

Rick had found the previous morning's route a good one. It skirted the edge of the town, giving him sprawling views of the valley, then cut into the city itself through some narrow streets until reaching a main thoroughfare. The few souls he passed were workers on their way to a morning coffee, or those who would man the machines to make it. He continued his loping stride through the middle of Orvieto, bending left and picking up speed as the route went on a slight decline toward the funicular station. This would be the furthest point before turning back on a loop that loosely followed the *ciabatta* shape of the city itself. As he had done the previous morning, Rick slowed and ran through a stone gate to enter the fourteenth-century *Fortezza* which guarded the southern cliff of the city. In a few hours it would be filled with children and mothers, and at this hour it offered Rick one of the few flat patches of grass on his run. He paused at the edge of the rampart to enjoy the valley view and catch his breath before starting back. As always on his morning runs, even in Rome, he enjoyed the peace of the hour. Here the bonus was seeing the sun start to glow behind the hills to the east. After running lightly in place to keep his leg muscles limber, he turned from the wall and took his first stride of the return run. Unfortunately, thanks to the incline, it would be the more difficult part.

The route brought him out at the plaza they had walked through the first evening after dinner. His legs enjoyed the first level ground since he'd begun his climb near the funicular station, and he slowed to a trot while passing the building which housed the city government.

"Signor Montoya."

Rick stopped and looked at a man who had emerged from the glass doors.

"Mayor Boscoli, *buon giorno.*"

Boscoli looked at the streaks in Rick's sweat shirt. "You appear to be at the end of your run. Can I offer you a coffee?"

"That's kind of you. Perhaps a juice instead."

"There is a bar across the street that all the city employees use."

They entered the bar and the mayor ordered a *spremuta* for Rick and a coffee for himself. The man behind the counter greeted the mayor with deference and gave Rick a quick glance without reacting to the outfit. Perhaps Boscoli brought joggers in with him every morning. Like in many such establishments in Italy, there was nowhere to sit, but it was early enough so that they had the counter to themselves. The barista worked quickly, dividing his efforts between squeezing Rick's orange juice and making the coffee.

"I understand you are visiting from Rome, Signor Montoya." The neon lights of the bar gleamed off the mayor's head.

"That's correct, we're up here for a few days to see the sights."

"I hope this investigation has not taken you away from your enjoyment of the city."

"We've been able to do both." Rick remembered LoGuercio's comment about the mayor being a political adversary of the cultural commissioner. "Signor Morgante, who I met in LoGuercio's office, has kindly suggested things to see."

Boscoli at first only nodded his head. "Yes, Morgante," he said after a few moments. "Did he suggest you eat at Lucia's Restaurant? He usually does that with visitors. His cousin owns the place. You might instead want to consult the guidebooks when it's time for lunch."

The coffee and juice arrived and sugar was added to both.

Rick had heard enough about Morgante. "How long have you been mayor?"

"Three years. I'm up for re-election in the spring. Unless the coalition dissolves, and that is always a possibility in Italian politics. I trust you follow Italian politics, even though you are American?"

"How did you know about my American nationality? Is my accent that noticeable?"

The mayor shrugged. "You are virtually without an accent." He downed his coffee in one gulp and patted the whiskers around his mouth with a paper napkin. "Do you think the inspector is close to solving this murder, Mister Montoya?"

Rick tried to read the face of the mayor. The use of "Mister" instead of "Signor" had an intimidating edge to it, which probably came with the office. Rick was familiar with his type: politicians who were all sweetness with their constituents but short with underlings and people who they decided didn't count. He'd seen them in New Mexico and Rome; the same animal speaking a different language.

"I wouldn't know, Signor Boscoli. My help to the inspector has been in interpreting, since a couple of the parties involved are Americans."

"You must have some sense of how the investigation is going."

"Even if I did, it wouldn't be correct for me to tell anyone, don't you think so?"

It was obvious the man didn't think so. "Of course," he said, and looked without subtlety at his watch. "I must be going."

Rick thanked him for the juice, they shook hands, and Boscoli walked quickly to the door. Rick got the eye of the barista and pointed to the empty cup and glass, getting a head shake in return. Apparently the mayor ran a tab.

◇◇◇

"Remind me again what the mayor looks like," said Betta. "He was only at our table for a minute, and I was looking up at him."

"Heavy set, a little goatee that makes him look a bit satanic, thinning hair." Rick was applying butter to a crusty roll in preparation for a thick layer of jelly. He was always hungry after his run, but today his appetite was larger than normal. She watched him over the top of her coffee cup.

Despite the chill Rick had experienced on his run, the hotel had not moved breakfast inside. The clients didn't seem to mind, given the view of the rooftops and cathedral, but they were more bundled up than the previous morning. Half the tables were occupied, and as usual he tried to guess the nationalities of the people at them. About half Italian, he thought. Two tables of Germans, the rest Brits and Gringos.

"If the long range weather forecast I saw on TV when you were dealing with the mayor was correct, this terrace may soon be closed for the season." She poured more coffee into her cup and added hot milk.

"There could always be…" Rick tried to remember the term in Italian for "Indian summer." He knew there was one, but it wasn't coming to him.

"*L'estate di San Martino*," Betta said, stirring sugar into the cup.

"Yes, that's it. Why couldn't I think of it?"

The smile showed her perfect white teeth. "Clearly you're losing your touch. You'd better quit your translator job and become a policeman, as your uncle is always telling you."

He grunted through a mouthful of roll. After swallowing, he said: "I should probably get paid, I'm working so much for the cops. But today, *Cara*, I will push the murder case out of my mind and leave it in the capable hands of LoGuercio. After I spent so much time with Paolo yesterday, today you and I will be together and do interesting things that have nothing to do with murder."

"Until something comes up."

"Of course, until something comes up." He watched as she carefully cut the rind off an orange and pull the pieces apart on her plate. His hand darted out and grabbed one. "I thought we might see another part of Umbria this morning and drive over to Todi. Does that sound like fun?"

"It does, Rick. I've never been there."

"Then Todi it is. Far from the murder case."

"And far from falling flower pots."

When they'd finished their coffee, Rick pulled back Betta's chair as she got to her feet and they walked to the glass doors. The British couple that had been in the sitting room the previous night was being seated at a table near by. Rick smiled at them and nodded.

"Mornin', folks."

All the flustered woman could come up with was "Good day." The man just stared.

◇◇◇

Betta won the coin toss and chose to be the driver on the *andata* to Todi, so that Rick would get the *ritorno*. That way each would be able to give their full attention to the scenery in one direction. It was only a few minutes into the drive, as the dark blue Lancia was barreling around a traffic circle, when Rick mentioned her speed.

"*Piano*, Betta. This isn't your brother's motorcycle. We're in no rush."

She said nothing and downshifted into third to slow their speed without the use of the brake. The engine voiced a disappointed whine. They followed the distinctive green A1 *autostrada* signs to drive away from Orvieto Scalo and on south. The road passed the entrance and toll booths, staying on the two-lane pavement alongside the highway. Rick watched the cars heading south on the *autostrada* and could not help noticing that Betta was keeping up with them. He kept silent.

A few minutes after passing the toll booths, their road bent left and in quick succession they passed over the Tiber and the highway. Then the road began to climb steeply, going through an area that would not be considered the most scenic part of Umbria. For most world travelers, central Italy was vineyards, art and Renaissance buildings. But the less picturesque infrastructure had to be put somewhere, and their car passed it now. Stacks of rusting metal and yellowed plastic pipe rose behind a menacing row of barbed-wire fencing. Old cars and trucks that had long ceased to run tried unsuccessfully to form a neat line. The fading letters on the building between them indicated a construction firm, but Rick doubted it had put up any structures recently. Farther up the road was another low building, but at least this one showed human activity, and its coat of paint was recent. They were past it before he could decipher the type of business.

The highway passed through scrubby bushes before opening a view of a dam which held back the Tiber to form the Lago di Corbara. Their road now ran along the lake, crossing one arm of it on a causeway before climbing into hills covered with low trees. Below them the water squeezed back to river-width as they drove over hills that looked down on its meandering course. A bridge took them to the other side just before the gorge softened into a river valley for the final kilometers to Todi. Betta slowed, turned off what had become almost a highway, and crossed back over the river to the town of Pontecuti. Here the climb began in earnest. The road sliced through the tiny town and started a series of turns through groves of olive trees, cutting back and forth to the delight of the driver. Rick could sense her disappointment when the hill leveled out and she had to turn onto a side road to reach the tourist parking area. They found a space at the end of a row and she turned off the engine. Rick happily unlatched his seat belt and stepped out of the car.

Despite the similarity in elevation between Orvieto and Todi, it felt colder. It may have been the cooler air blowing down the Tiber River Valley from Perugia, or simply that Todi's hill was more exposed, but the temperature was lower. They locked the car and walked toward the contraption that would take them up to the town itself. The lot was a third full, and the line of long spaces marked for tour buses had only one occupant. It would be filled in July and August, but now the tourist season was winding down, despite the near-perfect weather.

"*Mannaggia.*"

"What's the matter, Rick?"

He jerked his thumb at a car parked at the end of the row. "Let's hope there's more than one silver Mercedes in Umbria. The two American women's rental car is just like that."

"I'm sure it's a common model and color. And you promised you would stay away from the investigation today, so it couldn't be them, could it?"

They picked up a ticket and waited for the next ride up. Unlike Orvieto's antique funicular, the machine the *Todini* chose to carry their tourists up to the town was a rectangular glass and metal box that ran up and down a single, steep track. For the hearty, or those who didn't want to wait or pay for the next run, metal steps ran the length of the line. Rick looked up and saw the empty car slipping into its berth. They got on with five other people, and after a few minutes the doors sealed shut and they climbed through the trees. At the top was a paved area between a street and the wall, what would be called a scenic overlook in America. Benches and trees broke up the expanse, but not enough to block the view of the valley below and the hills in the distance. Rick and Betta enjoyed it for a few minutes before starting up the street into the *centro storico* of Todi.

Betta took out her red Umbria guidebook and read from it as they walked. The church of San Fortunato appeared high above on their right at the top of a long set of stairs, but they decided to continue on to the main square, the jewel of the town. They passed a couple tourist shops on the left, as would be expected for the route visitors took from the funicular into town. Rick remembered that Crivelli's other ceramics store was somewhere in Todi, but he expected it to be found in a more prestigious location. The street bent to the left after passing the town theater and narrowed to an almost car-width canyon before reaching the long, rectangular piazza. They stopped to survey the space before them.

To draw tourists, many town squares in Italy had become the site of summer theater and concerts, but Rick and Betta agreed that this one would work especially well for such events. It was small, almost intimate by Italian standards, and its rectangular shape lent itself to rows of chairs. The cathedral facade at the far end was the perfect backdrop for a concert, its raised steps the ideal place to set up a stage, and the buildings around the other three sides would help the acoustics and provide window seats for a privileged few.

"I wonder if the Romans had that in mind," Betta said, holding her book, "when they laid out their forum here a couple thousand years ago."

"It looks like there's nothing left from that time," Rick said as his eyes moved around the piazza. "Not even a couple columns. That's a shame."

"Still, it's quite spectacular." She read descriptions of the buildings around the square, starting with the three massive palazzi closest to them.

Rick listened and then they walked to one of them. "The thirteenth century must have been a prosperous time for Todi to get those three constructed. It couldn't have been cheap, and as we can see, back then they built them to last." He rapped his knuckles on the stone.

Betta snapped her book shut. "Let's go to the cathedral and work our way back."

Rick nodded and they headed toward the far end of the square.

"Rick!"

He looked up and saw Gina waving as she came down the stone steps of the Civic Museum. "So it was their car," he said to Betta. "Go ahead. I'll meet you in the Duomo in a few minutes."

Betta sized up the woman coming down the stairs. "That's all right, I'll wait. You can introduce me. I can practice my limited English, since you never let me do it with you."

"Don't start on that again. You know what I've told you about relationships fracturing when one person tries to teach a language to the other."

"I think you made that up."

Gina was dressed in the same outfit she'd worn on the funicular, making Rick conclude that she liked to pack light. She was almost out of breath, even though she'd been coming down rather than ascending the stairs. She looked at Betta and back at Rick.

"Hi, Rick. Thank you for what you did yesterday morning, it made it much easier to deal with what happened to Mom." She looked at Betta and back at Rick.

"Gina, this is Betta. You remember her from the funicular. Betta, Gina."

"I was going to ask about her when I saw you at the juice bar, Rick, and then I was so upset yesterday morning that I didn't ask then."

Rick wondered if Betta had understood Gina's rapid speaking style.

"How are you coping, Gina?"

"As well as can be expected, Rick. Thank you for asking. We decided to get out and see things rather than mope around the villa. My mother would have wanted it that way." She rubbed her nose with her fingers to prevent a sniffle.

"Where's Francine?"

She shook her head before pointing across the square. "She's over there drinking a cappuccino and nursing a headache. She got completely trashed last night in Orvieto. I had to drive us back to the villa, in the dark and all those winding roads with her carrying on. Rick, it was terrifying." She grasped Rick's arm without thinking and quickly let it go, the move not lost on Betta.

Apparently Francine had not told Gina that she'd seen Rick in the outdoor cafe the previous afternoon. So he wouldn't mention it either. "People show their grief in different ways."

Gina snorted as if Rick had told a bad joke, bringing a surprised look to Betta's face. "I'm beginning to wonder if it's in her to grieve at all."

This was a new side to Gina. "That's a pretty strong statement."

She glanced at the other side of the square, perhaps to be sure that Francine was still well out of ear shot. "Well, Francine will be getting some part of my mother's inheritance, given their friendship. I'm sure of it. Likely some guilt from the way she treated her."

"What do you mean?"

"Years ago, when Francine was about to be engaged, my mother had an affair with the man. There was no engagement after Francine found out. My mom always said that the man wasn't worth it, and that she saved Francine from a bad marriage, and Mom knew about bad marriages. But I think she felt guilty for what she'd done."

Rick thought about what Francine had said about guilt while drinking her wine the previous afternoon. Guilt seemed to be a big issue in Arizona.

"So bottom line, Rick, Francine will manage her grief just fine. I think she's now focused on the joys of being in Umbria, and I don't mean the museums."

Rick and Betta walked slowly toward the cathedral after saying their goodbyes to Gina.

"Were you able to get what she was saying? The woman talks fast and runs her words together."

"You met her at a juice bar?"

Rick couldn't tell if the question was mocking or serious. For sure it was annoying. "I forgot to mention that. When I was coming back from seeing Fabrizio the first time she was standing outside a bar. We exchanged a few words."

"Oh."

He decided not to explain Gina's comments about her mother and Francine. If Betta didn't understand them, it was her problem.

They crossed the piazza and went up the steps of the cathedral, then left the sunlight for the subdued darkness of its interior. After dipping hands into the stone font just inside the doorway and crossing themselves slowly, their eyes moved naturally to the altar before pulling back to take in the space in its entirety. Rick was pleased to spot what he regretted not seeing in the piazza outside: the columns that lined the nave had to be Roman. Over the centuries the Italians became masters at recycling building materials, and one of the most common examples was using Roman columns in churches. Besides the practical aspect of such re-use, there was also the symbolic message of Christianity taking the place of paganism. Italians loved symbolism. They walked to the front and sat in one of the pews. Betta pulled out her red guidebook and opened it to the pages on Todi. Rick looked around while she read silently.

"What should I know about the cathedral?" he said after a few minutes. "So far I like it. Nobody came in and ruined it with changes when Gothic architecture went out of fashion, thank goodness." It was one of Rick's pet peeves.

"To begin with, *si vuole*, it was built on the site of a Roman building."

Rick laughed. "You have to love the Italian language. So if we wish to believe it, the guy who wrote the book won't mind, even though it may not be true. Well, I for one am going to accept that we're sitting on top of a Roman foundation."

"I will too," said Betta firmly.

She read the rest of the section about the cathedral while Rick turned at the appropriate times to see what was being described. The biggest surprise, they agreed, was the painting of the Last Judgment which covered the entire inside wall of the church entrance. Neither had noticed it behind them on the way in, but now they walked back toward the door to appreciate its power. Christ sat on a throne at the top with the blessed, while down below the writhing figures of the damned struggled vainly with grotesque devils pulling them into the inferno. The location was intentional, a warning to the faithful as they left the piety of the church for the temptations waiting outside its doors.

Rick stopped to zip his jacket before they started down the steps outside. Clouds had moved in, and with them a light but chilling wind. Betta pulled the light wool coat she was wearing tighter.

"Can I see the map in your book?" Rick asked. Betta passed it to him. "Unless you want to go to the Pinacoteca," he said, holding the book open to the map page, "why don't we go down one of these streets, get on one that clings to the side of the hill, then work our way up to Via Cavour?"

"And avoid encountering the American women?"

He chose to ignore the inference of the question, as well as the tone. "Not just that. It will give us some good views, and we can't get enough of them. But mostly we can see another part of the town. No telling what interesting building we might come upon."

The small side streets were narrow, as expected, to the point of being wide enough only for foot traffic. They were also so steep at points that steps appeared in the pavement and metal handrails had been attached to the stone buildings on each side. Even with those walking aids, these would not be streets to be traveled on a snowy winter day. Winter would also wipe out the flowers in the window boxes, their colors made more brilliant in contrast with the street's canvas of gray stone. The alley emptied onto a level street that ran along the side of Todi's hill, a pleasant change after the steep descent. The hill on the left side of the street dropped off steeply, giving the houses on the right a perfect view of the valley below. A hundred meters ahead they found a long, rectangular pool under a portico supported by seven columns. Betta pulled out her trusty red book, did some searching, and found that the Fonte Scarnabecco, a public well, dated to 1241. Each capital at the top of its seven thin columns was different from the next, but the book wasn't able to tell them why.

"You were right, Rick. This is lovely, and if we hadn't come this way we would have missed it."

At the next corner they made a right turn and started climbing up another narrow street. They crossed under arches which appeared to have no purpose other than to brace the upper floors of the two buildings. The buildings were all residential, with wood doors at street level and small windows that offered only a view of another stone building across the pavement. It was a good way to get to know the neighbors, if nothing else. The street bent left and right before emptying on what the map indicated as the main street leading from the Porta Romana up to the main square. The main gates of Todi, like so many towns in Italy, were named for the destination reached by passing through them. Rick assumed there was a Porta Perugina at the north end of the walls, and a Porta Orvietana on the west. Where else would anyone be going to or coming from? Though as narrow as the one they'd just been on, this street was populated by a few shops as well as residences. The closer they climbed to the center of town the more commercial it became. Rick stopped Betta and pointed at a sign hanging above a doorway.

"There's the other shop of the guy I told you about, the one who taught the victim pottery techniques when she was a student."

"Studio Crivelli," Betta read. "There doesn't seem to be much to it. Let's go in, I'm curious to see his work."

"You go ahead. Crivelli goes back and forth between his two shops, and could be here today. I don't want to run into him again. But I'll be interested to hear what you think of his ceramics' designs."

It didn't take her long. Rick was standing a few doors up gazing through the window of a *salumaio*, realizing he was starting to get hungry. His eyes rested on a platter with thick slices of *porchetta*, stuffed suckling pig with rosemary and other herbs. It was a favorite of his in Rome, going back to roadside stands on Sunday trips to the countryside when he was a kid. Of course in Todi they would claim theirs to be the best in Italy.

Betta's voice jolted him out of his culinary musings.

"Your man Crivelli has found a style he likes and sticks with it. It must work, the girl there says he exports it all over the world. She gave me a card with his website so I can order."

"He wasn't there?"

"No. Unless he was in the back somewhere, creating art."

"My guess is that he has other people actually getting their fingers in the clay."

After passing a small square with a fountain decorating its back wall, the street leveled out and they passed the obligatory statue of Garibaldi, staring down at Todi from a tall pedestal. Dressed in his signature hat and cape, the Liberator folded his hands on top of his sword, unsheathed as if to signal he was ready to fight again for a united Italy should he be needed. They continued on and found themselves back in the main square, at the opposite end from the cathedral, the completion of a large loop. The question at that point was a simple one: go to the museum or go to lunch. Neither Rick nor Betta found it difficult to answer.

The restaurant they chose from the guidebook sat among the fields in the valley below the town. Enough Fall had arrived in this part of Umbria to allow the trattoria to have a few dry branches burning in a brick fireplace in the corner. The odor of the fire wafted lightly through the dining room, matching the rustic décor of wood and brick. They were early, just one other table was occupied by three men in leather jackets. A waiter gestured to the new arrivals, indicating that anywhere they wished to sit was fine with him. Betta chose a table close to the fire.

"This looks perfect," she said, rubbing her hands together as if it had been below zero outside. The waiter brought menus and turned over the glasses that had been sitting at each place. Rick ordered mineral water and a half liter of the house red, and the waiter scurried off.

"I've been turning over in my mind what Gina told me up in the piazza."

"I suspected that, Rick. Your head seemed to be elsewhere since you talked to her. Tell me again what she said, I doubt if I got it all."

"Well, to begin with, she thinks Francine will be getting some of her mother's inheritance. In addition, several years back there was some issue about a man they were both interested in."

Her eyebrows went up. "Really? All the money wouldn't all go to Gina?"

"She didn't think so."

"Both those revelations make this Francine woman a stronger suspect. But if the daughter gets most of the inheritance, she's a suspect as well. And she has no alibi."

"Nobody does; the murder happened in the middle of the night."

The water and wine arrived, along with a basket of warm bread that the waiter proudly noted had just come out of the oven. They turned their attention to the menu and decided, since they made their own bread in the place, to start with the *crostini di caccia*, toasts with pâté made from various things hunted. It seemed like an appropriate dish for a cool autumn meal. Staying in the same seasonal mood, they both ordered the fettuccine *al profumo di bosco*. Rick guessed that the "scent of the forest" on the fresh pasta would include, at a minimum, some type of mushroom. After the pasta course they would decide what else they wanted, if anything. He poured each of them wine and they tapped glasses.

Rick was bringing the wine to his lips when he heard the familiar sound of the Lobo Fight Song. He put down his glass and pulled his phone from his pocket.

"It's LoGuercio."

Betta shrugged and sipped her wine.

"Si, Paolo…no, we're outside Todi, having lunch…not at all, the food hasn't arrived yet." He looked at Betta, who was drumming her fingers on the table in what Rick interpreted as mock impatience. "Sure, I'll come by when we get back, I have some things I wanted to tell you anyway, since I ran into one of the American women…yes, that should be perfect, see you then." He closed the phone.

"Is there something new?"

"I don't think so," Rick answered. "He wants to go over where things are at this point. Right now he's going to see Signora Vecchi." He noted the puzzled frown on Betta's face. "She's the woman who ran the boardinghouse where our victim lived when she was a student here. I may not have mentioned her to you."

"One of many things you hadn't mentioned. But you can tell him what the daughter said."

Rick pulled a crust of bread from the basket. It was still warm. "Exactly. But the other thing Gina said I need to think about a bit more to decide how to translate it into Italian for Paolo. I was about to tell you."

"You weren't going to keep it from me again?"

He ignored the jab. "She said something about Francine, the other woman, not really showing much grief. But if I understood correctly, she also insinuated that Francine is, well, fooling around."

"Here? They just got to Italy a few days ago. Wait a minute. Do you mean…?"

"Exactly. The caretaker. Paolo's hunch that young Donato could be doing more than cutting the grass may be correct."

The waiter put empty plates before each of them and positioned the platter of *crostini* in the center of the table. Rick saw two kinds of pâté, a mushroom and tomato spread, and something else he didn't recognize but looked very appetizing. He also counted them.

"Thank goodness," he said as he motioned for her to take first pick. "It's an even number. We won't have to fight over the odd one."

Chapter Eleven

LoGuercio was not surprised to find that Signora Vecchi lived a mere two blocks from the police station. The town was so small that several Orvietos could fit inside the walls of his native Ferrara. When he was growing up, his preferred mode of transportation had been the bicycle, as it still was in the city for young and old. Unlike the many Italian cities that had been built on hilltops, Ferrara was flat and spacious, its streets straight and often wide. In Orvieto there were few bike riders, in part because of the inclines of some of the streets, but mostly because everything was close enough to walk. That's what LoGuercio had decided to do to reach the woman's residence.

He stopped when he got to the door. The two-story building had a plain front painted dark yellow, and its entrance was marked by a marble slab: Casa San Bernardo—1948. It was one of a few retirement homes in the city, one that LoGuercio guessed had been built to house the many widows caused by the war. The design was bland and institutional, with no hint of the fascist architectural style popular less than a decade before the date on the plaque. He pushed open the door and entered a wide reception area. A nurse looked up from a desk on one side and eyed him with curiosity. He was not a family member she was used to seeing. Her expression turned to surprise when he showed her his identification and asked for Signora Vecchi. She had trouble forming her words.

"But, I don't understand."

"I said I'd like to speak with—"

"No, Inspector, I heard you. What I don't understand is how Signora Vecchi knew you were coming. She told me this morning after breakfast that someone would show up to see her today. Since she has no relatives that I know of, I found it strange. And now you appear." She gestured toward open double doors on the other side of the room. "She's waiting for you in the visitors salon. She's the woman wearing a bright red sweater."

LoGuercio thanked her and walked to the doorway. The visitors salon was divided into a half dozen conversation areas, each with comfortable if shabby chairs. One was being used by two people who looked old enough to be residents, but they were chatting with a much older man who listened with a distracted smile. On the other side of the room, under a hanging light fixture that looked to be original to the building, Signora Vecchi sat on a wide couch. She looked up and smiled at the policeman. Besides the sweater, she wore a long black skirt, and her gray hair had been carefully put up in a bun. A hint of rouge shone from her cheeks below frameless glasses. LoGuercio walked over and took her hand in his.

"I am Inspector LoGuercio, Signora, I understand you are expecting me."

She smiled, but her eyes squinted at him. "Aren't you supposed to show me your badge or something?"

"Of course, sorry." He pulled his identification card from his wallet and she studied it, glancing from his face to the photo and back before returning it to him. He sat across from her.

"It took you long enough to find me. When I saw in the paper before breakfast that the murdered woman had attended the program here, I expected to see you this morning."

Of course, the newspaper. The morning's edition had run more details than he'd wanted to become public. Orvieto was small enough to walk everywhere, but the downside was that news often spread too fast.

"We were interviewing other people who knew the victim then."

"The paper said she was Rhonda something, a name I didn't recognize. But Rhonda wasn't that common a name, so I assumed it was Rhonda Davis. Was I right?"

"You were right, Signora." Normally this was the point when he'd say that he was the one who was supposed to be asking the questions, but he couldn't bring himself to do it. This was not the doddering senior he had expected, the woman was sharper than his own grandmother.

"So you remember Rhonda Davis. What can you tell me about her?"

"She was one of a few of the girls that I remember quite well." She folded her hands in her lap and looked past him into the distance. "The program was my whole life then, I'd just lost my husband and used what money he left me to buy the boarding-house. It was my good fortune that right at that time the university started the exchange program and needed a place to put the girls. I don't remember if Rhonda was here for that first year, but it was early on. She arrived already speaking decent Italian, unlike most of the girls. She'd been living somewhere else in Italy, I think."

"Milan."

She nodded. "Yes, Milan. So I was able to talk to her more than I could with the others."

"What did you talk about?"

"Just about everything. Living in Orvieto, the history of the place. She was curious about what it was like during the war, when I was a little girl. And politics. She was fascinated by politics. As you might expect for an arts student, she was very much to the left politically. It was just at the time of the worst turmoil in Italy—the student uprisings, the shootings, the kidnappings." She frowned and shook her head as if trying to shake the memory from her mind.

"Do you remember any of her friends?"

"Thought you might ask that. No, I can't recall anyone specific. I don't think she had a boyfriend in the program, but she had some Italian friends. Boys, I mean. Those girls didn't think I knew what they were up to, but I did. Nothing in my house, though, I saw to that. I didn't want the university to cancel the contract, so I was pretty strict about what went on there."

A middle-aged man in a dark suit and a frail woman walked slowly into the room and took seats near them. Signora Vecchi nodded at them.

"That's my friend Luisa," she said to LoGuercio in a lower voice. "Her son visits her every day. I never had children." Her sigh was short, a quick breath. "I suppose the American girls were like family to me. Who do you think did this, Inspector?"

The question brought him back to the matter at hand. "Unfortunately no obvious suspect has been identified. It could have been a random murder, but it would seem more likely there was some connection with the time she was here as a student." It was more than he should have revealed, but he was too tired to care. "Which is why your help in remembering something— anything—could be critical."

She rubbed her hands together. "I've been thinking about it since I read the article in the paper. Perhaps something will come to me. I've been looking at the photos to try to jar my memory, but it hasn't helped much."

"Photos?"

He had noticed a white album on the table next to her, but assumed it belonged to Casa San Bernardo. She picked it up and put it in her lap. "Back then everyone had a camera, and a real one, not a telephone." She patted the cushion next to her. "Come sit and I'll show you."

He did as he was told, and she opened the album. The photos were mostly group shots, though some pictures had a much younger Signora Vecchi standing with one or two of the students. Most were taken in front of the same building, which he assumed was her boardinghouse. LoGuercio found it interesting that styles had not changed radically in forty years. The hair was different, longer on the girls' heads and the boys' faces, but the clothing was essentially unchanged, especially the jeans. A few of the tee-shirts had words written on them, but the shots were too wide to be able to read them easily.

"I think this is Rhonda's year," she said after turning one of the thick, plastic pages. The inspector leaned closer. The photos were yellowed, like the earlier ones, but still clear. In one of the group photos Rhonda stood smiling in the front row. The next showed Signora Vecchi holding a pot, Rhonda next to her.

"She gave me that pot." She rubbed her finger over the plastic sheet of the album. "You know, I can't remember what happened to it. I think when I moved in here it must have been left behind. What a shame, I could have found space for it in my room."

At the top of the next page was another photo of Rhonda. She stood next to a bearded male who looked vaguely familiar to LoGuercio. Her arm was entwined in his and they both smiled at the camera.

"Who's that?"

"He was the pottery instructor, Crivelli. He had just been hired."

LoGuercio looked closer at the photo, recalling that Crivelli denied having any social contact with the students. One photo couldn't prove him wrong, but it was curious nonetheless.

She tapped on the photo. "Crivelli is still in Orvieto, I think. You should talk to him. The only other I can think of from that time would be Bianca." Her finger was now over another picture, a group shot. Bianca Cappello and Rhonda stood together in the back row. "But I think she moved to Milan."

"She's back in Orvieto, Signora. Runs a real estate business. I spoke with her yesterday."

"Yes. Yes of course. Now I remember. It's hard to keep track of people if they don't come by to see me." She closed the album and placed it carefully on the table. "You'll come back and tell me when you've solved the case, won't you, Inspector?"

"Of course, Signora." He took out a card and put it in her hand. "But if you remember anything else, please call me. Even minor details can be helpful." He stood up.

She held the card between her thin fingers. "Of course I will."

LoGuercio bent down to shake her hand and thank her for her help. She watched him as he walked to the double doors and out into the reception area. Signora Vecchi's friend, deep in conversation with her son, had never noticed the policeman.

◇◇◇

It was still early afternoon when Rick started to walk across Orvieto to the police station. He'd left Betta at the hotel with her book and received her blessing for his return to the murder case if he promised to stay away from terra cotta pots. Between his morning runs and walking to the interviews with LoGuercio, he was starting to feel like he knew his way around town, at least the main arteries. He found himself on the street he had walked with LoGuercio the previous day, recognizing the shoe store he had perused.

He was mulling over his suspicions about Gina and Francine when a man and woman rushed out of a store and walked toward him, arm in arm. Bianca Cappello and Livio Morgante. She looked up and noticed Rick, a shocked expression on her face. Morgante saw him and smiled.

"Riccardo, I think you've met Bianca Cappello?"

"I have," Rick answered. She nodded, but said nothing.

"Are you feeling better today, Riccardo?" Morgante turned to Bianca. "I spoke with Inspector LoGuercio this morning and found that he and Riccardo were called to the villa where the murdered woman was staying. Possible break-in. But they didn't find anyone, apparently."

"You're well informed," said Rick, not disguising his annoyance. "I didn't realize that you two were friends."

"It's no secret," said Morgante, squeezing her hand.

She smiled at the pharmacist, but to Rick the smile seemed forced. Or nervous. If their relationship was not a secret, what was her problem? Likely she didn't want to be reminded of the death of her old friend, and Rick was that reminder. If Morgante and Cappello were in a relationship, which was obviously the case, they must have shared their information about Rhonda's murder. Had Bianca not leveled with Morgante about how well she knew the victim, since that would make her a suspect?

Finally Bianca spoke. "The owners of two properties outside town want to hire me to rent out and manage their villas, so I need to do an inspection." She had assumed the tone of a businesswoman, though it didn't match the flamboyant way she was dressed. "Livio has agreed to go along for the ride."

"She promised to buy me dinner at a wonderful little trattoria near the villas. It was an offer I couldn't refuse." He patted her hand. "And have you and Betta been seeing the sights today?"

"We drove to Todi this morning and had lunch."

Morgante appeared stunned, but Rick realized it was for dramatic effect.

"Todi?" He swept out his hand. "With Orvieto at your disposal? I'm shocked. Well, tomorrow you will see our jewel. We are still confirmed for tomorrow morning at the cathedral, aren't we?" He turned his head to Cappello. "Bianca, I invited Riccardo and his friend to join us at the tour tomorrow morning. Since he's been so helpful to the police, I don't think the mayor will mind that I invited him, do you?"

"He'll only be annoyed that he didn't think to invite Riccardo himself," she answered.

"Betta and I are looking forward to it," said Rick. "I must not keep you, and Inspector LoGuercio is waiting for me. Nice to see you both. Enjoy your dinner."

They exchanged goodbyes and went in different directions. Rick had mentioned his appointment with LoGuercio to see what Bianca's reaction would be, but she betrayed nothing. The nervousness, or perhaps surprise, that she'd shown at first had been replaced by a studied calm. He put it out of his mind and continued on his way to the police station.

It was getting close to the hour when offices were closing, and it appeared that some workers were already heading for home. They joined students hoping to hook up with friends, pensioners out for a stroll following their afternoon nap, and wives making last-minute purchases for the evening meal. It was one of Rick's favorite times to walk the streets of an Italian city, when they were most full of life and movement. He passed the window of a *salumaio,* which was as inviting as the one he'd seen in Todi, though without any suckling pig. The place of honor in this shop was a basket almost overflowing with freshly made cheese tortellini. As he watched, a hand inside a white jacket sleeve reached down and scooped some of them into a small box. Rick wondered if they would be served that evening in broth or on a dish with a sauce. On he walked, coming to a toy store. It reminded him that it wasn't too early to think about birthday gifts for his two nephews back in Albuquerque. This was one of the advantages to having nephews: it gave him acceptable cover to browse toy stores and play with its wares. He looked at the display of toy cars and tried to recall what he'd given them last year. In his next e-mail to his sister he would have to ask; she would remember. He realized the time, reluctantly turned from the display, and continued to his destination.

The final few hundred feet to the police station were on a gravel path through a small and beautifully manicured park. It was a miniature version of the Borghese Gardens in Rome, complete with the tall umbrella pines that inspired Respighi. The rays of the afternoon sun were broken by the lanky trunks, casting long shadows across the grass and gravel. He stepped onto the path from the sidewalk which circled the park.

"Signor Montoya."

Luciano Pazzi, looking no different than the previous day, appeared out of one of the shadows.

Rick did not try to hide his annoyance. "Signor Pazzi, if I had anything to say to you I would have called."

"I suspected you would be coming to see the police again," the man said. "It is curious that they need the help of a foreigner to do their work." Pine needles crunched under his shoes as he walked closer. He stopped under one of the pines close to the path and turned his head upward. "Beautiful trees, aren't they, Signor Montoya? Legend says they were brought here by one of the popes when he passed through Orvieto. Homesick for Rome, perhaps."

"Listen, Pazzi—"

"I listen to people all the time, that's how I earn my living. But it is not a one-way street, I am often the source of information for others. Unfortunately I can't think of how I could be helpful to you, a tourist passing through Orvieto, so I have to rely on your sense of—"

He didn't finish the sentence. The crack of a gun sounded somewhere to Pazzi's left, and simultaneously a bullet thudded into the tree next to him. The man froze, and his mouth dropped open to reveal a row of crooked teeth. Rick instinctively dropped flat to the ground.

"Pazzi, get down!"

Another shot whizzed by, but fear had turned the journalist to stone.

"Pazzi!"

The third bullet found the lower part of the man's neck. He instinctively grabbed the wound as he fell to the ground on his side. Dark blood poured through his fingers and seeped around his shirt collar. He still stared in disbelief, but without focus.

Rick crawled toward Pazzi while he looked toward where the shooter must have been. He saw only trees and shadow, but as he reached the wounded man the sound of a car speeding off rolled across the grass. He also heard shouting coming from the opposite direction, where the police station stood.

Pazzi now could see Rick and was trying to speak. Blood trickled from the side of his mouth as he made the effort. Rick put his ear close and tried to understand the words, which came out in a rough whisper. Pazzi's mouth stayed open but his sightless eyes glazed over.

Rick looked up to see two uniformed policemen pounding along the gravel path toward him. Behind them was LoGuercio. Rick got to his knees and pointed toward the far end of the park.

"The shooter was over there, I think I heard him drive off," Rick called to the policemen, who had come to a halt at the sight of the body.

"Get over there and see what you can find," ordered LoGuercio, out of breath. He reached Rick and stared at Pazzi's now lifeless body. "Tell me what happened, Riccardo."

Rick rose to his feet and realized that his heart rate was higher than when he did his morning run. He took a few breaths before answering. "I was just starting through the park when Pazzi appeared. He was barely into his second sentence when we heard a shot. Pazzi froze and I hit the ground. The second bullet missed him and hit the tree, but the third did this. He died almost immediately after the bullet hit his neck, but I crawled over to him and he said something."

"And that was?"

"It was difficult to understand, since the bullet hit his throat, but I think he said '*sono morto*.'"

"'I am dead'? A bit dramatic, but certainly accurate." LoGuercio bent down and examined the body without touching it. "If the shot had been a bit higher he would have died instantly. Which might have been better for him."

He got to his feet and pulled out his cell phone. Rick stood silently while the policeman made phone calls. After three he punched off his *telefonino*.

"The crime scene unit is on its way, and fortunately the forensics person is too. She finished her work in Terni." He looked up to see one of the policeman trotting back toward them.

"We found one shell, Sir, in the street near the curb. Aurelio is guarding it until the area can be roped off. If there were other shells the shooter must have picked them up."

"I heard the tires of a car speeding off," Rick said. "The guy could have used the car roof to steady his aim."

LoGuercio walked to the tree and rubbed his finger over a small hole in the bark. "It looks like a nine millimeter slug, but I'll leave it to the forensic people to pull it out and tell me for sure."

Rick stood aside and watched as the park filled with officials and equipment. LoGuercio gave orders, including sending two of his men to the houses along the street to find if anyone had seen or heard anything.

Rick's phone rang and he fished it from his pocket and checked the number. It didn't seem possible that Piero could already have gotten news of the journalist's murder. He hit the answer button.

"Uncle, you called at just the right time, I'm standing here doing nothing and have time to talk."

"I wish I could say the same. I was calling about Vincenzo Aragona."

Rick's eyes stayed on the activity on the grass. "I'm all ears."

"It's very curious. His record appears to be clean, but I can't be sure."

"I don't understand."

"Nor do I. There is something missing, but how much and what it deals with, I don't know. Without trying to explain our arcane records system, Riccardo, I'll just say that I can detect a gap. Someone has removed information from his record."

"How could that happen?"

"You've heard me rant many times about the overlapping and often conflicting agencies of our security services. You know: *Polizia, Carabinieri*, anti-mafia, *Guardia di Finanza*, anti-terrorism, art cops; the list goes on and on. I suspect that someone from another branch lifted this material from Aragona's record."

"Which means they're investigating him."

"That, or someone in power has made it disappear."

"Either way, chances are that Vincenzo Aragona is not a model citizen."

"Precisely. But I will keep digging. I have some friends in the records office who might have a clue as to what happened. Listen, I have to go. Anything new on our murder investigation?"

"Only that now there's another one."

"*Non capisco, caro nipote.*"

Rick brought his uncle up to date on the events of the previous half hour. There was no equivalent expression in Italian for "dodged a bullet" or he would have used it.

"Your friend LoGuercio has his hands full. We should be ready down here for a request for assistance."

"That's a bit of a bureaucrat's reaction, Uncle. What about concern for your nephew?"

"Every time in the past when I've told you to be careful, Riccardo, something bad happened, so I won't say it."

After he ended the call, Rick saw that LoGuercio was walking toward him. He decided not to tell Paolo about his conversation with Piero. The man had enough on his mind.

"Nothing much more I can do here right now. Let's go back to my office and see if anything is happening in the other case." They started along the path to the station, leaving the crime village behind them on the grass.

"What did Pazzi say to you before the shots?"

"He was trying again to get something from me about the murder."

"Again?"

"He stopped me in the street in front of the hotel yesterday afternoon, having found out who I was after seeing me with you earlier. I told him I didn't know anything and if I did, I wouldn't tell him."

"Pazzi could be very persistent." He looked up. "Oh, great. News certainly travels fast in this town."

A car had stopped in front of the police station and Mayor Boscoli was getting out. He spotted the two men and strode across the street toward them.

"Another murder, Inspector? This is getting to be regular occurrence." He squinted at Rick. "And Signor Montoya is already involved. Again the victim is an American tourist?"

"No, sir," LoGuercio answered, "the dead man is Luciano Pazzi."

"Pazzi? That bastard? You'll have no shortage of suspects for this one, Inspector." He rubbed the stubble on his chin, as if considering what more to say. "Orvieto doesn't need this kind of publicity." His muttered words were more to himself than to the two men. He shook his head and walked back to his car while Rick and LoGuercio watched.

◇◇◇

LoGuercio wearily lowered his body into the chair behind his desk. His work area had been almost bare on Rick's last visit, but now it was cluttered with papers, empty plastic espresso cups, and multiple ashtrays. Light had begun to fade from the view through the large windows, giving the grass and ivy a dark green color that would soon be black. The policeman gestured Rick toward the chair in front of his desk.

"We have some news, Riccardo. The fingerprints found on the belt of the victim were not hers."

He opened a file, found a photograph, and pushed it across the desk. It was a close-up of a belt, its style something Rick had seen many times in New Mexico, usually on tourists. He recalled seeing it on Rhonda in the funicular. The large silver buckle's design, including turquoise insets, was matched in smaller size by silver disks along the leather. Santa Fe Style takes another victim, he could not help thinking.

"The prints were on the buckle," LoGercio said, "which fortunately was wide enough to provide a nice surface. They are checking them against Italian and Interpol records. Now I have to get the prints of anyone who could remotely be considered a suspect."

"Aren't their prints already on file? I would have thought that in Italy it's a requirement that everyone be fingerprinted."

LoGuercio lit a cigarette before leaning back in his chair, causing a slight squeak. "Surprisingly, the answer to the question is probably no. Only in the last few years, thanks to the European Community, have Italian citizens been required to get fingerprinted to obtain or renew their identity card, or get a passport. So most Italians, certainly those over a certain age, do not have their *impronte digitali* on record. And unless they need to renew their identity card, or get a passport, or get in trouble with us, they never will."

"Which would take in about everyone connected with this case."

"Correct. Maybe Donato has had some contact with the authorities, so he might be in the files, but I'll get his prints anyway. If nothing else, telling him when he comes in that he has to do it could elicit an interesting reaction. Can I offer you a coffee, by the way? Water?" He pulled out a cigarette and lit it.

Rick looked at the plastic cups on the desk and waved his hand. "No, thank you. It occurs to me that Rhonda, being wealthy, could have a maid or cleaning person back in America, someone who could have touched the belt."

LoGuercio nodded, his fatigue evident. "We should be hearing back from Arizona on that."

"Were the fingerprints a man's or woman's?"

The policeman shook his head and blew some smoke toward the ceiling. "There's no way to know. Age, they can tell to a certain extent, but gender, no. Prints will often show if the person works with their hands, like a carpenter, through little cuts and scars, though the tiny nicks tend to disappear over time."

"No scars on these prints."

"Precisely. So nobody is ruled in or ruled out until we get them in here to get printed."

Rick digested his Fingerprints 101 lesson. "What about the two American women? They'll have to come in as well. I can call them."

"That would be helpful. But don't tell them we need their fingerprints. I'm telling everyone that we need them in here to sign a formal statement."

Rick nodded. "In case someone figures it out that a print was found on the body and they then decided to disappear."

"Exactly." LoGuercio, realizing how messy his desk appeared, shuffled some of the papers into neater piles. "You said you saw the Americans today?"

"One of them, the daughter. Signora Linwood was also in Todi, but was trying to recover from her hangover. I didn't see her." Rick recounted the conversation with Gina.

"Interesting," said LoGuercio when Rick was done. "It seems that both the daughter and Signora Linwood could be beneficiaries of the estate of our victim. Indeed, very interesting. Linwood tells you yesterday that she thinks the daughter and mother had a bad relationship and now today the daughter says that her mother had an affair with her friend's future husband. It appears that each one is trying to implicate the other." He rubbed his chin in thought. "Are you sure these two women aren't Italian?"

"Not that I know of, Paolo. In other suspect news, I also saw Signora Cappello, on the way here just now. She was with Morgante and they were heading off for a tryst in the *campagna*."

"It couldn't have been much of a tryst if they told you about it. And I checked around; their relationship is not a big secret. Were they really going out to the countryside?"

Rick nodded. "She is checking on a couple properties, and dragged him along with the promise of an intimate dinner under a leafy pergola somewhere nearby. I may be embellishing it a bit. I told them I was coming here, and didn't get a reaction."

LoGuercio again got up from his chair, and walked to the window. The backyard was now completely in shade. "Something occurs to me, Riccardo. Could it be that Morgante's interest in the case is not just based on his concern for local tourism? Perhaps he's worried that his lady friend is a suspect, and is probing to find out if we're getting on her trail." He turned to Rick. "If you hadn't mentioned seeing them it wouldn't have come to mind."

"The other possibility is that she put him up to it, asking him to use his influence to find out how much progress you're making."

The inspector wiggled his index finger. "No, that doesn't work, because he came to the station to ask about the case before we told her the victim was her old friend."

"Unless she knew already, and only acted surprised."

LoGuercio thought about that one for a few moments. "They could both be in on it, she planning it and he doing the dirty work." He rubbed his eyes. "Let's get back to reality."

"Yes, let's. How did your meeting go with Signora Vecchi? Did she remember anything about Rhonda?"

LoGuercio returned to his chair, pulled out a paper, and then put it back into place. "I was surprised to find she was very coherent, and remembered quite a bit. Our victim made an impression back then, so the *signora* was able to give me a good sense of what she was like. Not very helpful in finding our murderer, but good for building a picture of Rhonda Van Fleet. And speaking of pictures, she had a photo album and showed me photographs from that time. There was one of interest, Rhonda Davis arm in arm with a bearded Crivelli."

Rick leaned forward. "Really? That *is* interesting. Do you remember what he told us?"

"Exactly my reaction. That he didn't socialize with the students. One photograph doesn't really prove anything, but it got me more curious about Crivelli."

He got up and leaned over his desk, retrieving a file at the far corner. After sitting back down he opened it and thumbed through the papers inside, finding the one he wanted. "Crivelli was politically active enough in the late seventies to have gotten himself into the records of the police, but back then we were paranoid about such things, apparently. Bombs going off around the country, kidnappings, that sort of thing, and most of the time it was politically motivated."

"Was he ever picked up?"

"There was a protest demonstration in the north that he was involved in that turned violent and he was arrested, but immediately released. Pretty standard for those years, I understand. Unfortunately they couldn't put everyone in jail, and many of the protesters came from prominent families. What I find fascinating is that our anti-capitalist of those years has become a wealthy businessman and prominent member of the community, dining regularly with the mayor. Fascinating, but not surprising."

Rick recalled a favorite quote from Shakespeare: "youth's a stuff will not endure." The bard was likely talking about just getting old, but somehow it fit in Crivelli's case. He was thinking how to translate it for LoGuercio when his cell phone rang.

"Montoya." He listened and looked at LoGuercio. "Yes, Francine...I'm with him now...I will tell him, but I'm not sure—wait on the line, I'll tell him now." He took the phone from his ear. "Signora Linwood says you can take the guard off the villa. They feel safe enough, and perhaps he can be put to better use. To solve the crime."

LoGuercio grunted. "She's telling me how to run my operation?" He flicked his wrist in disgust. "Certainly, whatever she wants."

Rick put the phone back up to his ear. "Done, Francine. But be sure to lock your doors well tonight, and keep your cell phone handy." He was tempted to tell her to stay off the wine, but decided against it. Instead he said goodbye and slipped the phone back in his pocket.

He snapped his fingers. "I forgot to tell her she needs to come here for fingerpr—I mean to sign a statement."

"Call her tomorrow and I'll send a car and driver to bring them both here. I'll use the corporal who they are so kindly returning to me." LoGuercio became lost in thought which Rick interrupted.

"What's your first hunch on the murder of Pazzi, Paolo?"

"Ah, yes, our second murder." He ran his hand through his dark hair. "I was thinking that the American woman is more of a story for the press. But the killing of one of their own, even though he was despised by most journalists, will be considered important to cover. Press freedom, professional solidarity, and all that. But who killed him? The mayor was correct, Pazzi was not a beloved figure among our civic leaders, he even did an exposé on Boscoli himself last year. It was some murky payoff or kickback, without any real evidence but filled with innuendo. Classic Pazzi. So I will reserve any guesses about who could have done it and hope that the ballistics or the neighbors can lead us in the right direction.

"There's a chance the two killings could be connected."

LoGuercio had been lighting another cigarette. He stopped and eyed Rick warily. "I haven't had time to formulate any theories in that regard, but it seems you have. Tell me."

Rick tapped his two index fingers together. "Isn't it obvious? Pazzi's been trying to find out who killed the American, and the murderer, knowing the man's reputation, either thought he was getting close or was afraid he would do so eventually. So he decided to get rid of him."

LoGuercio raised his index fingers now, and pointed them at Rick. "If that's a possible theory, then there is another one which is equally plausible."

"*Cioè?*"

"Just this: the killer needed three shots, so he couldn't be an expert marksman. It's possible that he hit the wrong person."

"He was aiming at me?"

"Well, you *were* looking into the murder, helping the police, and could be getting close." LoGuercio let the idea sink in, then broke into a smile, his first of the day that Rick had seen. "No, Riccardo, I don't think so. You were already on the ground and the guy kept shooting. He was after Pazzi, and as the mayor said, there are dozens of people who dreamed of doing him in. But your first theory could be the right one."

He looked at the stacks of papers on his desk and then at Rick. "You are correct in not wanting to become a policeman, Riccardo. I hope you and Betta will be doing something interesting while I sift through these. You did come up here to see Orvieto, after all, and not from the back of a police car."

"As a matter of fact we have decided to see the Pozzo San Patrizio." He glanced at the clock on the wall of LoGuercio's office. "We should be able to get there before it closes."

"An excellent choice, a masterpiece of Renaissance engineering. There's an aura about it that I've always found somewhat disconcerting, perhaps because of the story that gave it the name, but you'll enjoy it."

"Story?"

"Christ showed Patrick the way down to the gates of purgatory, so that the saint could descend with members of his flock who would see what awaited them if they didn't walk the straight and narrow. Apparently the name St. Patrick's well was given to any deep hole in the ground back then. And this one is quite deep."

Chapter Twelve

The afternoon sun had dropped low enough in the west to cast shadows on the tree-lined path that led from the street to the Pozzo San Patrizio. Betta held her guidebook in one hand, its red ribbon marking the page she had read to Rick on the short bus ride. The history of the structure—if a hole in the ground could be called a structure—was fascinating, but its design even more so. Two winding staircases intertwined in a double helix, allowing men to descend with empty buckets by one set and return to the surface with full ones by another. No army encamped below would be able to cut off the city's water supply, Orvieto could hold out almost indefinitely. The years of labor it took to cut through the hard *tufo* rock were worth it.

The view of the valley below drew them to the edge of the hill. The angle was slightly different from the one they'd seen at the end of the funicular ride bringing them up to the city. Todi, only twenty-five kilometers to the northeast, was hidden from view behind rolling hills, their green made darker by the fading light. Lights from farm houses to the north flickered on as shadow seeped into the low points in the terrain. They watched for a few minutes before turning back to the structure behind them.

"It looks like a silo sunk into the ground with only the top showing," Rick observed.

"Or one of those cement bunkers from World War I that you can still find on the sides of the roads in the Veneto. There was one just outside town my brother loved to play in. I was always afraid to go inside."

Rick took her hand. "You're not afraid to go in this one, are you?"

"Of course not, I'm looking forward to it. And at this hour we may have it all to ourselves."

They found themselves on the top of the stairwell beginning its spiral down to the cistern at the bottom. Rick ran his hand along the cold rock outer wall as he started down the steps. Dim lamps set in the stairway wall illuminated the route, but most of the light, such as it was, came from the skylight at the top of the well. The late afternoon light spread from the void in the center into the stairways through tall openings cut at intervals along the inner wall. Betta leaned over a steel railing at the first opening and looked up at the skylight, then at the pool of water almost two hundred feet below. The musty smell of ancient rock clung to the silent air.

"What a project this must have been," she said. "How could they have been sure to get water? There must be some underground stream that comes out below the cliff outside. Perhaps your friend Morgante can tell us."

Rick was now beside her, his hands on the metal bar, peering down at the water. "Let me go down to that opening and get a picture of you up here. It will give a good sense of the spiral design." He pulled out his phone and continued down the steps while Betta watched him pass one opening, then several more, until he had made one and a half turns. He poked his head out, camera-phone in hand.

"I'm not sure if there is enough light from the flash. Let me take one and we'll see." He held up the phone and moved it until Betta's head and shoulders were in the center of the small screen.

Rick was about to click the photo when the image blurred and he heard Betta scream.

He charged back up the stairs. It seemed to take him forever to reach her, and when he did she was huddled against the wall holding her hand to her head. Above her he saw someone dashing for the entrance and made the decision to pursue the attacker and tend to Betta later. She seemed to know what he was thinking and waved him up the stairs.

"I'm okay," she called to him as he took steps two at a time.

As Rick stepped through the doorway into the half light he sensed someone standing just to his left. His intuition was enough to dodge a sucker punch that glanced off the side of his head. He whirled and caught the man square in the stomach with his fist, causing the assailant to double over in pain. Then Rick grabbed him by the collar of a leather jacket and slammed him against the brick of the building. The man's eyes tightened shut with the force of the blow on the back of his head, and he was at the point of losing consciousness. Rick stared at the face in disbelief.

"Carlo—why you son of a bitch," he said in English. He was pulling his fist back when Betta appeared at the doorway.

"Rick, don't."

"What's he doing here?" Rick snapped.

The attacker slid to the ground holding the back of his head.

"He wanted to talk to me. I…I told him we had nothing to talk about."

"You knew he was here? Why didn't you tell me?"

"I didn't know he was here in Orvieto, I swear it. I didn't tell you because…" She rubbed her hands together and didn't meet his eye. "I didn't want to upset you."

"He was stalking you, and you didn't want to tell me because I would be upset? Betta, the man just attacked you."

"I didn't think…"

Rick noticed a tear running down her cheek, and then saw that a red bruise just below her black hair. "Are you all right?" He stepped toward her and put his hands on her arms.

Carlo took advantage of the opening to scramble to his feet and run up the path. Rick barely noticed the dark figure disappearing into shadows that now spread out under the trees; his attention was on Betta. He moved his hand to her forehead but stopped before touching it.

"Did he do that to you?" His head snapped toward the path but there was no sign of Carlo.

"When I fell, my head hit the side of the wall. I'll be all right."

As he took her in his arms he could feel his own heart beating fast. Exertion or anger? And if anger, was it more with Betta's former fiancé or with Betta herself?

◇◇◇

Fabrizio shuffled along the street, his arms weighted down by two plastic bags full of dinner. His mother would have been working all afternoon making sauces and simmering meats, but Tullia was content with ready-to-serve items from the *salumaio*. Well, that was fine with him, all he needed was minimal sustenance to keep mind and body together, and a bit of deprivation was good for a writer. Just bread and wine would be enough. Wasn't that some quote he'd read somewhere? Something about a loaf of bread and a jug of wine? He tried to remember. Byron? Boccaccio? One of those.

He returned his thoughts to the latest chapter of his book, which was also the first chapter. Getting started had to be the hardest part of writing, especially if you don't know what you want to write. He'd thought it would all flow smoothly from his soul, through the fingers, and onto the keyboard, but it didn't seem to work that way. God knows he was getting enough life experiences, so when did the inspiration from it kick in? He'd been toiling over that first paragraph for days, knowing that it would be the most important one in the book. He'd read that somewhere. Maybe he should go back and read more books on writing; perhaps that one wasn't enough. It didn't have many pages, now that he thought about it. Tonight he would ask Tullia for some euros so he could go to the little bookstore near them. It should have some titles about the writing craft. If not, he could go online and see what he could find about the subject. Problem was, the best stuff there was in English, and his English wasn't that good. Unlike his cousin Riccardo. Was Riccardo still in Orvieto?

He reached his building, carefully set down his bags, and pulled out his keys. The door had two locks, and since he had not been using either of them, he fumbled with one key trying to find which lock it fit. After more jiggling of keys he found that only one of locks was turned. After what had happened the previous night, Fabrizio had locked both when he went out, he was sure of it. That meant that Tullia was already there and had neglected to turn both latches. He closed the door behind him and hurried up the stairs.

"Tullia, sorry I'm late. The *salumaio* was packed."

Between the stairs and the bags, he found he was out of breath when he pushed open the door to the living room. He looked quickly around the room, walked to the small kitchen, and put down his bags on the counter. Smiling, he tiptoed to the door of the bedroom and slowly pushed it open.

Tullia was not in the apartment.

He walked back into the living room and was about to start putting away the groceries when he noticed an envelope propped against his computer. After staring at it for several seconds he picked it up and loosened the seal. Inside was a single sheet of paper, its typed message signed in a hurried hand.

◇◇◇

It had been an especially long day for the head nurse at Casa San Bernardo, and the problems had begun before she arrived at work, thanks to her demanding mother. The nurse had barely clocked in when the first crisis happened, a broken elevator. Breakfasts had to be taken up the stairs on trays to residents who could not manage the walk down. Then Signor Rossi had one of his seizures, unfortunately in front of several others, and had to be taken to the hospital. A mix-up in schedules meant she had barely fifteen minutes for lunch, and no break in the afternoon, even for a coffee. At three o'clock Signora Minoti fell again while trying to get out of her wheelchair, and just after that Signor Rossi's son, a lawyer in Rome, called to demand an explanation of why his father was again in the hospital. Weren't they giving him proper care?

The nurse rubbed her forehead and turned her attention to the numbers on the clipboard. Numbers—that was all that was important to her bosses, and maybe it was better that way. The details of those real stories of the Casa San Bernardo, the small and large human tragedies, were better left untold in the monthly reports. Numbers were preferable to individual stories. Signor Rossi would become a number in the rows of statistics at the end of the month, a cipher under the category of ambulance calls. Yes, it was better that way. Numbers were better for everyone.

She finished the entries in the ledger and returned the clipboard to its nail under the counter. The foyer was quiet, as it usually was at this time in the late afternoon. The residents would be starting to awaken from afternoon naps and realize that it was almost time for dinner. In the kitchen it was anything but quiet as the staff prepared for the evening meal, but the walls were thick enough to contain the din. She looked at her watch. Another fifteen minutes and the night shift nurse would arrive so she could go home. After all that had gone on this day, the evening would have to be easy in comparison, even if Mother was still having issues.

She came out from behind the counter and walked to the double doors leading to the sitting area, her heels clicking on the stone tiles. It was getting dark outside, time to turn on the lights in the other room and set up the chairs for the evening games of cards. It was the duty of the next shift nurse, but with nothing going on, she could do it, and it would make her own shift go more quickly. She walked through the doors and saw that the room was not empty, as she'd expected. Signora Vecchi had a visitor. The two of them sat in the sofa looking intently at a photo album, the same album she had shown to the policeman that morning. How nice for Signora Vecchi, thought the nurse as she walked over to turn on the light switch. The woman doesn't get any visitors for months, and now she's had two in one day.

◇◇◇

"*Dove vai*, Donato?"

"I have to go out, Mama." He cursed to himself. He had been sure she was in her room asleep since it was well past the end of her usual programs. Instead she'd dropped off again in front of the TV and woken up when he came down the stairs. She was in the habit of turning off the sound when the ads came on, and now the remote was in her lap.

"You'd better get ready for bed, Mama. You know what happens when you fall asleep in that chair, your back hurts the whole next day."

She turned her head and smiled at her son. The screen flickered in front of her. "Yes, dear, you're right. You'll be careful, won't you?"

"Of course, Mama. *Buona notte.*"

He slipped out the door and descended the steps into the darkness. A few stars were visible above the house, and a cold wind was blowing off the field behind it. He looked around to see if there were any lights in the windows of the neighbors, but saw only dark behind the glass. No need to wake anyone. He pointed his key at the car, causing the interior light to come on and popping the door lock. When he got inside, the engine started easily. He steered the car around the house and out to the road, just as he'd done other nights. Seeing no cars in either direction, he eased onto the road, and after shifting into second gear he finally turned on his headlights and speeded up.

He couldn't get the phone call out of his head. The visit by that policeman was not something he needed in his life at this point. If his boss found out that the cops were talking with him, he might ask even more difficult questions than the inspector had. He couldn't afford to lose the job now—it paid well and he was just getting to enjoy it. And now this call. Come in, we need to talk with you again. Jesus, what did that mean? Did they really consider him a suspect in this murder? His hand got clammy on the steering wheel at the thought. How could the cops think that?

He rounded a curve, the beams of his headlights brushing the trees on the other side of the road. Still he hadn't passed another vehicle. He thought about turning on the radio to his favorite station, but stared at the road instead.

Calm down. Concentrate on what you're going to do tonight.

Five minutes later his breathing steadied, and he pressed the radio button. The silence of the night was broken as the speakers behind him pounded a beat that was matched in violence by the rap lyrics.

◇◇◇

Betta took off her reading glasses and put the book in her lap. Dressed in a loose fitting tee-shirt and light sweat pants, her preferred sleepwear, she adjusted the pillows between her back and the headboard of the bed. She sat cross-legged, the red toenails of her bare feet matching what was left of the day's lipstick. Rick sat at the room's small table, clicking away at his laptop. He too was barefoot, wearing jeans and a red tee-shirt emblazoned with a picture of Louie Lobo.

"Rick, you've barely said a word since dinner. Are you still angry with me?"

He looked up from the screen and his eyes went immediately to her forehead. "I'm trying not to be, but it will be difficult to forget what happened until your bruise heals."

He *was* trying, but the sting of betrayal was still there. Betrayal may be too strong a word, he thought, but trust was key to a relationship. He could not help wondering if trust had been lost when she decided not to tell him about Carlo contacting her. Would he have done the same thing in her shoes? Impossible to say; he wasn't an Italian woman. What bothered him was the thought that she might be keeping other things from him. Or would in the future. He tucked away his doubts and brought himself back to the murder.

"Betta, I keep thinking that nothing is happening in the case, and we're going back to Rome tomorrow afternoon."

"And you want to be in on it when Paolo catches the murderer."

"Of course."

"You want to be a successful police detective without being a policeman."

Rick shrugged. "Why not? It's worked before." He turned the chair, stretched his legs so that his feet rested at the bottom of the bed, close to hers. "I thought women only did their toenails in the summer, when they wore sandals. Are you going to paint yours all winter?"

Before she could answer, his cell phone rang. He looked at the number. "This should bring some good news. I hope." He hit the button. "Fabrizio?"

"Yes, Riccardo, it's me."

"No more break-ins, I hope?"

"I'm not sure."

Rick closed his eyes tightly and opened them. "What do you mean by that?"

"Well, I got back to the apartment, thinking Tullia was going to come over, since she said she would. When I got upstairs I found a note from her."

"She has a key to the place?"

"Of course, she's paying the rent."

Rick glanced at Betta, who was able hear both sides of the conversation. "What did the note say?"

"That we shouldn't see each other for a while."

Rick gave Betta a thumbs-up, and she shrugged.

"Well, Fabrizio, if that's what she wants—"

"But I don't know if it is what she wants."

"You're not making sense, Cousin. You're not sure if there was a break-in, and you're not sure that what she wrote was what she meant?"

"No, no. What I'm not sure is whether she even wrote the note. It started "Dear Fabrizio," and she's never used that name with me. Since we met she's always called me Fabi."

"So you think—"

"She either didn't write it, or was forced to write it and used that name to tell me that she was doing it against her will. I tried calling her cell phone but she doesn't answer. Riccardo, I know where she lives, I'm going over there."

"Don't do that," Rick said sharply. Then, in a more measured tone: "I don't think you should do that, Fabrizio. Whether she wrote it of her own volition, or was forced to by her husband, she clearly needs time to work things out. You can't interfere. Did you leave a message when you called?"

"Yes. To call me."

"Then leave it at that."

A few seconds passed until Fabrizio spoke. "I suppose you're right. But if I don't hear from her by tomorrow afternoon, Riccardo, I'm going over there."

"We'll talk about that tomorrow. Sleep on it, Fabrizio. Or should I say Fabi?"

After hanging up with his cousin, Rick leaned back and put his hands behind his head. "I sense that Fabrizio was looking for an excuse not to act, and despite his bravado, he was pleased I was able to give it to him. My guess is that Vincenzo forced her to write the note, but it is just as possible that she didn't need any more convincing to know she should end the affair."

"From the look I saw on her face yesterday, she might have been convinced then and there."

"So let's hope Fabrizio will now pack up his computer and do his writing at home in Perugia. Which reminds me that I should check my laptop e-mails."

He took his feet off the bed, tucked them under the table, and brought the computer back to life. She watched him for a few moments before retrieving her book and reading glasses. Silence returned to the room. Betta finished a chapter and was starting the next when Rick's voice took her away from the plot.

"*Ecco.* This is interesting. I just did some searching and found the website of our victim. Very well done, she must have hired a first-class web designer. Lots of pictures, easy to use, lets you order her pottery online. On the 'About Rhonda Van Fleet' page it makes her seem like the most prominent potter in Arizona, and perhaps she was. Her designs are not exactly what appeals to me, but there must be a market for it. All those rich folks from the north who go to Phoenix for the winter want to bring back some piece of local art, what better than a brightly decorated bowl or pot?"

Betta had again set aside her book and glasses. "So her wealth came from her artistic ability as well as her skill in finding rich husbands."

"Some of it. She might have used her divorce money to set up the shop, like a hobby, and it didn't actually pay for itself. That's what one of the American women told Paolo and me when we interviewed her. It's impossible to tell from this website if it was a successful business, but it certainly looks like a serious operation. But there is something very intriguing here that you have to see."

The expression on Rick's face was intriguing enough. Betta hopped down from the bed and padded to the table.

She bent over and looked at the computer. "Oh, my God."

"An interesting coincidence, isn't it?"

"Rick, the decoration on her pottery is virtually the same as what I saw in Crivelli's shop in Todi. The same wide strokes, the colors, everything."

Rick clicked the mouse and more photos moved across the screen. "Or Crivelli's pottery is an exact copy of hers."

She put her arms around his shoulders and squeezed. "Rick, you've found a motive for Crivelli. All these years he's become rich with a style that he copied from her. Then she shows up in Orvieto and they meet by chance in the piazza in front of the cathedral. He realizes that if she finds out what he's been doing she could sue him to get a share of his wealth, or at least ruin his reputation."

"I'm not sure, Betta. It doesn't seem like a strong enough reason to commit murder. Having met Crivelli, I would guess that he'd try to reason with her, or even more likely, try to buy her off."

"He may have done just that when they met that night, but it could have turned ugly. They argue, he kills her."

"As much as I'd like to buy that theory, it doesn't go with my impression of Crivelli from when we talked to him. Vindictive, cunning, yes—someone who resorts to violence, I don't think so. But we'll know tomorrow, before the afternoon when we get on the train to Rome."

She had moved from behind him to his side, so she could lean in to see the screen better. "How will it be resolved tomorrow?"

"The fingerprint I told you about, remember? Crivelli, and the other suspects are going to be coming in to sign a statement, not knowing that they're going to have their prints taken. If there's a match with the print on the buckle, he's our man."

She leaned to get a closer look at one of Rhonda's bowls, even though it took up most of the screen. Her shoulder brushed his chest and he got a whiff of her perfume.

"Betta, there's nothing I can do right now about this case. I certainly don't want to have it spoil our little holiday more than it has already. Let's forget about it until tomorrow."

She put her arm around him. "You're right, Rick, you need something to take your mind off it."

He looked up at her face. His hand moved up to her forehead at the same time she looked down at his head and brushed her fingers over his bruise. They simultaneously recoiled from the pain.

"Maybe we should stay clear of each other's wounds." He slipped his hand under her tee-shirt, and his fingers brushed her soft skin.

She took in a quick breath. "Yes, there are better things to do with our hands."

Chapter Thirteen

It had been an uneventful run, especially in comparison with the previous morning's encounter with the mayor, but that was fine with Rick. Something about the silence of the morning made Orvieto appear even more ancient than it did the rest of the day. The lack of people helped, allowing him to concentrate on stone and sky, aspects of the town that hadn't changed in centuries. Before the day's engine fumes and other modern odors infiltrated the streets, the air remained as it had smelled early in the city's history. He took in deep gulps of it as his running shoes slapped the stone.

The route took him a few blocks from the police station, bringing his mind back to the murder case. Was it possible that Betta's instincts were right, that Crivelli was the murderer? That would tie everything up in a nice bow, but somehow it didn't seem right. The one person he'd woken up thinking about was Donato. He wished he'd gone along to interview the man, to get his own impression, but from the way LoGuercio described him, the caretaker sounded like a two-bit thug. Motive? If Donato was involved, it had to be either a romantic encounter that went bad or someone else put him up to it. Bianca Cappello just didn't have any kind of motive. On the contrary, she was a good friend of the victim. Unless Rhonda had stolen a boyfriend from Bianca, but that seemed like weak gruel, motive-wise. Which brought him back to the American women. No, he couldn't envision either of them meeting Rhonda at the bus stop and committing murder. Certainly not Gina.

He was rounding the corner onto the hotel's street when he felt his mobile phone vibrate inside the zipper pocket of his sweat shirt. He stopped, trying to catch his breath, and looked at the number. It was not someone he wanted to hear from, but he had to talk to him sooner or later.

"Uncle, you are up early."

"I knew you would be up, Riccardo. Have you finished your run?"

There was something in Piero's voice that made Rick uneasy. "I'm on the last few hundred meters."

"Something has come up in your murder case. I just got off the phone with Inspector LoGuercio, but I wanted to call you too."

"You have my complete attention, Zio." He wiped sweat from his face with the sleeve of his free arm.

"The fingerprint found on the victim was identified."

"That's great news, who is it?"

"Perhaps I should not have used the word 'identified.' It is a print taken from a revolver connected to a crime that took place in Milan in 1979. Two people robbed a bank, or at least two people were observed, both armed with pistols. A bank guard was shot but survived. Leaflets found at the scene indicated that it was the work of the Red Brigades. I assume you know about them?"

"Of course. Urban terrorists, the ones behind the kidnapping of former prime minister Aldo Moro."

"That's right. You were born too late to have witnessed the years of lead, as they were called. The two robbers wore ski masks, so there was no useful identification of them by the witnesses."

"Both were men, though?"

"The report I read said that even their genders weren't a sure thing, but one of them was found dead of gunshot wounds, a male in his early twenties. A gun was found nearby, and tests confirmed it was the one used on the guard as well as to kill the accomplice. It was also the one that had your fingerprint. The second gun seen in the hands of the bank robbers was never recovered."

Rick wondered if the sweat on his neck was left over from the run or had appeared as his uncle was speaking. "So this guy, or this person, robs a bank with another Red Brigades operative, and afterward blows away his accomplice."

"And takes all the *lire*, about half a million in today's euro. That money was never found."

"So we may be trying to find a former bank robber and murderer."

"It appears so."

"And now—let me guess—you want me to be careful."

"How did you know?"

◇◇◇

After his shower, Rick sat in the breakfast room with Betta, thinking that in twenty-four hours he would be enjoying a cappuccino at the bar around the corner from his apartment in Rome. Dino, the pro behind the bar, knew exactly how Rick liked his cappuccino; just the right amount of milk with the correct proportion of *schiuma* on top. With a warmed *cornetto*, there was no better breakfast. The coffee here at the hotel was fine, but it couldn't beat Dino's.

He looked at Betta, who was reading the final pages of the paper, and wondered if he had done the right thing telling her about his uncle's call. He knew he could trust her completely, and he knew Piero felt the same about her. She was in law enforcement, after all. What was it that was bothering him? Just like in Bassano, they were a team; so what was it? The incident with Carlo at the well? Her reasons for keeping the secret were obvious: not wanting to upset Rick, hope that the problem would go away by itself, and the assumption that she could handle it by herself. It wasn't that she wanted to deceive him, it was that she wanted to preserve their relationship. He couldn't blame her, he felt the same way. Perhaps that was it, perhaps deep down he wasn't ready for this serious a relationship. The thought, for some reason, made him cough.

"Are you all right, Rick?" Betta peered over her glasses, her eyebrows slightly knitted.

Rick tapped his chest with his fist. "Something went down the wrong way. It will pass. Anything in the news about the murder?

"*Un bel niente.*" She was wearing a more sober outfit than the previous day—a skirt with a long-sleeved blouse—for the visit to the cathedral later that morning. "Tomorrow, if all goes well, it will be all over the front pages of every newspaper."

"I certainly hope so," he said as he pulled out his cell phone and looked at the time. "We still have an hour before we meet Morgante and his girlfriend, as well as all the civic leaders, at the Duomo."

She folded her paper. "Please Rick. Girlfriend? She's probably old enough to be your mother. But after hearing you describe her, I'm curious to see what she's really like."

He was inserting his phone back into his pocket when it rang. Out it came.

"Montoya."

"Rick, this is Francine. Someone broke into the villa during the night, we just noticed it when we were making breakfast."

"Are you sure they're not still there?"

"We've been in all the rooms. Rhonda's must have been what they were most interested in, but some items from the living room are missing."

"Okay, I'll call the inspector and we'll get there as soon as we can. Don't touch anything." He thought about the other woman, and added: "Try to keep Gina calm."

He hung up and translated for Betta. Then he used his phone again for a short conversation with LoGuercio.

"He'll be here in five minutes. At least this confirms that the first attempt was not just a random burglary."

"The real question, Rick, is if this time the burglar found what he was looking for."

"Since we don't know what it was, we may never find that out." He held the phone in his hand and tapped the table as he thought. "Damn. It looks like we'll never get that tour of the cathedral. I'd better call Morgante and tell him." He took out his wallet, found Morgante's card, and dialed the number. "Damn again. It goes right to voice mail."

Betta held up a hand to stop him. "Rick, we can't cancel again. I'll go, and you can join us when you're finished."

"That would be great. The man has been very accommodating, and we can't simply not show up without calling him. It shouldn't take that long at the villa. I may even get there in time." He stood and gave her a peck on the cheek.

She whispered in his ear. "Promise me you'll stay away from the flower pots."

◇◇◇

"I hope this is the last time we have to make this trip, Paolo."

Rick once again held tight as the car made top speed down the hill, the same driver at the wheel. The blue lights on the roof flashed, but the siren barked only when needed to pass another vehicle. In the distance a dark blanket of clouds covered the hills and dumped heavy rain, but fortunately on their patch of Umbria the sun reflected off dry pavement.

"As do I, Riccardo." The inspector watched the trees and bushes whipping past the car window. "I regret taking you away from your visit to the cathedral. I'm sure Signor Morgante is an excellent guide." LoGuercio was lost in thought for several minutes before punching his open palm with his fist. "I curse myself for taking the guard off the villa. The woman caught me in a moment of frustration."

"It may have a positive side, Paolo, you could find a fingerprint or some other evidence that leads you to the killer."

LoGuercio would not be mollified. "I doubt that."

They sat in silence as the car shot past a truck, barely avoiding an oncoming motorcycle. The police driver muttered something under his breath.

"Your uncle called you about the Red Brigades connection with the fingerprint? He told me he was going to."

Rick nodded, and expected the policeman to go on, but instead LoGuercio was lost in thought.

Rick's image of the Red Brigades was stamped by a stark, black-and-white news photo he saw years after it was taken. The crumpled cadaver of former Prime Minister Aldo Moro huddled in the open trunk of a car, surrounded by horrified police and other officials. The picture had the drama and pathos of a Renaissance painting depicting the lamentation.

After several minutes LoGuercio continued. "The Red Brigades held the classic belief that the political ends justified the means, but their means involved a viciousness not seen in Italy in decades. One of their favored techniques of intimidation, or ways of making a political statement, was knee-capping. Public figures who spoke out against them were confronted, always in broad daylight, and shot in the legs. Naturally the incidents were reported everywhere, which played into their hands. My uncle, a magistrate of some renown among the judiciary, was one of their targets. He bled to death on the sidewalk when he was attacked."

LoGuercio had been staring out the car window as he spoke, but now he turned to Rick.

"I tell you this so that you know we are dealing with an especially vicious individual. The *brigatisti* were devout believers in a religion of violence to create chaos. The person we are looking for may be older, and now wants order rather than chaos, but is still capable of violence."

"The shooting of your uncle must have made a deep impression."

"I was very young, but it was traumatic for the entire family. And it was one of the reasons I decided to become a policeman, to hunt down such people."

Rick hoped that LoGuercio's personal history with the Red Brigades would not cloud the man's judgment in trying to solve this case. Or worse, once the murderer was caught would Paolo find a place and time to even the score for his uncle? From his next comment, it seemed that the policeman was reading Rick's mind.

"That was a long time ago, Riccardo. We have to focus on the present, and my job is to find this person and bring him to justice."

Rick tried to measure the sincerity in LoGuercio's words. Working on the case, now up to two homicides, had taken its toll on the man. There was a noticeable change in him over just these few days. The stress of his job being on the line was starkly visible in his face and voice.

"I agree, Paolo. Let's go over where we are at this point."

The inspector nodded silently, and waited for Rick to start.

"The way I see it, it narrows us down to two suspects, since Donato's age disqualifies him He was barely an infant when the Red Brigades were operative."

"Problem is," LoGuercio interrupted, "by ruling out people of a younger age, it rules in a large swath of the city's population. Why, half the people at your private showing at the Duomo fall into the demographic of those who could have been Red Brigades operatives in the seventies, starting with the mayor himself."

"Don't say that, Paolo, with Betta there among them."

LoGuercio waved a hand. "Never mind, what were you saying about two suspects?"

"The first is Crivelli. His political activity may have gone beyond the demonstrations you found in his police file into something more serious. The general location for him during that time period is correct, in the north, so he could easily have been active in Milan. As far as this murder is concerned, I discovered a possible motive last night when I got online."

LoGuercio snapped his face toward Rick. "What was that?"

Rick explained the striking similarity of styles between Rhonda's and Crivelli's ceramics. "Definitely not a coincidence, but whether it would be a reason to murder Rhonda Van Fleet is something else entirely."

"It's the best motive we have so far," observed LoGuercio. "And there is something else that moves Crivelli to the top of the list."

Rick held on as the car swerved around a curve. "Really? Tell me."

"Signora Vecchi, the woman who ran the boardinghouse, called me this morning. She said she spent the night trying to decide if she should call and finally concluded that she should. It seems that Crivelli paid her a visit in the afternoon, something he'd never done before. Claimed he wanted to tell her about the death of Signora Van Fleet. They reminisced about the old times, and she showed him the same photo album I saw. He was very interested in seeing the pictures, she said."

"Did he ask her about your meeting with her early in the day?"

"She made the mistake of bringing it up herself, so she doesn't know if he knew already. But he asked her about it."

"Somehow, knowing Crivelli as we do, I doubt if his visit to the woman was motivated by benevolence."

"Nor do I, but like you I have trouble picturing him as a murderer. But the fingerprint will tell the tale. Your other prime suspect, I assume, is Bianca Cappello?"

The descent from Orvieto's hill had ended. The flat, if curved roadway allowed the driver to accelerate. There was little traffic to slow them down.

"Yes. Bianca was in Milan at the time, taking care of a sick grandmother, she claims. If I recall, the Red Brigades had women as well as men among their ranks. We certainly can't rule her out."

"But her motive for murdering the American?"

Rick nodded. "True, nothing obvious comes to mind. The only possibility I can think of is that Rhonda knew about Bianca Cappello's Red Brigades past, though not the bank robbery, and Cappello thought it might now somehow come out. At this point in her life she's an upstanding citizen, and would be ruined if it was revealed she had that on her record. As serious for her, on a personal level, is that her friend Morgante, given his position in the city, would almost surely break off their relationship."

"The same could be said about Crivelli if he's the *brigatista*. If Rhonda knew about an involvement with the Red Brigades, he couldn't let that become public either."

Rick shook his head. "I don't think Crivelli would have revealed that kind of information about himself to a student back then, unless they were in a more intimate relationship than he lets on. But Cappello and Rhonda were contemporaries, and good friends. Bianca could have opened up to her over a bottle of wine at that time, wanting to talk about it with someone who would be sympathetic, but afraid to talk to another Italian. My guess is that Rhonda wasn't exactly politically conservative herself in those days.

"True."

They were just passing the spot at the side of the pavement where the body had been found. The crime tape had been taken down, and a woman stood waiting at the bus stop, checking the screen of her cell phone. If she was aware of what had happened there only forty-eight hours earlier, she didn't show it. LoGuercio looked at the woman and checked his watch.

"Crivelli will be coming to my office in about an hour and a half. He's part of that cathedral visit, along with everyone else of importance in Orvieto, so I couldn't get him in earlier. I told the sergeant, if I'm not back, to ask him to wait until I return, which I'm certain won't make him happy. Cappello is scheduled for about a half hour after that, since I didn't want them chatting in the waiting area and comparing notes, so I hope this doesn't take too much time and gum up the works. If we are delayed too much I'll call the station and have them put Crivelli in another room. Damn this robbery."

The car slowed and pulled into the dirt road leading up the hill to the villa. In less than a minute it skidded to a stop next to the Mercedes. They got out and walked to the doorway as it was being opened by Francine.

"Thank you for coming so quickly," she said. "Please come in."

LoGuercio voiced a "good morning," in English and stepped through the doorway, followed by Rick. In the living room Gina sat on the couch clutching a coffee mug. The two women were each dressed, as the other morning, in a kind of exercise outfit. Neither had put on makeup, and their hair looked as if it had not been touched since leaving the pillow.

"Tell them, Riccardo, that I'm just going to make a general inspection of the crime scene, but a team is on its way to do a more thorough check of the building for fingerprints and other evidence. Find out what they noticed was missing, and then we can look at Signora Van Fleet's room."

Rick interpreted while Francine took a seat next to Gina and grasped the younger woman's free hand.

"What is missing from here," Francine answered, "is a small vase that sat in that niche." She pointed toward the wall. "We had all admired it when we arrived at the villa, especially Rhonda since she is of course into ceramics. From the way it was displayed, with a light over it, we thought it had some value. Apparently the thief agreed."

"Anything else?"

She pointed to another part of the room. "The books on that shelf had been disturbed, but since we didn't look at them at all since we got here, we don't know if any are missing. Burglars don't usually steal books, I would think."

LoGuercio had been writing in his notebook. "I would not be surprised, Riccardo, if taking the vase and shuffling the books was a diversion to make it appear as a real burglary. There is no doubt in my mind, and I trust in yours, that this has to be related to the murder. So where is the woman's bedroom?"

When Rick asked, Gina spoke for the first time and pointed to a door at the far side of the living room. Their bedrooms were on the next level, a few steps up, but Rhonda had taken the one on the ground floor. "Her room is the other side of the villa from ours, which is why we didn't hear anything."

Francine seemed to be about to say something, but then just nodded in agreement. Rick and LoGuercio walked to the door of the bedroom and pushed it open.

It was immediately evident that the person who had come into the room during the night was looking for something, but the search had been done carefully, so as not to make noise. The drawers of the two dressers were open, the clothing in them left in a jumbled mess. Empty suitcases that Rhonda had likely stored somewhere else now lay open in the middle of the floor. The mattress was slightly ajar and the pillow had been pushed to one side. The burglar was not trying to trash the room, but no attempt was made to hide the search either. The two men surveyed the clutter without touching anything.

"He could have found what he was looking for or not," said LoGuercio. "We won't know from looking at this place. The forensic crew will go over it, but I doubt if they'll find anything. Anyone who watches TV would know to wear gloves. Let's see if we can get more information from the women." He turned and walked back to the living room, followed by Rick. Francine and Gina were still sitting on the sofa.

Rick took the lead. "What can you tell us about last night? Did you go into Orvieto for dinner?"

Francine gestured at Gina, indicating she should answer.

"No, Rick, we ate here. We'd gone to a little store a few miles down the road and bought some cold cuts, cheese, and bread, as well as a bottle of wine. We came back here and had that. I was pretty exhausted, with everything going on, and went to bed early. I think the cool weather has also worn me out, and it makes for good sleeping weather. I didn't hear anything, but I'm a very sound sleeper."

Rick interpreted and then turned to Francine. "Anything to add?"

She acted like the student who didn't want to be called on by the teacher. "No, that's what happened. I stayed up a bit longer, read a few pages from a book, and went to bed myself. Dropped right off."

"Same story," Rick said to LoGuercio.

The policeman was leaning against the fireplace, not hiding his impatience with the situation. "I have to call the station, excuse me a moment." He walked to the doors to the patio, opened them and walked outside.

Francine watched him leave and got quickly to her feet. "Rick, can I talk to you in the kitchen for a moment?"

"Sure," Rick answered.

She motioned toward an arched doorway and the two of them left Gina staring through the glass doors at the policeman talking on the cell phone under the pergola outside. The kitchen combined modern practicality with the feel of a country house. Tiles formed rows on the walls behind the counters and stove, their colors matching the rest of the room's décor. Instead of an Italian espresso pot on the stove, a shiny American-style coffee-maker sat on the end of the counter, next to a set of mugs. There was a dishwasher, but the sink was full of cups and silverware. In the center of the room stood a butcher block table and four metal stools. Rick decided that if the renters were serious cooks they could work very well in this kitchen, but doubted that happened very often. Not with all the good restaurants just up the road in town.

Francine pulled a glass off the shelf and uncorked an already open bottle of wine. She held up a glass and gave him a questioning look.

"Too early for me, Francine, but it looks like you need something after this break-in. Go right ahead." He noticed that, ironically, the label was Sonnomonte, the vineyard owned by Vincenzo Aragona. As the dark red wine flowed into her glass something else occurred to him, but his thought was interrupted by her voice. Before speaking she had looked back toward the other room, as if to confirm they were out of earshot of Gina.

"Rick, is Donato a suspect in all this?"

The question took him by surprise. "I, uh, don't think the inspector has ruled anyone out, if that's what you mean. Do you have reason to think he should be a suspect?"

She shook her head quickly. "No, no. That's not what I meant. It's just…" She glanced again back into the room before answering. "Rick, I feel like I can talk to you about this. You see, Donato told me the police want to talk to him again. The inspector had already talked to him once, and now—"

"Wait a minute, Francine. When did Donato tell you this?"

Her eyes were wide, but blinking quickly. "You might as well know. He was here last night, after Gina went to bed. You won't tell the inspector, will you?"

"The forensics team will be here soon and they will find his fingerprints." He didn't point out that, being the caretaker, Donato's prints around the villa would be expected.

Francine turned pale. "Oh God, you're right. Then you must tell the inspector that he was in my sight the whole time he was here."

Rick didn't want to think about that one. "You saw him drive away? What time was that?"

"Yes, he drove off after midnight. Closer to one, maybe. I saw him go down the driveway."

So that was before the break-in took place, Rick calculated. But Donato could have come back, knowing both women were out for the night. Why would he do that? If he'd wanted to take something from the villa, he had a key and could have come during the day, when they were out seeing the sights. No, it made no sense that Donato would want to rob the place at all. Unless the guy was working for someone else; but again, why break in at night? Rick was trying to figure it all out when he heard the door to the patio open and close. Francine smiled weakly at him and they walked into the other room. Gina was in the same place, but now she was staring at a small book in her lap. Tears welled up in her eyes.

LoGuercio had not noticed. "The forensics team is on its way," he said to Rick as he and Francine appeared from the kitchen. "Before they get here, I'd like these two to look over the bedroom to see if by chance they notice what might be missing. Without touching anything, tell them. Any personal items they think Signora Van Fleet brought to the villa that aren't there now."

"In a second, Paolo." Rick walked to the sofa and sat down next to Gina, putting his arm around her shoulder. He tried to think of something he could say that would comfort her, but nothing came to mind. The book on her lap, he saw, was a photo album. The pictures in it were yellow and faded, but the faces were unmistakable.

"Where did you get this, Gina?"

She found a tissue and blew into it before answering. "It was Mom's. She showed it to us the day we arrived, and I was looking at it in my room last night before I fell asleep. Look at how happy she looked then, it's no wonder she wanted to come back one last time." She gulped when she realized what she'd said.

Rick took the small book and slowly turned the pages. Rhonda Davis smiled up from the plastic, either by herself, or in groups, sometimes in front of some recognizable landmark. The Pantheon in Rome. Perugia's ancient fountain. The Arno seen from the Ponte Vecchio. He saw many photos around Orvieto, of the squares and buildings that were now familiar to him. He turned another page and his hand froze. A photo showed Rhonda in front of the unmistakable facade of Milan's Duomo, flanked by two men. Rick was sure this one had been taken by a professional photographer, one who wandered the piazza catering to tourists. It was black and white, its tones crisper than the others on the page. Three pigeons perched on Rhonda's arm and one was pecking at the bird seed in her hand. Instead of looking at the camera, she was grinning at the handsome man standing on her right. It was the third person in the picture, the other man, whose face had jumped off the page. Rick carefully pulled the photograph from the paper, closed the album, and got to his feet.

"Paolo," Rick said, "I think we may have found what the burglar was searching for."

Chapter Fourteen

In the first decade of the fourteenth century, nearly twenty years after construction of the great cathedral of Orvieto had begun, the city fathers were in a panic. How could the structure, as designed, hold the weight of the walls and roof? They had heard stories of other churches crumbling to the ground, often with great loss of life. They wanted Orvieto to become famous for its intact cathedral, not for a disaster while trying to build it. A relatively unknown architect from Siena, Lorenzo Maitani, was brought to Orvieto, made a citizen of the town, and given charge of the project. Surprisingly little was recorded in the local archives about Lorenzo, save that he kept his position until his death twenty years later. Clearly he was a major influence on the eventual design and decoration, including the bottom tier of the spectacular facade. It was that part of the church which has always brought tourists to Orvieto, visitors who then sent the colorful image around the world in postcards and photographs. But Maitani's true genius was in the interior of the cathedral, a space which displayed a symmetry and balance but which most visitors took for granted. That may have been just what the leaders of Orvieto in 1310 wanted.

"Most tourists spend much of their time staring at the facade," said Livio Morgante, "then quickly walk through this magnificent expanse to get to the frescoes of the chapel. *Che peccato* that the part of the cathedral where Maitani's genius truly shines does not get the attention it should."

Since they were the only people in the church, he spoke in a normal voice, which echoed off the stone floor and walls. In the piazza the sun was starting to warm the air, but inside the night cold still clung to the stone, and everyone in the group, including Betta, kept their hands deep in the pockets of their wool coats. The priest had let them in the side door and scurried away to get warm, disappearing through an opening somewhere near the transept.

The number of people in the tour was what Betta had expected, given what Morgante had said when he gave them the invitation. The tourism chief had introduced her to Bianca Cappello, but the need to start the tour had prevented her from meeting others. Just as well, since she didn't want to shake the hand of Vincenzo Aragona. There were other women besides Bianca, but most of the group was male. Betta looked around, trying to guess which of them was Crivelli, but couldn't decide.

Everyone listened as Morgante explained how the massive columns played their structural role while drawing together the other architectural elements of the apse, including the half-circle window niches and the towering ceiling. The group's eyes moved as Morgante's narrative shifted from one feature to the next, and everyone stayed politely silent as he spoke.

They walked to the middle of the transept, the central point of the cross the building itself formed. Morgante explained the design problems that the site had brought to the architect, forcing him to set aside exact symmetry in the face of practical considerations, and how he managed to hide it from the eye. The group walked a few steps up from the cathedral floor into the San Brizio Chapel, which held the most important artwork in the city—the frescoes of Luca Signorelli. Morgante was just beginning his speech about the paintings when the faint sound of the side door opening and closing reached their ears.

Betta was relieved. Rick had made it after all, and had only missed a few minutes of Morgante's presentation which was, she decided, the best she'd heard outside of her university art history lectures. It had the advantage of being less academic and more passionate. The man truly enjoyed being a booster for his city, and he did it well. She listened to the footsteps approaching the chapel and recognized the click of Rick's cowboy boots. But there was more than one set of footsteps. Morgante stopped speaking and looked toward the chapel entrance causing everyone else to do the same.

Rick and Inspector LoGuercio walked the distance from the side door and came up the steps into the chapel. Their eyes searched the crowd, looking quickly from one face to another. Betta tried to follow Rick's gaze, but it moved too quickly. She watched as Rick leaned toward the policeman and said something in his ear. LoGuercio, his eyes still moving through the people, shook his head quickly.

When she saw the policeman, Bianca Cappello, who was standing near Morgante, had moved closer and taken his hand. He smiled down at her before addressing LoGuercio. "Inspector, you are able to take time away from the investigation to join us for some culture. How nice. We were just about to gaze upon Signorelli's masterpiece. It depicts the day of judgment, as you know."

"How appropriate," said LoGuercio.

Morgante's eyes moved from the policeman's face to Rick's, and back. "I don't understand, Inspector. The painting's subject is a serious one. If you were attempting to make light of it…"

"Not at all, Signor Morgante."

Bianca's hand clutched Morgante's arm, but the man didn't appear to notice. He looked at LoGuercio, his face showing his usual calm. "Then I will go on with the description of the work."

"I am not here for culture, Signor Morgante," said the policeman, "but in search of a murderer."

The effect on the people was immediate, only the sacred surroundings kept them somewhat subdued. Instead, they turned to one another and spoke in low voices, stealing looks at the policeman as they did. Every one of them knew about the murder of the American, and almost certainly the news of Pazzi's shooting had spread even faster. It was Morgante, taking back his role as leader of the program, who eventually said what they all were thinking. Letting go of Bianca's hand, he stepped forward.

"Inspector, surely you don't think anyone—"

A woman screamed, and the crowd parted like a human curtain. In the middle stood Vincenzo Aragona, a dark pistol in his hand. Every eye was on the weapon, which he waved rapidly, causing some men to drop to the stone floor. Rick stared in horror, then pulled Betta to his side. LoGuercio's hand moved slowly behind him.

"Don't try to get your weapon, Inspector, unless you want yourself or someone else shot."

"Signor Aragona," said LoGuercio, "be reasonable. Put the gun down." His voice was soothing, but Aragona was in no mood to hear it. Instead, he continued to wave the pistol and stepped clear of the group.

"I will not be arrested. I know how to use this."

Morgante watched the gun as it swung back in forth, pointing in the direction of the Signorelli frescoes. "Vincenzo, what are you doing?"

"I'm not going to let them make an arrest." The nervousness gone, his voice had turned to steel.

"Vincenzo, please." It was Morgante again. "Remember where you are." His eyes raised to the decorations of the chapel ceiling. Every inch of space between the ribs of its vaults was decorated with biblical characters, angels, and saints. Frozen in paint and mosaic, they looked down with solemn faces at the scene playing out below.

"I don't give a damn where we are. I'm going to walk out of here, and not even the almighty can stop me." As he spoke, he waved the pistol in the direction of the priceless frescoes high above them.

Morgante gasped and lurched forward, grabbing Aragona's pistol hand while the others watched in silent fear.

"Everyone get down!" shouted LoGuercio, rushing toward the two struggling men.

Morgante had taken hold of the barrel and tried to pull it out of Aragona's hand. "I can't let you—"

His words were cut off by the explosion of the pistol. He froze and stared blankly at Aragona while his free hand grasped his blood-stained shirt. His mouth moved, and no words came out, but he continued to cling tightly to the gun barrel. Aragona tried to pull it free, but Rick leaped at him and landed a blow on his neck. Stunned, the man staggered and let go of the pistol. The grip banged on the stone floor, but the muzzle was still in Morgante's hand. LoGuercio pulled out his service pistol and pointed it at Aragona's chest.

Seeing that the chapel was now safe, Morgante finally loosened his grip on the weapon. It slid out of his hand and rattled across the floor, coming to a stop near the altar. The harsh odor of the discharged gun mixed with the sweet smell of incense.

Three uniformed policemen charged into the chapel, weapons raised.

"Sergeant, get an ambulance," LoGuercio called out. "Corporal, handcuff this man." Two of the policeman followed his orders while the third stared at the man cradled in the lap and arms of a sobbing Bianca Cappello.

Morgante's eyes looked past her face and stared at the ornate walls of the chapel. "How…could he?" His words came in short gasps. He looked past her at the wall that held Signorelli's masterpiece. "This is…the jewel…of Orvieto."

Tears poured down her cheeks. "I'm so proud of you, Livio."

Rick looked back at the cream of Orvieto society. Most of them were on the floor, still stunned, but their heads were lifted, trying to decide if it was safe to get to their feet. Rick walked to one person who had wedged himself behind a large woman made larger by a fur coat.

"It's safe, now," he said to the man. "You can get up."

LoGuercio had been in a corner of the chapel talking furiously on his cell phone. He snapped it closed and rushed over to Rick, giving a quick glace to the man on the floor.

"I just spoke with the crime scene crew at the villa, Riccardo. The two women decided to take a drive instead of standing around waiting for them to finish. Our man from the photograph appeared and the crew leader told him where they'd gone. We don't have a moment to lose." He stuffed his phone into his pocket.

Rick called to Betta. "I've got to go. See what you can do to comfort Bianca, she may be in worse shape than Morgante." He ran behind LoGuercio, catching up with him when they got to the patrol car. "Paolo, where were the two women going?"

Their backs pressed against the seats as the driver shot off.

"The Etruscan tombs. It looks like you're going to see them after all."

◇◇◇

The *necropoli* of Orvieto were not the most famous of the burial sites in what had been the territory of the pre-Roman Etruscan federation. That honor went to Tarquinia, where colorful wall paintings illustrated the festivities that awaited the deceased in the after life. In contrast, these tombs were drab, stone crypts, monotonously similar. If there had been paintings on the walls of the tiny rooms, they had long ago succumbed to the elements. If art had been placed on the shelves with the dead, it had been plundered ages earlier, along with the burial urns themselves. What was left were low rows of gray stone structures, their flat roofs covered with earth and overgrown by grass and weeds. It was, as LoGuercio had said, a city of the dead, but the dead had disappeared centuries ago. The grid of tombs and pathways squeezed together on a plot of land below medieval Orvieto. A thicket of bushes and small trees grew between the necropolis and the base of the city's escarpment, its steepness tempered by shrubbery and rounded boulders. High above, the walls and spires of a fifteenth-century church loomed at the edge of the city, young in comparison with the low stone structures below.

The two police cars careened off the road and came to a stop in the parking lot. Only four other vehicles were parked there, including the silver Mercedes. LoGuercio jumped out of the lead car and gathered the men around him.

"When we get to the tombs, spread out and start working you way up the paths. If you see the American women, get them back here and out of danger. If there are any other tourists, tell them to leave immediately. Remember that this man is dangerous, so don't try to take him down by yourself. Call for backup and wait until it arrives. Let's go."

As they started up the path, he pulled Rick aside. "Riccardo, you stay with Sergeant Grecco. When we locate the American women, you'll be the one to explain to them what's going on."

Rick thought about protesting his role, but realized it made sense. LoGuercio's record was already a problem, he didn't need the injury of the nephew of a high-level police official added to it. He and the sergeant did as they were told, and ended up taking the last path among the tombs. They walked slowly along the gravel, looking into the darkness as they passed each crypt.

On the drive down the hill Rick and LoGuercio had talked about the man's reasons for following the two Americans, and the conclusion was clear. The killer was determined to destroy all evidence that linked him with his past, which is why he was searching for something among Rhonda's belongings that could have done just that. She may even have told him about the photograph before she was killed. But he couldn't be sure that Rhonda hadn't told her daughter everything. Mothers always confide in their daughters don't they? And then there was Francine.

All of that was going through Rick's mind as he continued up the slightly inclined path between the stone. He quickly decided that it was useless to check each of the tombs. There was no reason for their quarry to be hiding in one, since he didn't even know the police had arrived and were searching for him. Rick stepped up his pace, leaving the sergeant peering into stone doorways. It was when he got up to the end of the row that he heard Gina's voice. He turned the corner and she was there, framed by Orvieto's hill, talking with a large man in a dark suit. The man's back was to Rick, and he was speaking to her in a low voice while he edged closer. Gina's face showed puzzlement, or perhaps fear.

"Is this what you were looking for at the villa?"

Mayor Boscoli spun around and faced Rick, who was holding up the photo he'd taken from the album.

"You?"

"Gina, quick, get out of here," Rick shouted, hoping that Boscoli's English was not good enough for him to understand. It worked, she broke down the hill before the mayor could react. Instead he glared at Rick.

"What have you got there, Signor Montoya?"

"A picture of you and Rhonda Davis in Milan. I assume that the third man in the picture was her friend, the one who tragically died soon afterward?"

"You appear to be well informed for someone who is not a policeman."

"Rhonda held the secret of your Red Brigades past, so she had to be eliminated. What did you do with the money from that bank robbery, Mr. Mayor? Perhaps you just salted it away to use in your political campaigns?"

Rick was trying to keep the man occupied until LoGuercio arrived to take him prisoner, but he could see from the look on Boscoli's face that he knew. His eyes focused behind Rick before looking up at the town high above him. Without a word, he turned and rushed into the thick bushes behind him. At that moment the sergeant appeared at Rick's back.

"Was that him?" the policeman asked, his gun drawn.

"It was," answered Rick. "Is there a way to get up to town from here?"

"A path, a rather steep one, runs up to the town," said the sergeant. "The Etruscans used it to carry their dead here for burial. It is closed to the public."

"Find LoGuercio. Tell him Boscoli is climbing up to the city."

The man turned and ran down through the tombs. Rick watched him go and then looked where the mayor had gone. It was a break in the shrubbery, a narrow path barely visible. He jogged toward it while looking up at the hill trying to find the route, but saw nothing among the rocks and trees growing from the patches of dirt between them. It would be considered an easy climb back in New Mexico, he thought, remembering the various trails up to Sandia Peak above Albuquerque. And given his experience with climbing, it would be easier for him than for Boscoli. He brushed through the bushes and soon found himself at the base of the hill. A wooden barrier marked the beginning of the trail with a sign on it warning of the danger, as well as a fine for anyone tempted to risk it. Rick skirted the barrier and began his ascent.

Almost immediately he knew that Boscoli had just preceded him; on the stretches of soft dirt, fresh footprints were visible. Their deep heel marks indicated that the man was running, and Rick picked up his pace. He was above the top of the trees now, with a clear view of the grid of tombs and paths below. He saw some of the other policemen, but did not spot LoGuercio. Gina and Francine were nowhere to be seen, but he guessed they had been taken to the parking lot. He returned his attention to the trail, which was becoming steeper and more narrow. It bent back sharply and started to climb in the other direction, making Rick think it might continue to criss-cross all the way up to the city. He carefully chose his steps and clutched pieces of rock or vegetation as he climbed, just as he had learned to do in the mountains of New Mexico. The path cut back once again and widened slightly. Rick took advantage of the easier footing to look back down. The parking lot was visible, and he could make out the two women standing beside two uniformed policeman. He was straining his eyes to find LoGuercio when something flashed.

Rick instinctively jumped back and held up his hand, but it was too late to avoid the steel blade which cut into his palm with a searing pain. Boscoli reeled back, knife in hand, to strike a blow at Rick's body, but stopped when his shoe slipped on the rock path. He fell, dropping the knife and clawing at the ground as his large body slid slowly toward the edge. Rick stared at the knife while holding tight to his bleeding hand. Boscoli saw his eyes and lunged toward the blade, but the effort only pushed him back, and he slid slowly off the path, trying desperately to stop his fall. Most of his body was over the cliff when his hands grasped a thin gnarled vine.

"Montoya," he gasped. "Don't let me fall." He turned his head and saw only sharp rocks far below.

Blood dripped from the fingers of Rick's good hand as he held it over the gash. "I would, Mr. Mayor, but to do that I'd need two hands and one of them, you'll notice, is cut badly."

"I'm the mayor of Orvieto, you must help me."

At that moment a familiar voice was heard behind Rick.

"You also murdered two people and were about to murder another." LoGuercio looked down at Boscoli, whose hands were turning white from gripping the vine.

"Thank goodness you're here, Inspector. Get me up." His tone returned to that of someone used to giving orders.

LoGuercio didn't move. He glanced at Rick's hand and the knife lying on the ground before his eyes bore in on the man hanging over the edge. "A different weapon from those used by most Red Brigades operatives back then, isn't it, Mayor Boscoli? I thought you used guns when you went after the people you disagreed with, like professors, politicians, and of course magistrates."

Rick didn't move.

"That was long ago, Inspector," Boscoli pleaded. "You see what I've become. One must eventually put away one's past."

"That is easier for some people than others, Boscoli."

The policeman reached down and picked up the knife. He stared at it for a moment, then with a vicious blow sliced the vine, sending Orvieto's mayor crashing to the rocks below.

Chapter Fifteen

Gina sat on the lone bench at one end of the parking lot, staring at the ground, her shoulders covered by Francine's arm. Rick knelt in front of them. LoGuercio, a lit cigarette in one hand and his cell phone in the other, stood next to a Toyota SUV parked near the Mercedes. The trunk of the Toyota, and its four doors, were open. The medical crew, having patched Rick's hand, had gone to retrieve Boscoli's body.

"I can't believe what my mother went through back then." Gina shook her head violently as if trying to rid it of her thoughts. "It must have been a nightmare. Why didn't she ever confide in me about it? I had a right to know."

Francine rubbed the woman's back. "Your mother didn't see it that way, Gina. She had witnessed something very ugly, something that scarred her, and she didn't want to pass that scar on to you."

"Francine's right, Gina," Rick said, getting to his feet. "She didn't want you to become bitter."

She looked up at Rick. "Mom was bitter, all right. If I had known why, it would have been easier to accept the way she was, the way she treated me. All I can think of now is how she suffered."

"But she worked through it," Francine said, "and she moved on. That's what you'll do."

"I don't know if I'll have the strength."

Francine squeezed Gina's shoulder. "Of course you do.

Rhonda always told me how proud she was of you, what you did on your own to start your life in Santa Fe."

"She did?"

Rick stepped back, deciding that it was a good time to leave the two women alone. He walked to where LoGuercio was standing. The policeman saw Rick and finished his call while pointing at the open trunk.

"There are some dark spots which could be blood stains in Boscoli's Toyota. It looks to have been cleaned but I'm sure we'll find something to indicate the body was carried in it."

Rick looked inside the vehicle and glanced back at Gina, still huddled on the bench. This was not something she needed to know.

"Thank you for talking with the American women, Riccardo. How are they coping?"

"As well as can be expected. I didn't say that Boscoli was intending to murder them too, but I'm sure they understood the danger. I also gave them an abbreviated version of what happened here when Rhonda was a student, leaving out the most violent details but keeping to what I think are the facts. I didn't say that she was actually part of the Red Brigades."

"Which may well be the case. It's likely we'll never know the full truth."

Rick's eyes moved slowly from LoGuercio's face up to the cliff path and back. "You sound like you'd prefer that the truth never come out."

LoGuercio's hollow eyes looked at Rick. He crushed his cigarette under his heel and glanced at his watch. "I have to get back to the Duomo. Are you coming with me?"

Rick nodded. "I want to see if Crivelli is still on the floor hiding behind the woman in the fur coat."

◇◇◇

The Piazza Duomo, as always, was filled with tourists, but they divided their attention between the famous facade and the commotion taking place on the south side of the church. The cordoned-off street was crowded with official vehicles, their flashing lights bouncing off stone and stained glass. Several policemen moved in and out of the side door while others stood around talking in low voices, smoking or staring at the church. The ambulance carrying the wounded-but-stable Morgante, with Bianca Cappello at his side, began to pull out, its siren starting a low wail. Rick, Betta, and LoGuercio stood on the long strip of grass that ran along the side of the church, watching the vehicle slow at the corner and start down the hill.

Betta turned back to LoGuercio. "When you came in you were looking for the mayor?" She was still trying to understand what had become a complicated scene inside the church.

"That's right," said LoGuercio. "Riccardo found the photograph so we knew he was almost certainly the one who killed Signora Van Fleet. He was supposed to be among the people getting the tour but when we got inside we couldn't see him. I thought at first he was in the back of the group. When I said we were there to find a murderer, the last thing I expected was to have Aragona pull out his gun. We weren't even focusing on Pazzi, but somehow assumed the two deaths were related, and that once we got the mayor, the other crime would be solved as well."

"I know why Aragona killed Pazzi," said Rick.

"I think I do too, Riccardo, but you tell me your theory first."

Betta threw up her arms. "Well?"

"I saw something when we were at the villa this morning," Rick began. "I can tell by the look on your face, Betta that you don't see how something there could have anything to do with Aragona, but it was a bottle of wine that Francine was pouring. The label was Sonnomonte, which is Vincenzo Aragona's vineyard. The name was churning in my head when we found the photo album and had to go rushing back to town to find the mayor. But now I realize what it was about the name that bothered me. I told you that when Pazzi lay on the ground he said to me '*sono morto*,' but he wasn't really saying those words, that he was dying."

"He was saying Sonnomonte," Betta said.

"Exactly. I'm sure Pazzi was preparing one of his exposés about Aragona's business dealings, and getting close." Rick turned to LoGuercio. "Remember you told me that the *Guardia di Finanza* had set up shop in your offices? It would not surprise me if they are investigating the same irregularities. Selling cheap wine to other countries inside high-priced bottles would be my guess. That seems to be rampant these days and I've read that EU authorities are clamping down."

There was also the gap in Aragona's police file that Uncle Piero had mentioned, likely information removed by those same *Guardia di Finanza*. But Rick decided to keep that information to himself since Paolo knew nothing of the Fabrizio caper. Things were complicated enough.

LoGuercio was smiling. "I reached the same conclusion, but didn't need a wine bottle to get there. I called the *Guardia* when we were down at the tombs. They didn't want to tell me what they were investigating, but when I told them we had arrested Aragona they admitted it was his wine sales. They were not happy to find that Pazzi was also onto the guy, but a wine scandal would be just the kind of story that Pazzi would be digging up. It wouldn't surprise me if he had approached Aragona directly and tried to get some payment for keeping it out of the papers."

"So the two murders that you were sure had to be connected were in fact totally separate."

"Betta, thank you for pointing that out," said LoGuercio. "But Aragona may have hoped we would want to connect the two, and by walking by at the right time, Riccardo helped."

"Or the wrong time." While looking in Rick's eyes, Betta reached over to squeeze his hand. He recoiled. "Sorry, wrong hand." she said quickly. "How long did they say the bandages will stay on?"

"As long as I can get your sympathy, I keep them on."

"*Cari amici*, I should be getting back inside," said LoGuercio.

"And we must get ready for our return to Rome," said Betta. "When will we see you there, Paolo?"

LoGuercio gave them each a warm *abbraccio*. "I will appear at some point when you least expect me, just as Riccardo did here in Orvieto."

Betta and Rick walked to the square and took a final look at Maitani's masterpiece. The tourists had tired of the activity on the side of the church and returned to their normal vocation: taking pictures. A small swarm of school children next to the right door were the only group without cameras or phones. While their teacher, a nun, talked, they stared intently at the figures carved in the stone above them. The section was another depiction of the last judgment, no doubt placed there by the sculptor as a Bible lesson for the mostly illiterate population of the time. It was a terrible scene, filled with demons, serpents, and souls writhing in agony.

"I wonder what the sister is telling those kids," said Rick.

"She's a nun, she's saying what you'd expect her to say."

"We'd better go to mass this week."

They walked through the square toward their hotel. Another group of school kids passed them, these a bit older and led by a teacher dressed in civilian clothes. Another teacher in the rear, working like a border collie, kept the stragglers in formation. She shooed two boys who stopped to stare at the stuffed head of a boar hanging from a food store window. Rick was watching the show when he looked up to see a scowling face doing its best to avoid recognition.

"Signor Crivelli. May I introduce my friend Betta Innocenti? Or did you meet in the Duomo before all the excitement? Betta, this is Signor Amadeo Crivelli. I think you saw his work in Todi yesterday."

Crivelli shook Betta's hand, annoyed at being forced to show some manners. "My pleasure, Signora." He turned to Rick. "I really must be on my way. I'm expecting a major buyer from Belgium."

Rick put on his most sympathetic face. "Business is business, Signor Crivelli, but if you have a minute you'll enjoy hearing this."

Betta looked at Rick with a curious smile.

"I could certainly use something to take my mind off what went on earlier."

"Well, it was this. I don't understand police procedures, but I know the inspector worked tirelessly to find the perpetrator of this terrible crime. He's been accumulating mountains of evidence." Rick paused for effect. "He told me he uncovered something interesting, and though of course it is of no consequence now, you of all people will find it amusing." Rick glanced at Betta.

"And, *Mister* Montoya, what would *that* be?"

"In researching the victim, Signora Van Fleet, he found an amazing similarity between the designs of her ceramic pieces, and, well, yours. Isn't that a curious coincidence?"

Crivelli swallowed hard. A bead of moisture formed on his cheek and seeped into his white beard. "That is curious, to be sure. Must have been something I taught her those many years ago." He attempted a nostalgic smile, the professor remembering his prize student. "I must make a point of complimenting Inspector LoGuercio for his work." He quickly shook Betta's hand and then Rick's. "Well, I should be on my way, I don't want to keep an important client waiting."

They watched him hurry down the street.

"Rick, you could have told him you were the one who discovered the similarity."

"It's more fun this way."

◇◇◇

The door to the funicular opened with a pneumatic hiss and the people inside pushed through. Rick followed Betta, rolling their bags behind him, down the ramp to the station door. The temperature outside was warm enough so that they didn't need their coats, but there wasn't room in the suitcases, so they wore them. A few taxis stood idle in the small square, their drivers reading newspapers while they waited for fares. One looked up, but when nobody approached his car he returned to his reading. Rick and Betta crossed the square and entered the railroad station. Just inside was a coffee bar, its machines giving off their beckoning caffeine fragrance. Rick stopped before they reached the escalator to the parking lot.

"Would you like a coffee to stabilize you for the drive back?"

"No thanks, Rick, but you go ahead. I think I'll go check out the magazines. Are you all right with both bags?"

"Leave them to me."

Betta wandered off to the newspaper kiosk, and Rick walked to the small bar that was squeezed against one wall of the station. There must have been trains about to arrive or depart Orvieto, since at least ten people stood sipping espressos and other drinks. It was impossible to tell whether they were going to head north toward Firenze, south to Roma, or points in between such as Arezzo or Terni. Rick guessed that two young girls drinking glasses of white wine were students. A group of four men in suits listened to a fifth as he made some point that, judging by his waving arms, was extremely important. Other people were by themselves, nursing their coffees and staring at the bottles behind the bar. One of them, a large duffel bag at his feet, was Rick's cousin.

"Taking a trip, Fabrizio?"

The lad looked up, startled. "Riccardo. I didn't expect to see you. You must be going back to Rome."

"I am, indeed." Rick tipped the two suitcases upright and ordered an *espresso macchiato* from the man behind the bar. "This is a strange place for you to get your coffee, Cousin." He looked down at the duffel bag. "With luggage?"

Fabrizio's sigh came from deep in his soul. "I'm going home, Riccardo."

"I'm glad to hear that. Why the change of heart? Certainly not from the sage advice offered by your cousin."

"Huh? Oh, no, it wasn't that. Something…happened."

Rick's coffee came, and the barman poured just a splash of hot milk into the tiny cup. "Unburden yourself, Fabrizio. It will do you wonders." After stirring in a spoonful of sugar he took a sip and waited.

"You think? Well, Tullia called me a couple hours ago. Something terrible happened to her husband. She was too shaken up to tell me exactly what. Apparently he's going to be away for a while."

"That sounds serious."

"Right. I said I'd come over immediately but she told me not to. She'd already called her sisters, who live up north, and they were on their way to Orvieto. She didn't think it would be a good idea to have me around. Can you believe that, Riccardo?"

"That she'd called her sisters before calling you, or didn't want you around?"

"Both, I guess." He stared into the mirror at the other side of the bar. "I'm just surprised she wants a couple women to comfort her rather than me."

The kid has learned nothing. "That's called family, Fabrizio."

Fabrizio nodded. "Funny you should say it, because that's just what I was thinking. And that's why I decided to accept what Tullia said and just go back to Perugia. Family *is* important, and the only way I could really understand that was to be away from home for a while."

The kid has learned something. "You won't regret your decision."

"I hope not."

"And, you've also learned other things about, well, life."

"I'll say, Riccardo. I've learned a whole lot, that's for sure. I don't know when I'll use it in a book, but you'll read it sometime." He looked again at the clock. "Listen, my train is due, I'd better get to the track. Great seeing you." They gave each other cousinly hugs.

"Give my best to your parents."

Fabrizio rolled his eyes, picked up his sack, and walked away. Rick was still shaking his head when Betta appeared, a magazine in her hand.

He raised his hand to get the attention of the barman. "Betta, we're going to have a prosecco for the road."

Chapter Sixteen

Uncle Piero's restaurant selection was tied to a police investigation at the north side of Rome's *centro storico*. A woman had been found dead in an apartment at a bend in the Tiber across from the Palace of Justice. The location was ironic, since the deceased was the estranged wife of an undersecretary of the Justice Ministry. Any similar case would have brought in a precinct detective, but at the request of the minister himself, Commissario Piero Fontana was assigned to investigate. He was not happy, but now pushed work from his mind to enjoy lunch with his nephew, their first since Rick had returned from Orvieto. They sat in La Campana, which had started life as an inn, and now claimed to be the oldest restaurant in the city. As befitted an establishment that had been on site for almost half a millennium, the menu was Roman. As was the clientele.

Rick observed that no one in the room was dressed more elegantly than his uncle, despite Piero having come directly from a crime scene. No surprise there. Today a bright paisley tie over a dark blue shirt contrasted with a subtle glen plaid jacket that could have had elbow patches but didn't. A solid red handkerchief peeked from the jacket pocket, picking up the colors of the tie which would soon be covered with a white napkin.

Normally Rick and Piero skipped anything resembling antipasto and went directly to the pasta course, but one of the specialties here was the *carciofi alla giudia*, artichokes fried to a crispness that made them crunch at the bite, so they succumbed.

For *primo*, Piero tried to talk Rick into joining him again, with *tagliolini con alici e pecorino*. Rick, not a fan of anything with anchovies, opted for the *spaghetti alle vongole*, always done to perfection at La Campana. The choice of a main dish, if there was to be one, would wait until after the first two courses. The seafood in the pasta choices called for a white wine. Assuming that Rick had tasted enough Orvieto Classico on his trip, Piero selected a bottle from another part of Umbria, a smooth Montefalco Bianco. They were halfway through it when the waiter removed their empty artichoke dishes.

"Riccardo, I think you can take at least partial credit for your cousin's decision."

"How do you figure that, Zio?"

"You are family to him. He said he came to the realization that family is important. You being there helped put the thought into his thick, young head."

Rick chuckled. "That's a bit of a stretch. More likely is that he saw the handwriting on the wall when Tullia invited her sister to stay with her. He saw that it was over."

"Perhaps they were both looking for an excuse to end it. Let's hope so, for Fabrizio's sake."

Piero took a drink of his wine. "What I hope is that the knowledge the boy learned from the experience was not solely carnal. Some his age are mature beyond their years, while others give the impression they will never grow up. I fear that your cousin is in the latter category." He waved his hand. "But I would rather talk about the exploits of my other nephew."

"We're back to the murder case."

"Exactly."

The pasta arrived, suspending the conversation momentarily. Steam rose from both the fettuccine and the spaghetti as the dishes were placed in front of them, and with it their delicate aromas. The waiter added a small plate for Rick's empty clam shells and retired. Grated cheese was neither expected nor offered.

"We did some digging into Mayor Boscoli's past," Piero said after his first bite. "There was a period after he graduated from the *liceo*, and before the university, that was a blank. It coincided with the time of the Milan bank robbery. After getting his degree here in Rome at La Sapienza he went back to Orvieto and opened a practice. He also started investing in real estate."

"Paolo said Boscoli owned a lot of property in town. So how can a guy fresh out of the university afford to buy buildings? Family money?"

"That was my thought as well. No, he came from modest means. While it is impossible to know if the money he used to buy the property in Orvieto was stolen, I think it's highly likely it came from the robbery. The records of the sales only show the amount, not how it was paid. It could have been in small bills for all we know."

"And since he's dead, we'll never find out. What is happening with Aragona?"

"He's incarcerated here, but it may be a while before he comes to trial. He hired a lawyer who I thought only worked for Mafiosi, and he doesn't come cheap."

"He can afford it. That's for the homicide charge, which don't include his problems with the *Guardia di Finanza*. By the way, were they responsible for the gap in his criminal file?"

"They were. And the word is they were about to stage an early morning raid on his premises. The *Guardia* loves pre-dawn raids. He was shipping wine to Germany under his expensive labels but the bottles contained something of much lower quality. Surprisingly, some German must have noticed. So he has a separate set of lawyers for each case. When it's all over, there will have been a large transfer of funds from Aragona's accounts to the legal profession."

"I wonder if Tullia had her money in a separate bank."

The policeman shrugged.

"The one hero in this was Morgante," Rick said, "and he will benefit the most."

"The pharmacist who took the bullet in the cathedral?"

"Right. LoGuercio tells me he is now the town hero for protecting the cultural patrimony of the city. With the removal of

Boscoli, the town council unanimously voted him in as mayor, even those who were in Boscoli's coalition. There's talk of him running for parliament in the next national election."

The dish next to Rick's pasta plate was filling with the empty shells at the same rate that the spaghetti was disappearing into his mouth. Piero filled his nephew's wineglass and returned to his pasta. He was about to speak when a balding man being led to his table by the waiter tapped him on the shoulder. Piero nodded in a formal way and the man continued through the room. Rick guessed it was a politician, but Piero didn't say, instead returning to the subject at hand.

"That ceramics artist who was a suspect?"

"Crivelli," Rick said.

"Right, Crivelli. From what you said, I can understand why you thought he might be the murderer. The revelation that he had stolen his basic style from a student would have, at the very least, made him the laughing stock of the other potters in Umbria."

"Interesting that you bring that up, Zio. I spoke to LoGuercio a few days ago, and he mentioned Crivelli. The man sent him a note of congratulations for solving the murder, along with a small ceramic pot. Paolo is using it on his desk as an ashtray."

"To keep LoGuercio's lips sealed, it should have been something considerably larger. I doubt your friend will ever have any problems with Crivelli."

"With what Paolo's got on him, probably not."

The empty dishes were picked up by the ever-attentive waiter who stood with them in his hand and posed the expected question.

"*Per doppo?*"

Rick exchanged glances with his uncle and asked for menus to help them decide. The original good intentions were cast aside and both of them decided to have another course, though one was lighter than the other. Piero, having admired the asparagus on display when they entered, asked for *asparagi alla parmigiana*. Rick opted instead for the *calamari fritti*. His justification was that one should always order what a restaurant is known for, and fried food was a specialty at La Campana.

Piero handed over his menu to the waiter and turned to his nephew. "You can give me a few bites of your *calamari*. You ate well in Orvieto, I trust?"

In Italy, that was always a rhetorical question, but Rick nodded.

"Riccardo, I considered inviting Betta to join us today."

Rick had been about to take a drink of wine, but now slowly replaced his glass on the table. "Inviting Betta? To *our* lunch?" He held up his hands. "Don't get me wrong, I love being around Betta. But Zio, with Betta we wouldn't be able to—I don't know—to talk about things like we always do."

Piero appeared to be enjoying his nephew's discomfort. "Have we said anything today that you wouldn't want to share with Betta?"

Now Rick did take that drink of wine. "Well, I can't think of anything off hand. But having her with us would change the atmosphere."

"For the better, in my opinion."

"What about discussing your cases? We couldn't really do that with an outsider present. Could we?"

Piero gave the question some thought and looked at Rick over his half glasses. "She passed all the tests and background checks to get into the art police. I don't recall that you, dear Nephew, have ever had a security check by the Italian authorities." He rubbed his stubby beard as his brows knitted. "Perhaps I've been bending regulations by talking about my cases with you."

Rick held up his hands again, as if warding off an attacker. "You've made your point."

The *secondi* arrived. Piero's asparagus was arranged neatly on the plate, a thin crust of browned cheese contrasting with the green of the stems. Lemon slices framed Rick's stack of crisp calamari. He picked up one slice and his fork, squeezing the juice over the squid.

"*Buon appetito,*" Piero said as he took his utensils in hand.

"Altrettanto," Rick replied, still thinking about Betta's possible inclusion in their periodic lunches. Since they had returned from Orvieto, Rick had attempted to push the incident with Carlo from his memory, but it nagged at him. As much as he tried to convince himself that Betta had meant no harm, and she believed she was doing the right thing, he was still stung that she'd kept it from him. The scar on her forehead had healed, but the tiny pang inside Rick was still there.

"Zio?"

"*Si*, Riccardo."

"About Betta."

"*Si.*"

"Let me put this as succinctly as I can. If she were to be included in our lunches, it would signal to her that our relationship has gone to a new level. I'm not sure if I'm ready to take that step."

"We've had dinner together. Several times."

"Not the same."

Piero patted his lips with the white napkin and smiled. "I think I understand. And of course I will honor your wishes."

"Thank you, Uncle." He took a piece of calamari that was small enough not to need cutting and put it in his mouth. The soft inside was the perfect foil, in taste and texture, for the crunchy breading.

"Your friend Inspector LoGuercio appears to be back on the track for advancement." Piero carefully sliced one of the asparagus spears, but held it on his fork while he continued. "Resolving two murders in a matter of a few days did him no harm. And the fact that one was connected to terrorism, albeit from decades ago, gave him even more notoriety. He may even be left in Orvieto to run the operation rather than send in someone else, since he was so successful there." He tilted his head at Rick. "Perhaps the new mayor will request it, and our bureaucracy pays close attention to local politics, when it works in our favor."

Rick had been curious about LoGuercio's future, but had

avoided bringing it up. "It would not surprise me if Morgante has put in a good word for Paolo."

The commissario finished a bite of his asparagus as well as the wine in his glass. "There were people in the central office who had thought the man may not have been cut out for police work, but after this their view has changed. He's proved himself."

Rick rubbed the narrow strip of bandage still covering part of his hand. He looked at Piero before his eyes moved back to the plate in front of him.

"Uncle, are you ready to taste my *calamari*? As always, they are excellent."

Author's Note

As with the previous books in this series, this one takes place in an Italian town which I've had the pleasure of visiting many times. Its proximity to Rome made Orvieto an easy place for us to get to on a weekend, either by car or train, both routes running parallel to the Tiber River as it runs south out of Umbria into the region of Lazio. Like almost any town in Italy it has a rich history, in this case stretching back to the Etruscans and flowing through the Roman era to medieval and modern times. Much of Orvieto's history is evident as one wanders the city's streets, especially the relationship it had with the papacy, starting with one of the few papal palaces found outside of Rome. It was not by chance that Clement VII took refuge in Orvieto after the sack of Rome in 1527. Equally evident for the casual visitor is the city's rich artistic tradition, especially in the field of ceramics. I have described the cathedral in some detail on these pages, but there are other churches worth visiting, as well as museums of various kinds. The Pozzo San Patrizio, the wonderful double helix-staired well built as a defense against sieges, should be part of any tourist itinerary to the city.

Nearby Todi, which appears in this book, is another gem of southern Umbria. It is your classic Umbrian hill town, with steep streets that keep both inhabitants and tourists in shape. Todi's main square is one of the loveliest in Italy, boasting a symmetry and charm that make it look like a theater set. (In fact, one scene in the movie *The Agony and The Ecstasy*, with "pope" Charleston Heston riding into "Rome," was filmed there.) The delightful town of Bolsena, on the lake of the same name, finds its way into another chapter of the book. It is one of many small towns, including Bagnoregio just to Orvieto's south, that make this corner of Umbria so appealing to the visitor who wants to get off the usual tourist track.

Normally in my books I do not mention restaurants by name, even though in many cases the places described are ones where I've dined. I made the exception here with Rick and Piero's lunch at La Campana. This venerable establishment was a favorite eatery of ours the years we lived in Rome and one we always go back to on return visits. It is hidden on a small side street near the river, but well worth searching out if you want to savor genuine Roman dishes.

My thanks go to readers and friends who clamored for more Rick Montoya. I am also indebted to the many people who helped me with this book. Once again my son provided technical advice, in this case regarding firearms. (Sorry, Max, that I couldn't include hidden Nazi gold or zombies in the plot. Maybe the next one.) *Grazie mille* to my good friend Guido Garavoglia, who helped out by researching fingerprinting requirements in Italy. Also in the realm of fingerprints, I am grateful to Jane Benavidez of the Pueblo, Colorado, Police Department for her mini-seminar on the subject. And, as always, my wife, Mary, was the source of ideas, encouragement, and advice. Without her this book could not have been written.